Joanna Nadin

ur   Nadin is the author of more than seventy books for
l ʼn and young adults, including the bestselling Rachel
aries, the critically acclaimed *Eden* and *Undertow*, and
ꓵegie-nominated *Joe All Alone*, now being adapted for
ꓳn. A former broadcast journalist, political speech-
and special adviser to the Prime Minister, she has a
ꓵ the concept of self in young adult literature, and
ꓹ in Creative Writing at Bath Spa University. She lives
with her daughter.

Anthony McGowan

ny McGowan is one of the most widely acclaimed
-adult authors in the UK. His books have won several
awards, and been shortlisted for many more. He has
ritten highly regarded adult fiction, as well as books for
er readers. He has a PhD on the history of beauty, and
ught philosophy and creative writing. He lives in
n with his wife and two children.

Everybody Hurts

Joanna Nadin

& Anthony McGowan

ATOM

ATOM

First published in Great Britain in 2017 by Atom

1 3 5 7 9 10 8 6 4 2

A CIP catalogue record for this book is available from the British Library.

ISBN 978-0-349-00291-0

Typeset by Hewer Text UK Ltd, Edinburgh
Printed and bound in Great Britain by Clays Ltd, St Ives plc

Papers used by Atom are from well-managed forests and other responsible sources.

Atom
An imprint of
Little, Brown Book Group
Carmelite House
50 Victoria Embankment
London EC4Y 0DZ

An Hachette UK Company
www.hachette.co.uk

www.atombooks.co.uk

For Rosie and Millie

SOPHIA

Once upon a time, I made a list of things I do not believe in. There were a bunch. Hey, I'm a cynical kind of girl. But these, in no particular order, were my top five.

1. A benevolent God. Or any kind of God, really. But benevolent really is the icing on the cake of bulldada.
2. That anyone named Rainshine Wilson, Yuffy or some Nigerian guy called Professor Mahuba can any more cure a brain tumour than they can bring back the dead or enlarge my non-existent penis.
3. Fake tan.
4. Conspiracy theories (no, the FBI did not cause the tsunami, blow up the twin towers or force Backstreet Boys to reunite).
5. Love at first sight.

If you believe in that last one – the whole eyes-meeting-across-a-crowded-room shit – you might as well start arguing for the existence of the tooth fairy, Santa or Jesus. It just goes against science, as well as the law that unless you share some basic grounding in music appreciation then you're pretty much doomed to failure. And I know that both of you liking the hidden track on some obscure Deaf Beats album doesn't mean you're fated, but it's better than basing an entire relationship on the fact your stomach lurches because of the way his hair falls into his eyes. What if it's just indigestion?

Lexy said I was being provocatively cynical (she found that one on a blog). And I know she thought it was just the tumour talking. But then she would. Because she counts on life playing out like it's Hollywood-scripted and has fallen in love more times than she's fallen off her latest diet. Jesus, she spent the whole of GCSE year looking for her Heathcliff; worked her way through half a dozen boys from the wrong side of the tracks in the hope one of them would have leading man potential. It's Leeds, I said, not Hollywood. You're not going to find a hero working down Kwik Fit.

Besides, Heathcliff's a jerk. And love is blind at best, and a deceit at worst. The idea that we're all half formed, lost without a boy by our side, or preferably one step ahead of us, opening doors and fighting wars? Screw that, I said to anyone who would listen. There's nothing missing from me. I'm whole, complete, and I can open my own doors and clear my own pathways. Thanks all the same. No, *The Great Gatsby* is where it's at. Just fine dresses and gin and everyone playing at being someone else. Love in West Egg is so clearly an illusion, and if you think for a minute you can cross that great divide in disguise or otherwise then you're a fool; nothing but a beautiful fool.

Until I clocked him. And he clocked me. And my steadfastly cynical world was tilted swiftly off its axis, and I landed – bruised, bewildered – in a bed of bloody roses.

I didn't see that one coming.

Not on a wet Friday afternoon in March against the Dettol-scented backdrop of a hospital canteen.

Not with a boy nearly a year younger than me and a whole record collection short of anything resembling taste.

Not with a boy like him at all.

But then love, like I say, is blind.

And I, it turns out, am a fool after all.

MATTHEW

Friday

'This is the worst idea you've ever had.'

Me, Jango and Corky were halfway up the long hill leading to Mickey's – meaning St Michael's Hospital – so I had a bit of a wheeze on when I said it, like I was blowing it out through a mouth organ.

And it was the truth. I mean about it being the worst idea Jango had ever had. The absolute total literal effing truth, despite the fact that Jango's last stroke of genius was to take a long, green, foaming slash in Mr Harris's welly boots, which he'd left outside his tent on our geography field trip to Pately Bridge.

I admit though that Jango showed his true greatness in what followed. Harris lines up the whole year in that field, half quicksand and half cow shit, and he screams at us that unless whoever did it comes forward the trip will end NOW and we'll go back to school and spend the next month in DETENTION. Jango then does this huge act of looking around, like he knew exactly which other twat it was who'd done the deed, and he tuts as if disgusted that they are too chicken to own up; so lacking in honour and courage that they'd rather see the whole year slapped down than just take their punishment like a man. And then, still rolling his eyes, he steps out of the line and says, 'Me, sir, I done it,' but with the sarcasm dripping off him like runny shit off a stick.

So Harris goes red, then some other colours including purple and a sort of pale green, not unlike the piss colour with which Jango has filled up his boots, and he knows everyone's laughing at him, but he can't do anything about it. And he sort of yells at Jango for a while, you know, just noise, really, and then says, 'This had better not happen again,' and that was it.

Back on the road to Mickey's, Jango stopped in a most dramatic way. He's got this long face that makes him look like he ought to be playing the piano in a concert hall with everyone watching him in silence until the applause breaks out. Anyway, he looked at me with his fiery black eyes, and I knew I was in for a special 'you've been Jangoed' moment.

'We've been through this four hundred and seventeen effing times. Up there . . .' he pointed one of his weirdly long fingers at the dark gothic edifice of St Michael's . . . 'is a hospital full of sick people. Most of them are old and ugly and smell like they're already dead. Some of them, however, are kids. And there is one ward specially devoted to teenagers. Teenagers with deadly effing diseases. Diseases that are going to put them in severe risk of totally effing dying.'

'But, Jango—'

'And elementary general knowledge, such as you are supposed to have stored in that mega-brain of yours, tells us that half of those teenagers are gonna be girls—'

'Jan—'

'And we all know – know for a total fact – that there is a list of things that every teenage girl wants to do before they ultimately and utterly snuff it. They want to swim with effing dolphins. They want to watch the sunrise over Mount Kilimaneffingjaro. They want to ride in a stretch limo with Taylor effing Swift. And they most certainly and without the least iota of effing doubt want to get right royally effing laid. And that's why we've committed the grievous effing offence of bunking off on this fine Friday afternoon, when we should be enjoying the delights of double PE with that sadist Fricker.'

'Yeah but—'

'*But* me again and I'll butt *you*,' said Jango, and he's enough of a psycho for me to know that he meant it, even if he's also enough of a friend for me to know that it'd be one of his playful headbutts that doesn't smear your nose all over your face like jam on a scone.

'Because the thing is that – and this time feel free to effing contradict me because such clearly is your wont, and here I'm genuinely interested to hear your views – we have not the least chance of ever getting our cherries popped collectively, individually or any combination thereof, have we—'

'Jango—'

'When I want your effing opinion I'll ask for it. Except actually I won't because I'LL NEVER WANT YOUR EFFING OPINION. And now my thread – I've effing lost it. No, wait, yeah, there I was . . . because just look at us. I said, LOOK AT US! There's Corky here who c-c-c-c-c-c-can't say a f-f-f-f-f-f-flipping thing because of his st-st-st-st-st-st-st-stammer. And there's you, effing genius, but with a face even your own mother would happily trade for an effing baboon's ARSE—'

'F-f-f-f-f c-c-c-c-c,' said Corky.

'Language, Corky, language. And then there's me.'

Big pause here, while Jango gave me and Corky the eye, the eye as black as a black cat locked in a black box falling into a black hole in hell.

'And. Then. There's. Me.'

And Jango raised up his leg – the bad leg, the short leg, and on the end of it that effing big shoe; the big shoe that scares the living shit out of everyone who sees it; the big shoe that he wields like Thor's hammer in fights against the hardest wankers in our school or any other school. And that big shoe of Jango's can settle any argument. It's the big shoe that could stomp down on the Gordian Knot, and crush it like you'd crush a beetle or the sad little toes of a Year 7 midget.

'And so,' says Jango, the big shoe down on the floor again, replaced in the air by his long, jabbing finger, bony as the twig stuck out through the bars by little Hansel, 'he's dumb, you're ugly – not to mention scared shitless of the opposite sex – and I've got an effing BIG SHOE. So what sort of chance do we stand of getting to play the beast with two backs, unless it's from, by which I mean *with*, some poor girl who's reckoning on shuffling off the old mortal coil, and who doesn't want to do it, i.e. the shuffling off, unloved, which is to say un-popped, eh. Eh? *Eh?* EH?'

'OK, Jango,' I said. What else could I say? 'You're a knobhead, Jango.' I suppose I could have said that. And it would have been true. But not the whole truth. And the whole truth about Jango, well, that would take a book.

So that was why we were strolling up the road to Mickey's, me in my trainers, Corky in his boots and Jango in his one big shoe. It was because we thought we might get some action from the dying girls on the fabled Ward 4W.

I didn't want to be there. I'd have given all the money in my special hiding place at the back of my sock drawer to be anywhere else. But I could no more go against the will of Jango than I could decide that today would be yesterday or tomorrow today.

And, anyway, what if he was right?

What if there was someone there who ... needed me? Someone kind. Someone beautiful. Someone sad.

But no. I was thinking like Jango. No, not like Jango. Nobody thinks like Jango. I mean that I was drifting away from reality, just like Jango.

And on we trudged.

SOPHIA

Friday

There are some pretty choice things about being almost dead.
Like:

1. Being so wasted that the only time you leave your bed
   is to stick your head down the toilet and hurl up your
   Cheerios for the second time that morning.
2. Catching sight of yourself in the bathroom mirror when
   you're rinsing out the sweet and sour taste of multi-
   grain vomit and having to admit that your skin's unique
   Pantone shade is Zombie Movie Extra.
3. Coming to on the floor of the refectory and realising
   that you've peed yourself in front of the rugby first XI
   and Mr Hamner from tech who's been at the top of half
   of the sixth form girls' to-do lists since he arrived out of
   teacher training last September.
4. Accepting that, however hard you bargain with God, or
   Allah or whoever, the floor is not going to open up and
   swallow you, just like you never got those 34C breasts
   or the pony you prayed for.

So, yeah, all of these I could happily live without (ha ha – pun intended). But the worst bit isn't so much what it does to you. It's what happens to everyone around you. It's like they hear the word 'tumour' and some kind of chemical reaction goes off inside them. Even when it turned out to be the good kind – well, the better kind: benign, growing in minute, shuffling increments, meaning it's sat there inside me like a slow-mo half-hearted time bomb that might tick-tock and go off, might just wind itself down – all they can focus on is the 't' word, so that they can't look at you without plastic smiles and cow eyes that barely hide the pity behind them. Some brave face. It looks more like a clown. Which would make my mother the grand ringmaster.

I get why she does it. I mean, having a kid with any kind of growth – a wart or a melanoma would do it, especially one that can't be sliced off or out – doesn't fit into her neat, iCal, five-year-plan world. Not that I ever did. I mean, the litany of things about me that don't dovetail in runs longer than the snagging list for the builders who redid the kitchen. There's the hair, which just doesn't do that glossy Pantene swish, which isn't helped by my phobia of GHDs and scissors and, well, product of any colour, smell or price range. But, you know, it's just hair. Plus wearing a dead woman's dresses possibly doesn't help. So they're Grandma Ellington's, not some random corpse's. Plus I'm recycling, so yay for the polar bears. Only polar bears don't really register in the White Anglo-Saxon Protestant world. And then there's the almost-deadness. Which even I admit was kind of a step too far.

At first she went into textbook tiger mother mode: googling quacks and snake oil cures; begging, then threatening my dad to move us back to the States with its shiny hospitals and even shinier doctors. He told her she was overreacting (she was), that she wasn't helping (she wasn't), and that he'd read a paper on this, and what she needed to do was to 'normalise' (cue more cereal vomit) things. Only it turns out this wasn't such a great alternative. Because instead of being the centre of attention I'm now one all-singing and all-dancing elephant in the room. In a black tutu and Chucks.

Or maybe not even that. I'm a wine stain on her Jaeger skirt, or a grey hair in her ash-blonde bob. And instead of tears I get that fake, Colgate smile and twenty minutes on Julia Wills-Beckton's cellulite.

So obviously there was no way I was going to let her come with me to the hospital that afternoon.

'Lexy can come with me,' I say. 'She's on a free all afternoon.' (Aka experimenting with Daddy's drinks cabinet.) 'Plus she wants to.' (Massive understatement.)

'But . . . she won't know what to ask,' Mom protests.

Unbelievable. 'I know what to ask. I'm seventeen, not seven.'

'Yes, yes, I know. But, oh, Sophia . . .' She trails off, and I wait for them . . . yes, here they were, the full-on Friesian eyes.

11

'Dad?' I plead.

'Let her go,' he says. 'It'll be good for her. Won't it, Soph?'

'Exactly.' *Ding ding.* Round one to Sophia.

'I . . .' But she can't think of anything, or at least anything that won't escalate the tiny ink stain to a full-on Merlot all over the cream carpet crisis.

'Thanks, Daddy.' I pull on my fake fur coat and my best poor-little-rich-girl voice and kiss him on the cheek. He waves it off absent-mindedly, his head already back in his book. Then, before Mom can write out a list of points to raise with Dr Gupta, or smear me with antibacterial gel, or force me to put on a full protective bodysuit, ruining my ensemble, I am gone. Game, set and match.

So that's my family fully freaking me out. But I can rely on my friends, right?

Think again.

'I don't know what to say, Soph,' they say. Or, 'I'm totally here for you, babes.' Only they're not. Oh, I mean at first they are, because you're a novelty, like some freak-show documentary merboy, or Flick Cameron in Year 11 who showed the class how she could bend her legs behind her head and got asked out five times in as many minutes. But then you start saying no to vodka at parties, and then missing parties altogether, and next thing you know they've shrugged you off like last season's maxi dress.

Except Lexy. For her, this whole deal is a wet dream come true. The only thing that could notch it up to full-on multiple orgasms is if she were the one who was possibly dying. (Did I mention that? Not probable, just possible. Which is a whole different ball game to me and Dr Gupta, but not, like I say, to Mom and Lexy and the entire Penn student body.) Will (I'll explain later) says Lexy has a pathological need to invent drama in her life due to being born to two accountants. Personally I think it's a diet of eighties films, trash romance novels and Diet Coke, but hey, the result is the same.

'Darling!' She hugs me and pulls me into her room, as if she's about to tell me she's the one on the wait list for the afterlife. Then she makes me sit down on her bed (four poster, with canopy, natch), which only confirms that the news is grave, at least in Lexy Land.

'I saw Lucas this morning,' she says, adopting her sympathetic police-officer-at-the-door-of-murdered-teenager's-parents tone.

I feel myself flinch, but reckon she'll put it down to meds or a minor seizure. (Oh yeah, a side effect of having a tangerine-sized lump in my head is that it pushes down hard on my epilepsy button, which, like, WTF? Couldn't it pick the bit that makes me happy or horny, or think I'm Elizabeth Taylor?) Instead, I effect as much nonchalance as is possible when discussing your ex who dumped you six months after diagnosis and immediately slept with Claudia Dawson aka Saucy Dawsey, whose only growths are her 32DDs. 'And?'

'He's split up with Dawse. Well, she chucked him. Apparently she thinks he's still into you. Which, like, is so obviously true. You were his first, which is, oh god, it's like *Romeo and Juliet.'*

Which it really, really isn't. But I don't like to shatter her illusions completely. Plus, the nonchalance has kind of been kicked out of me by the word 'split'.

'He dumped me,' I remind her quickly.

'Yeah, but, it was hard on him, wasn't it. Your . . .' dramatic pause, laboured intake of breath . . . 'illness. Only he's had time to think.'

I know for a fact that at this point she's picturing him in his bedroom reading Sartre and crying to some old Leonard Cohen CD, which is so far from the truth (for a start he only reads football magazines) that I have to resist the temptation to laugh.

'And he's thought what, exactly?'

'Well, he didn't actually say as much but, obviously, now he'll come to his senses and realise his place is at your side.'

Seriously, she actually talks like that. 'Maybe I don't want him "at my side",' I say.

'Oh. My. God. Are you mental?'

'Yeah, that's what happens with a brain tumour,' I deadpan.

And here they are: cow eyes, only unlike Mom she manages to squeeze out real tears (practised religiously for her career at the RSC by watching *The Railway Children* twenty-seven times in a week so now, like Pavlov's dog, even the thought of 'Daddy, oh my daddy,' can make her well up) and the full hand over mouth 'I should never have said that' thing. Normally this is my cue to apologise (don't even start). But I can't do it. Not this morning.

'I have to go,' I say instead.

'But I'm coming with you, aren't I?' I can see the panic in her eyes. 'You need me, don't you?'

And the thing is, I do. I mean, I like her, love her even. And she's always been there. She was there when I first got airdropped into England – into Mallory freaking Towers with the added horror of teenage boys – at the age of twelve. And she was still there when I'd dropped the accent like an ill-fitting shirt, or most of it. When everyone realised being American was no more exotic than just mispronouncing tomato, and I became just some girl with hair and an eclectic taste in mothballed dresses. She stayed. So I'm grateful and all. But some days Lexy is just too much. Too much noise. Too much drama. Too much Lexy. And so I lie.

'I'm meeting Mom there,' I say. 'Sorry, that's what I came round to tell you. Dr Gupta said.'

'Oh—'

'Next time,' I add, before she can get in a 'but I'll just stay in the corridor, I won't even come in I promise, and then when you come out you can just cry on me and I won't ask anything or say anything I will just, like, be'.

Only she can't just 'be'. Not ever. Because she can't last five minutes without needing to Instagram the 'be'ing or post it as a status update or at the very least turn it into a scene in

15

the imaginary movie of her brilliant career. And so that's how I end up in St Michael's without a parent or guardian or drama queen of a best friend to keep me on the straight and narrow. So if you think about it, it could be fate, or it could be their fault. Whichever, what happens next is the beginning of the rest of my (albeit potentially shortened) life.

MATTHEW

Friday

We nicked some flowers from the graveyard of the old church halfway up the hill. They weren't the greatest flowers in the world. Mine were – well, I don't know the names of all the flowers, but they were once pink and white, and were now mainly brown. Jango had done better – he'd thieved a little rose in a little pot from the little grave of a little old lady. Corky had two daffodils. Perky enough, but, you know, just the two of them, which was a bit of a giveaway. Like who ever goes into a flower shop and says, 'Just a daffodil, please, love. No, hang on, I'll splash out – make it two!'

So we reached Mickey's, and marched through the car park, and then went through the big front door, which has a stone arch over it, because the entrance part is really old, although most of the rest of the building is concrete and glass. It was mental in there, with people rushing about, and then that hospital smell made up of the stuff that comes out of you when you're sick mixed with the stuff they put into you when you're sick with an added layer of the stuff they use to clean up the stuff that comes out of you when you're sick.

There was a reception area with some women behind a desk, but Jango ignored them and went up to a big board on the wall, full of 'clinic this' and 'clinic that' and different wards and all kinds of other stuff.

'Four W,' he said. 'Effing got you. It's four because it's the fourth floor and it's W for west, elemental, my dear Watson. Off we go, boys and girls, off we go.'

So we got in a giant lift with a load of other people in it. None of them looked very happy. But you wouldn't, would you? We stepped out at the fourth floor thinking it would be right there, you know, in front of us, but corridors went off in all directions. We went one way and then another, past waiting rooms full of old people and mothers wrestling with toddlers with snotty faces.

Finally, there it was. A double door with 'Ward 4W' written on it, and a poster of Justin effing Bieber visible through the glass on the wall on the other side.

Jango cranked his face up to full-on demonic, rubbed his hands together and did a little sort of evil dance.

'Our victims await,' he said, in a horror-film voice. Then he walked towards the door with his arm out, ready to burst through to the other side like a rock star hitting the stage.

But Corky wasn't moving, except for his head, which he was shaking from side to side.

'What's up with you?' said Jango.

Corky squeezed his eyes shut, trying to get a word out.

'Don't say it, Corky. Don't say an effing word. I know what you're like. You make me ashamed. You reckon that the girls in here with cancer and that are gonna be repulsive, faces eaten up with tumours and their insides all rotted away. You reckon that if you kiss one of them you're gonna end up with bits of lip and tongue stuck to your face, like you've snogged a corpse or a zombie. Well, I'm telling you straight, I'm disappointed in you, Corky. Disappointed and, let me tell you, angry. It's time to rise above your base feelings. What we're doing here is an act of generosity. It's an act of effing LOVE. Now, sort your shit out, and let's get lovin'.'

'F-f-f-f,' said Corky.

'Good man, Corky, good man.'

And then, with his long coat flapping, the little pot of roses in his hand and Corky and his two bent daffodils in tow, Jango pushed through the double doors and entered the secret world of Ward 4W.

Me?

Well, I let the doors open and then swing back closed again, with me still on the outside, looking in at the poster of Justin B.

I reached down into my pocket and felt the clank of six fake one pound coins. Then I did a neat heel spin and headed back down to the ground floor of Mickey's, where I'd spotted a sprawling great canteen area full of the sort of crap food that puts people in hospitals in the first place.

SOPHIA

Friday

The thing about hospitals is that they're not just there to do their business – you know, the pills and the poking and the cutting open and the sewing up. They have a whole subplot going on, which we shall call 'there but for the grace of God'. Because the clean white corridors and the smell of Dettol and despair conspires to create a giant game-show set, and each passer-by is a potential patient. You size them up, looking for symptoms, guessing which bit of them failed, guessing their sentence. Are they dying, or just buying grapes and Lucozade for someone who is? (Which, while we're on the subject, what is that stuff about? It's frick-fracking evil. I want full-fat Coke and a Krispy Kreme or just don't bother.)

Don't tell me you don't do it. Even I do it, and I'm guaranteed to be on the losing team. Though I can usually get away with fooling the audience for a few rounds at least.

'Still got your hair,' says Dr Gupta when I walk in. 'You're one of the lucky ones.'

I finger the long, dark blonde mass that still reaches halfway down my back. That Mom begged me to bob so I could

20

'get used to the idea', and which I'm pretty sure Lexy willed me to lose, to add to the whole cancer-chic vibe.

'I should probably buy me a lottery ticket, huh?' I reply.

He ups the stakes: 'Or take up poker.'

Thank the god I totally know doesn't exist for Dr Gupta, who is the one person who can actually laugh at this thing. I guess to him I am lucky. And he has a point: I could be so much worse. I could be one of the kids on Ward 4W with the scarves and the wigs and the odds so long not even one of the losers who hang round Ladbrokes on Argyle Street would stake a dollar on them coming through. So, yeah, if you don't know me, you might just think I'm anaemic or anorexic or whatever the diet of choice is these days at Pennington High. You might even think I'm normal.

So, when I walk out of Dr Gupta's office, I'm feeling lucky. Not out-of-the-woods, throw-away-the-meds lucky, just 'the chemo's worked, it's shrunk, you're not going to bite it anytime soon'. Which is lucky enough not to have to get home and tell Mum to start picking out her hat and canapés for the wake. Lucky enough to risk a drink in the hospital canteen while I work out what I think about Dawse banning Lucas from her La Perla G-string.

Which isn't much, I decide as I suck Pepsi (why, St Michael's, why?) through a plastic straw. It happened two weeks ago according to Lexy, and he still hasn't texted or IM'd or posted some barely cryptic status.

JOANNA NADIN and ANTHONY MCGOWAN

Which is exactly when my phone beeps. Which, like, what the frick-frack? My heart has already taken its second battering of the day before I realise it's probably just Mom keeping tabs or Lexy, one-thumbed typing because her fingers are crossed for major drama.

Or, better, Will. Who Lexy has obviously messaged in her endless need to share the pain.

'You had a lucky escape, doll,' it reads. Will doesn't do LOLs or ROFLS or even ironic smileys in a turban. He says they're a sign of intellectual bankruptcy. But then he wears orange suede loafers, so he's in no position to comment on what is and isn't bankrupt.

Another text pings through. 'Plus he probably has chlamydia and a penchant for cheap perfume so quarantine him, or I'll be forced to come and corral you myself.'

'I should be so lucky,' I type back.

Now Will, he really is one of the winners. Fully in remission and moved away to a new life in Leighton Buzzard (or Leighton Bollocks as he not-even-jokingly refers to it). Which of course Lexy took as a personal affront. Her first GBF, with full-on cancer, and he gets better and promptly pisses off down south, and not even to Shoreditch. As far as she was concerned, he had deliberately lowered her stock value.

He replies. 'You're mine anyway. We'll both wear Dior and adopt seventeen children, which we can pick from the Boden catalogue.'

I smile as I slip the phone back in my bag and suck up the last dregs of now warm pseudo-Coke and wash-back. I should go, I think. Face the music. Or at least the Radio 4 and the rictus smile. And that's when I see him.

Sixteen, or seventeen, I guess. A plastic drink in one hand and tray of trans fats in the other. Just visiting, I think. Either that or he's got a real death wish. Bowel disease, maybe. Or heart failure. But then I figure it's probably just me who takes such deep satisfaction in defying my mother's endless macrobiotic diet plans and vitamin water, so I start on round two (*ding ding*), which is: who is he visiting? And I've just got it down to a confirmed bachelor (i.e. gay) uncle with a tropical disease he's picked up in Goa, when I realise he's looking at someone across the room and smiling.

And that someone isn't a gay uncle, or a straight aunt, or even some pallid and sickly girlfriend.

That someone is me.

MATTHEW

Friday

I was in the queue for McDonald's and I sort of looked around, like you do, not really taking anything in, just letting your eye slip over things. Then my eye got itself caught, like when you snag your jeans on a barbed wire fence, and there was a shock to it as if the barb had gone through into the flesh.

She was sitting by herself, staring at nothing. And that was hard, because there was something wherever you looked: grey-faced relatives of sick people; gaudy signs for the fast-food joints; rampaging toddlers streaming snot and rage; tired hospital workers in loose green pants. But somehow she had bored a tunnel of nothing through it all, made a zone of emptiness, and put her face to it.

It took me a couple of seconds to understand exactly what I was seeing. Her hair was a bit of a mess, and there was a lot of it to be messy. I couldn't even say properly what colour it was. Brown missed it by a mile, but it wasn't blonde either. It was a sort of golden grey. Dirty blonde? Is that it? I don't know. I've never really got my head straight on the words for hair. And her clothes. I didn't really understand them, either.

She didn't look like any of the girls at school. She wasn't a goth or emo or chav. But nor was she one of those girls who aren't anything, you know the ones with flat shoes and glasses who are good at French and maths. She was definitely *something*, but the something she was didn't fit into any category that I knew. It was almost as if she'd invented her own look, or rampaged into the past to steal it. Different layers. A black dress. Sounds boring, but this wasn't a boring dress. It was like some kind of shadow. Not evil but, I don't know, like it came from some place beyond good and evil. Shit, no, that makes her sound like a goth, and she wasn't any kind of goth that I recognised. Then I don't know, some sort of a silken thing floating over the top. Then over the back of the chair I saw the collar of a coat in pale fur. No, fake fur, had to be. But that dress. Nothing fake about that. Like it was made of bone. Something held tight within. Like a maze. Was there a way in?

But I didn't think much about her clothes or her hair, because what got me – the barb, the splinter, the glass – was that face. It should have been all wrong. Everything was too big. Her eyes, her nose, her mouth – especially that mouth. It was so wide, and it curved up at the ends as if she were smiling, even though I could see that she wasn't smiling, no not smiling at all. A dolphin mouth.

And in that moment of seeing her – not even a second, but some tiny fragment of a second, I knew all kinds of things. I knew that it was a face that I'd been looking for without realising it. Seeking it in other faces, in all the usual shit of clouds, stars, whatever. I knew that it was the face that had been created for me. No: wrong way round. It was the face that I had been created for. But I also knew that there was something fatal in that face. And I knew that something terrible would come of this.

I don't know why I thought that. Maybe it's because of me, what's in *my* head. Maybe it's because that – I mean the feeling of tragedy and doom – is just always part of this feeling. And I didn't want to give it, the feeling, a name – the obvious name – because I knew that it was stupid. But also true.

Last year in English, Miss Standish read out a poem to us. Everyone fancies Miss Standish, so we all listened, instead of just talking and fighting. The poem was called 'Leda and the Swan'. It was about how the Greek god Zeus disguised himself as a swan and did *it* with a girl called Leda. Miss Standish had to explain it to the class, which made them all . . . well you can imagine the racket. Animal noises, whoops and stuff. Jango did a sort of impression, I mean of a swan *doing it*, and it was one of the funniest things I've ever seen, with his arms flapping and the whole middle of him thrusting in and out, and even his neck seemed to grow long, like a swan, and he made this noise, a sort of frustrated whine, because everyone knows that swans don't really make noises, and this got the frustration of wanting to make a noise when you're doing it but not being able to.

And I was laughing with everyone else, but I was still thinking about the poem, and the point of it – that this thing they did, the swan-god and the girl, ended up with a burning city and dead heroes and horses with their guts spilling out.

I can't remember who wrote the poem, or any of the actual words, and I didn't let anyone know that I thought it was amazing, but I did.

And now I was looking at this face, and I could see the smoke from the burning city and smell the blood of the horses.

Except, no, that was just the shit burger. Because while all this was in my head I'd got to the front of the queue, and ordered and paid with the fake pound coins in my pocket.

I'd been hungry, but now, when I looked down at the filth on my tray, my hunger was gone the way a fox goes when you glimpse it by the bins at night, and it sees you, and then it slips into nothing before you've had time to breathe. And the space of the hunger was filled with embarrassment.

I thought about the girl, thought about what she'd think of the tray full of dead grease. She just wasn't a burger kind of girl. A vegan, I reckoned, from the strange, alien look of her. Or maybe she just ate sushi. That would be a dolphin thing. Or she lived off nothing but the smell of flowers, the way butterflies do. So I walked it over to one of the bins they have, the ones with the flapping door, slid my filth into the black throat and stacked the tray on top with the others, making the pile wobble like a drunken accordion.

And then, still not really thinking, I walked over to her table.

Why? Was it in spite of the blood and smoke, or because of them?

It didn't matter. Suddenly I was right there, looking down at her, and she was looking up at me. And her face didn't have any kind of expression on it, hardly even surprise, and I realised that even if she had filled up my consciousness the way helium fills a balloon, I still didn't really exist for her at all. I was just a shape stealing her light and air.

SOPHIA

Friday

Like I said, of all the things I don't believe in, love at first sight is up there in the top five. The thing is, it's not even 'at first sight' that's on shaky ground here. Maybe I don't believe in love at all. Because whatever I had with Lucas so wasn't it. At the beginning I think I just liked that he liked me. And at the end I just thought no one else would like me again.

But even in the good bits I didn't once look at him across the body-packed, sweaty dance floor at Jimmy's, or his straight-out-of-*Elle-Decoration* bedroom, or a crowded, boiled-food-smelling canteen and feel this ... strangeness. This warmth. This ... this ... recognition? Is that what this is?

Maybe that's all this is, I think. Maybe I know him from school. From the ranks of Hollister hounds that trail Lucas like he's hunt master or fox. Or the tortured wannabe poets that slouch along the wood-panelled corridors like the world weighs so heavy on their seventeen-year-old shoulders, *The Catcher in the Rye* sticking pointedly out the back pockets of their skinnies.

But this boy doesn't fit in either picture. His clothes don't try to say anything; they don't need to. Jeans. Black jacket. A

T-shirt. It's the sort of T-shirt that should have had a band on it, but there's nothing. A void. Maybe he isn't into music. So there goes the shared love of eighties Manchester indie. And I don't know where he belongs, or who with. Will would say— Oh, frick-frack Will. And the obvious railroads in, complete with bells and whistles and a can-can chorus. He's gay, I think. Of course. Because my life is not directed by John Hughes. Or even whoever it is who mistakenly dedicates their life to bringing the Hallmark-quote wonder that is Nicholas Sparks to the big screen. It's some straight-to-DVD eye-rolling farce.

Only not of course. Because he just doesn't look . . . gay. I mean, his hairstyle isn't one. His shoes are just . . . shoes. They're not some statement, on fashion or anything. 'We don't all go round advertising our life partner preference with quality footwear,' Will said once. Only as I said, Will wears orange loafers, and his last boyfriend, Caleb, had a pair of custom Docs with pink skulls and crossbones glue-gunned on the sides, which kind of negates that point.

He's still looking at me. Into me, even. Like, even if I don't have a goddamn clue who he is, he seems to know who I am. Or wants to know who I am? I am so not good at this. I wish Will were here. Lexy even. Although I'm pretty sure what she'd say. Take your pick from:

1. This is totally like *Romeo and Juliet*.
2. This is totally like any Brontë novel.

3. This is totally like, oh, you know, the one with the guy from *Gossip Girl* and thingummy with the tits.

But it's not like *Romeo and Juliet* or a Brontë novel or the one with the guy and the girl. It's not even like the farce. Nope, then it turns into the made-for-TV afternoon special it really is. You know the kind: mothers searching for the kid they just had to give up at birth only to find out they're on the kidney wait list and, oh, what do you know, the mother's a perfect match – the trash that takes up the tear-jerking slack in a schedule otherwise devoted to shopping and reality shows. Because his eyes drop from me. He looks down at his tray, and then away, off to the far left. He thought I was some-one else, I think. Some girl he was meeting. Or one that died, maybe. He thought for one brilliant, shining minute that I was her. Only I'm not. I'm me. And he's disappointed. And well, who wouldn't be? I wish I were someone else about 99.9 per cent of the time.

Only then the Channel 5 special segues back into farce again because, get this, he walks over to the bin and tips the whole lot – burger, drink, whatever other greaseproof-wrapped parcels of pure, palate-pleasing joy he's got – straight in.

I can hear Lexy in my head. 'Oh. My. GOD. He's anorexic. Or bulimic. Or BOTH.' And then, 'Or mental. He's off the psych wing. It's, like, totally . . .'

And then she lists a whole primetime schedule of back-to-back black-and-white weepies. But it's not any of these. It's not like anything I've seen before. Because then he clatters the tray on to the stack on top, and turns back towards me with this look of fear and joy and pure, roll-the-dice-and-go-for-it determination. And I think he's not gay or anorexic or depressed. He's just a boy taking a chance.

'Mother of all that is holy,' says the wannabe-Catholic (it's just so much sexier than agnostic) Lexy in my head.

Only Lexy's not here. I am. And he's walking towards me. Me. Not an uncle or a boyfriend or some other girl, dead or alive. Me. And, mother of all that is holy, he's going to speak.

MATTHEW

Friday

'Is, er, anyone sitting here?' I said, the dumbest thing you can say, the dumbest thing anyone has ever said.

I read something on the internet once about how you chat up girls, and one of the things it said was that you should never ask a question like that. You should make a statement, be challenging, get their interest by being mischievous. But I hadn't done any of those things. I may as well just have unfurled a big banner with a finger pointing towards me, and 'LOSER' written on it in purple paint.

And she could have said at least eight different cutting things back, putting me down, ripping the piss, making me feel smaller than an atom. 'If I throw a stick, will you leave?' That sort of thing.

And she waited a beat or two, so that I thought it was coming, and I was doing that thing where you put on a hard face, while the middle of you, the inside of you, is turning to sludge. But what she said . . . it was . . . *kind*.

'Not yet.'

It took me a second or two to realise that she hadn't told me to fuck off.

Not yet.

No one sitting there *yet*, she meant.

She meant that there could be someone sitting there, *soon*.

Someone that was *me*.

And I was looking at her face the whole time, and I saw now that it wasn't blank, it was just that the stuff going on there was too subtle for a kid like me to get without working it out, like a maths problem, or one of those poems that doesn't make sense until you read the notes. And now I could see the little lines of amusement around her eyes, and the faintest movement at the corner of her mouth.

And my brain was sort of stuck there, and I might have spent the rest of my life looking at that face, finding new things to be amazed about each day, each week, each month, each year.

But then some still-just-about-sane part of my brain realised that I was looking like a weirdo, I mean just standing there and not saying or doing anything. And looking like a weirdo is the thing I least most want to do, partly because it's my biggest fear – I mean looking like a weirdo.

So I sat down. But not until I'd pulled out the chair in a clunky, uncool way, making a clatter and then a scrape like nails on a blackboard, although there haven't been blackboards at school since my dad was there.

But suddenly I was at her level, just a few centimetres from her, and I could smell her, I really could, smell the shampoo in her hair and the soft aroma from her clothes.

And now I was here I couldn't just go on saying nothing. It had to be something funny. Maybe something about hospitals. Doctor, I can't feel my legs. That's because we had to amputate your arms. No, that's crap. Hospitals, huh, these people are sick. No, that's not even a joke. Man goes for an examination.

'You've only got ten to live,' says the doctor.

'Ten what?'

'Nine . . .'

That's sort of funny but not . . . right . . .

And then I was speaking.

'You look like a dolphin.'

Had I really said that?

Oh Jeesus.

'I mean your mouth. Or a swan.'

Oh, god, no. Why hadn't I just sat at another table and ogled her, and then walked home and thought about her and hated myself for chickening out? Because that would have been better than this.

But something was happening to her dolphin mouth. The smile that wasn't a smile was turning into a smile that was a smile.

'Well, I haven't had that one before. But you have to decide which it is. I mean, I can't have a mouth like a dolphin, and a mouth like a swan. Anyway, that'd be a beak, wouldn't it?'

Her voice was even better than the rest of her. She didn't sound like any of the girls I knew. She sounded like she was

JOANNA NADIN and ANTHONY MCGOWAN

in a play, or on the telly. Not just posh, but dark and oh, I don't know, like something you'd pour on your food, I mean to make it better. It was so beautiful I could barely make out the words in the music.

Mouth. Beak. Focus.

'Oh, god, I'm sorry. I didn't mean to say that out loud. I was just over there, and I looked at you, and I thought *dolphin*, and then I thought *swan*. I haven't, I mean, I don't usually . . .'

'I can tell.'

Still she was smiling. This was going so much better than it should have done. I ought to have been on my way down, smoke and flames filling the cockpit, the fields spiralling up to meet me. Scrabbling to open the canopy. But it's stuck, and now my hands are on fire, and the parachute has opened up inside the damn thing, and I'm suffocating as well as burning.

It was my turn again. The internet thing had said never ask ordinary questions, because that puts you in the wrong zone. What would be an ordinary question in these circumstances? Why are you here? Are you sick? Do you have any interesting diseases? Is your granny dying? I could see how they were either offensive or boring or boringly offensive.

What's your name? That would be harmless, but also boring. Guess. Guess her name. Rumpelstiltskin.

'What?'

Oh, jeez . . . I didn't really say Rumpelstiltskin out loud, did I? I didn't think so. I think it was just that my lips moved.

Which was almost as bad. No, maybe worse. If I'd said Rumpelstiltskin then I would have had to explain it, and that would have got us talking. She might have found it cute, but I was just opening and closing my lips like a fucking fish. And not one of the smart fish.

'I was wondering what your name was.'

'Oh. It's Sophia. People call me Soph.'

That was so easy. She'd just told me, like it was nothing. Now I knew her name. Don't Native Americans think you own their soul if you know their name? No, that's somebody else, and it's not names, it's photos. But that didn't matter. I'd just invented a new culture, a culture of me, and now I owned her soul. Except that was a bit creepy. Better not to mention it to Sophia. Soph. Sophia. Soph.

I could see that she was looking at me in a new way. I was supposed to do something. I needed someone here giving me instructions, someone with words to spare. Jango . . . Oh, Jesus, no, not him. She'd have already called the police or hospital security, or the guys from the mad ward, if there was one.

No, it was me. I mean what my name was. Is.

'I'm Matthew,' I said. 'Matt, usually.'

'Who's sick?' she said, her face back to that neutral half smile that wasn't a smile.

I was still being gormless, and it took me a second to remember again that we were in a hospital.

'Oh, you mean, why am I here? I'm having a mild heart attack.'

JOANNA NADIN and ANTHONY MCGOWAN

It was the first thing I'd said that was meant to be even a bit funny. Except I realised that it wasn't just funny. Heart attack. Heart breaking. Love hearts.

Almost invisibly, the last tiny bits of smile left her face, the way the warm goes when you leave the kitchen door open.

'Oh, that's a shame,' she said, deadpan. 'Except, well you're in luck.'

'How's that?'

'I can do CPR.'

I was out of my depth. I knew it. She knew it.

'Don't you need those electrical things? The wadyacallits . . . paddles.'

'I do it old style. Acoustic . . .'

I'd been assuming that Sophia was my age, or maybe a bit older, but now I wondered . . . 'That what you're doing here, then? Are you, like, a nurse?'

She shook her head. 'Just visiting.'

And then her face changed again, and I did for a second think she was going to call for help, but it was just the beginnings of a laugh.

'Sorry, Matthew . . . you said Mathew, didn't you? I don't know what I'm doing, really. I've had kind of a funny day. But, I . . .'

And then her eyes moved from me, drifting away over my shoulder, and I thought I'd just lost her interest, even though I was sitting near enough to her to reach out and stroke her face.

'You!'

The voice, hash and shrill, came a moment before the hard tap on my shoulder. I turned round to see a woman in an orange uniform and a man in a polyester shirt and brown trousers and orange tie standing behind me. The voice belonged to the woman.

'This is him,' she said to the man. 'He bought a meal, and paid in the pounds.'

The man, who looked like he'd rather have been some-where else, held out his hand.

'Recognise these, sonny?' he said, without any enthusiasm.

I shrugged. But already I could feel a blush coming over me like a huge hot cloud of burning dust.

'Looks like money to me.'

My voice cracked a little. I could feel my back grow clammy. I began to curse Jango and his fucking scams.

'These are all fake. See, you can scratch the gold colour off.'

The man used the edge of one coin to score the surface of another. Underneath the gold you could see the dull silver of the soft base metal.

'I don't know anything about it,' I said.

But I did.

The deal was this: Jango got the coins from someone he knew for thirty pence each. They were totally shitty fakes, and it was hard to get even the most stupid shopkeeper to take them. So he used to hang around Sainsbury's and go up to people who were putting their shopping trolleys back in the conga line, and say, 'Can I have your trolley?' and he'd give them a pound, a fake one, and people would usually take it, and not check. Then he'd wait till they'd cleared off, and he'd put the trolley back, getting a good pound out. It's sort of money laundering for cretins. It takes all day to change your money, and you could probably earn more by just looking on the ground for lost pennies, let alone getting a real job in Nando's or wherever. But, anyway, Jango, obviously, couldn't be bothered doing it all by himself. So he'd either beg us to do a few for him, or just sell the coins on to us for fifty pence. Which was why I'd had a pocketful of them.

'Sorry,' I mumbled. 'I didn't know.'

'How could you not know?' said the girl in the uniform. 'You had six of them. You don't just have six fakes on a fluke.'

'Where did you get them from?' asked the man.

'Petrol station,' I said. I don't know why.

'Petrol station?' The man now looked a bit more suspicious. He could probably tell that I wasn't driving about the place in a Mercedes Coupé. 'Look we're going to have to contact the p—'

'Here,' said the girl. I mean *my* girl. I mean Sophia. Soph. Sophia.

She was in her bag. In her purse. She took out a fiver and a pound coin and thrust them into the hands of the man.

He looked down at the money, and back at Sophia, and then at the hard-faced girl who, even though she was only a burger flipper while he was the manager, was clearly the dominant one.

'Don't take that,' said the girl. 'He's a . . . what is it . . . thief. A smuggler. No, I mean a forger. One of them.'

But the man was already wandering off, staring at the good money in his palm. The girl followed, but looked over her shoulder at me and mouthed something obscene that I didn't catch.

'Thanks,' I said, not knowing how to feel or what sort of voice to use. This hadn't gone according to plan. Not that I'd had a plan. I mean, if I'd had one, it wouldn't have looked much like this. 'I'll pay you b—'

'You better get out of here,' she said to me, her mouth twitching again, like a dying fluorescent tube, going from smile to not-smile, smile to not-smile. 'That woman's on her phone. She's probably calling the Feds. What with you being a big-time forger and all.'

'But what about you?'

'I'll be OK. I don't even know you. I've never seen you before. You could be anyone.'

'But you paid the bill . . .'

'Because I took pity on you.'

I knew that this was meant to be the conversation she'd be having with the police – if they even bothered turning up, which I doubted. But it felt too close to the truth to be comfortable.

'But to pay you back . . . I'll need to . . . can I have your number?'

41

She looked at me carefully. The smile light wasn't flickering any more. It had stopped. At *off*.

Then without saying anything she started to write on a napkin. She folded it in half, reached across the table and put it in my hand – pretty much as she had done to the doofus with her money.

'Run,' she said, 'before it's too late.'

I got up. I'd spent the entire encounter not knowing what to do, and that wasn't changing anytime soon. I needed a line, something crisp to leave her with. And she looked at me, as if she was expecting it, too. But still, I had nothing. Not any words, anyway.

So then I did it. The thing I'd been waiting all my life to do. I leant across the table, put my right hand on her left cheek and kissed her on the lips.

SOPHIA

Friday

When you're dying, or almost dying, or even just possibly heading that way in the fairly distant, the first thing everyone's just chewing their gel nails waiting for you to do (apart from get God or start wearing wigs) is name them in the last will and testament. Which, in case you're wondering, Lexy gets the Dior heels even though she'll never squeeze her size sixes into them further than her big toe, my annotated *Gatsby*, because that's the only way she's going to scrape through English lit, and my iTunes catalogue, by way of an education. You're welcome.

But the second thing? Write a freaking bucket list. A one to ten, in no particular order, of swimming with dolphins (which we will so come back to in a minute), shaking hands with an outsized mouse at Disneywherever (though Paris is kind of cheapskate, but thanks for the offer, Aunty Fiona), and, the biggie, the pinnacle of last breath wishes: falling in love/getting laid (depending on gender/age/tendency to watch too much daytime TV). Because, who wouldn't want their violins and roses moment when they've got tubes hanging out of their arm and possibly pee hole and can't even keep a bagel down?

Only the thing is, when you're actually there, in that bracket of potential untimely exit, dolphins and Disney aren't really the top of any list. Not for me anyway. Lexy said I was crazy. That I had to ride a camel or fly to Paris or at least have an orgasm without the aid of my own right hand. But when I tried to think about it, I realised it wasn't about the grand gestures. It was the small stuff that counted, at least during chemo. The being able to actually digest a Yorkshire pudding. The reading more than four pages of a novel, or even a trashy gossip mag, and not falling asleep, or forgetting what it even is you're reading in the first place. The watching Thom try to fit a square brick into a round hole for the bazillionth time.

Oh, did I mention that? I have a kid brother. He's three. Born ten months after diagnosis and you don't need to be a mathlete to work out that my mom was lining up a replacement or some kind of walking talking organ donor. She swears it was an accident but, believe me, there is nothing accidental in my mom's life. I'm pretty sure she planned the birth around my bouts of chemo to keep the vomit level in the house down to a minimum. She must have been pretty disappointed when Thom came out and we didn't even share genitals let alone a blood group. Plus, what was she expecting him to donate? His brain? But that's not really the point.

The point is that love – or sex – didn't figure. Not after Lucas. I just didn't . . . care enough. Not any more. I figured that I was lucky to be here at all and I'd take roast potatoes over true romance. Love was uncharted territory. Here be dragons, I thought. And I've never been much of a dragon slayer.

Only I swear, in these two seconds, three, however long his lips are on mine, I get it. I get what Lexy's always chasing. I get what the films are always selling. And I get that whole Heathcliff thing, even if he definitely looks like a Matthew. And some kind of cluster bomb goes off inside my royally messed-up brain and all these thoughts are scatter-gunning out. Like:

1. Did I brush my teeth this morning?
2. Why did he have six fake pound coins? Is his dad some kind of small-time big-dreaming gangster? Because Lexy would so love that.
3. Lexy would love this. She'd say it totally *is Romeo and Juliet*, even if he does say I have a dolphin mouth.
4. What the frick-frack is a dolphin mouth?
5. Dolphins can't do this with their mouths.
6. His dad must be a really bad gangster though because seriously who tries to fake pound coins with model paint?
7. And he doesn't look like the kid of a gangster because nothing he's wearing is fake. Nothing about him is fake.
8. So who *is* this boy?
9. And how dare he just kiss me? He doesn't even know me.
10. But don't let him stop. Not yet.

Only, somehow, impossibly, at exactly the same time, in those same two seconds, everything halts – all the words and the thoughts and the smell of hospital food and the small talk that hides the big truth – and it all shrinks down to those few centimetres, those tiny touchpoints where his fingers hold my face, and his lips meet mine. And I can't hear or smell or see any more (because, oh yes, I close my eyes); all I can do is taste (gum – Doublemint) and feel (my heart skipping a beat; no, that stuff is not made up). And, oh sweet baby Jeebus, it feels good.

It's two seconds of perfect. Three, tops.

And then it's over. Because he pulls away, tries and fails to smile, and does exactly what I told him to do. He runs.

And I wish to – I don't know – the Wizard of Oz – that I hadn't said that. But more than that, I swear, hand on heart, on my own messed-up, in-the-balance life, that I wish what I'd written down on the napkin was my actual honest-to-dog phone number.

Not some kind of *Scooby Doo* X-chase.

MATTHEW

Friday

I'd forgotten how to walk. I vaguely recalled that it involved moving your arms and legs, and so I tried that. It might have been OK if I'd had an hour to get the hang of it out in the desert or in the middle of a field, with just a cactus or a cow to miss, but here there were chairs and tables and other people's feet to get past, and so I crunched and clattered and stumbled my way out of there with all the grace of a fat clown riding a drunk moose. And even when I made it out of the canteen I was still lost in the hospital, and it was like the sort of crazy house you get at crap funfairs, with slanted floors and skewed walls, and mad mirrors that give you back to yourself as a giant or dwarf or fat man or bug-eyed alien.

But at last I was bursting out through the swinging doors of Mickey's into a new world. Hadn't it been raining when we'd come up the hill? Hadn't there been grey clouds low enough to stick a damp tongue in your ear? Well now the universe was so bright it looked like it was made out of fireworks and lasers, and my mind was dazzled by it, as if I'd been living underground for years.

I couldn't believe what I'd just done. Even going up to her was out of my comfort zone. The truth was, my comfort zone was more or less entirely limited to what was in my head. Outside that, everything was a sharp stick, with shit on the end of it. And I'd walked over and talked to her, like it was the kind of thing I did every day. Not just that. I'd bent down and kissed her. Kissed her. Bent down and kissed her. On the lips. On her human lips.

My legs were working better now, and I began walking back down the long hill. But it was a kind of walking that was dangerously close to skipping. Which wasn't a good idea in this part of town. Or any part of any town. And thinking about it made me forget again how to move. So I stopped, right in the middle of the pavement, like furniture dumped off the back of a van and left there to rot.

Then I remembered the piece of paper she'd given me. The piece of paper now damp in my sweating hand.

I looked at it, smoothed it out, looked at it again. And now I was remembering the way she'd written it – I'd hardly noticed it at the time, but it must have got in my head somehow. I saw that pen of hers. A heavy silver fountain pen. It looked old. And her fingers, and her nails. Clever fingers. Perfect nails – painted, but short, not talons, but not bitten stumps, either. And now I tried to focus on her writing. Confident, clear. Not like my scrawl, scratchy and angular, like someone tracing around static electricity.

Numbers.

For a second I forgot what they were, and thought it was some complex code, each number meaning a letter or a feeling or a touch. One for I love you, two for a caress. Jeez, I was effing nuts. Numbers. Telephone number. That was all.

But not all.

In place of two of the numbers were Xs.

07737 7X51X8?

I gawped at the figures, trying to compute the significance of this. And then it hit me. She was blowing me off. Without those two numbers I could never call her. It was just mockery. Piss taking. No, not even that. Piss taking would at least have involved some active thought. But she was just shooing me away, like you would a fly or a sore-covered trash dog. She'd seen this massive loser standing in front of her, and found the most efficient way to get rid of me.

Except for the kiss.

That didn't fit in with her just getting rid of me. I wasn't an expert on kissing, but it didn't strike me that she hated it. But I could have been wrong. Like I said, I was no expert. In fact she was precisely the third person I'd ever kissed. The first was Amanda Huggins. It was in Year 6. Amanda was famous for liking to kiss. She'd stand in a corner of the playground, and boys would go over to her – sometimes literally forming an orderly queue – and then get thirty seconds of lip action. I got goaded into joining that queue one day, by some other kids saying I was gay if I didn't. When it was my turn Amanda looked up at me, and I closed my eyes and lowered my head.

It seemed I'd been lowering my head for an awfully long time, and I still hadn't made contact, so I opened my eyes, and saw that she'd moved her head, so her lips were next to my ear.

'I don't want to,' she said. 'I've got sore lips.'

Then, at going-home time, I was putting my coat on by my peg in the corridor, and suddenly she was there, and she sort of made a little leap, like a salmon, and kissed me, and then she was away down the corridor, and she said, 'My lips don't hurt any more,' as she ran, without even turning around. I thought she might kiss me again after that, but she never did, and nor did she let the other boys kiss her any more, but I don't know why.

The second time was last year, at Corky's sister's party. Corky's sister is in the year above, and she isn't like Corky. She's good looking, blonde, cool, and in with the in-crowd. Corky was allowed to bring one friend, and he didn't even tell Jango about the party, which was a good idea, because he'd have crashed it like a plane flying into a tower block. So I was there with Corky, skulking in corners, trying to get hold of some of the booze that was going round, maybe even getting a bit high on the odd whiff of spliff.

And then I found myself on this baggy old sofa, and the bagginess of it meant that the person sitting next to me was sort of slumped against me, and I realised that it was a girl. And the next thing I knew we were snogging. Well, I think that's what you'd have to call it. I wasn't even sure at times which part of her face I was on. But it was . . . nice. I could feel her hair falling on my face, and she made little noises – soft noises. She tasted of cider and another sweet taste that I couldn't figure, until I realised it was cherry lip gloss. And I was going to talk to her about cherry-flavoured things, about how they're much nicer than actual cherries, so they must have got the formula just right, the artificial cherry formula, I mean. Unlike banana-flavoured things, where the formula's all wrong, and they taste much worse than actual bananas. But I never got to say any of that stuff, because she stopped kissing me, and said into my ear, 'Get me some drink.'

So I hauled myself out of the sofa, like someone trying to get out of quicksand, and went to find some booze. It took me a couple of minutes to locate a can that wasn't being swigged out of or used as an ashtray, and when I got back, the sofa was occupied by some other kids, not my girl. I wandered around trying to find her, but I didn't know her name and couldn't remember what she looked like, because I'd been close up and had my eyes shut most of the time. I couldn't even find Corky. So I went home.

So that was me and kissing.

Until today.

Not much, but it was enough for me to know that she had definitely kissed me back. Not going at it like she was eating a burger, like the girl at the party, but enough to know, like I said, that she didn't hate it. There was even a tiny hint of tongue. No, maybe I imagined that. You can imagine things, when you're kissing. In fact that might be the best part of it, the imagining. So maybe there was no tongue, but there was something. Something in the softness of it. She hadn't tasted of cherries or any other kind of fruit. Fruit-flavoured lips were for kids. She wasn't really a kid at all. What she tasted of was lipstick – proper lipstick. And then the other taste. The taste of . . . person. The human taste of the human mouth. A human mouth mingled with my human mouth.

Oh god.

So she kissed me back, definitely kissed me back.

Then why the blow-off with the numbers? I looked at the napkin again.

07737 7X51X8?

And then I did some basic maths. If I replaced the Xs with numbers, how many tries would it take me to get the right one? For a few seconds I was thinking thousands, millions even . . . Then I got my brain working. Ten possibilities for the first number, ten for the second. Ten times ten. One hundred. Max. That was so doable. And I realised why she'd done it. It was a test. And so perfectly judged. Having to dial maybe a hundred numbers would put off some chancer. And a thousand numbers would put off almost anyone else. She had thrown me a lifeline – but one I'd have to reach for.

Well, I was all for reaching.

Somehow I'd got walking again. Faster now, flying, almost. Flying home. Still the air was so bright it seemed to fizz like Coke. I'd been *outside* myself, like a blurry after-image, my body and my soul a few centimetres apart, but suddenly I was back in my body, fitting it properly, and I could feel every cell, every molecule singing and zinging. Even the people I went past looked good. Gone were the grey faces, the hunched backs, the bad feet. These were beautiful people, floating through a beautiful world. They looked like ballerinas doing that tiptoe thing, moving without trying. No, like skaters, when you see them gliding over the ice, and you can't work out how they're doing it, how they're getting their . . . what is it? *Propulsion.*

Except it wasn't them moving but me. And now the world was utterly still, and I was the only thing moving, because they were frozen, and I was liquid metal, flowing all over and through them.

My god this felt good. This just-having-kissed-someone feeling. Not some little kid who kissed anyone. Not some drunk girl at a party who didn't know who I was. It was this girl, this mystery, this thing of pure thought, this . . .

'Oy! Fucknuts, stop.'

SOPHIA

Friday

It's not like I haven't been kissed before. By no less than four different boys. Which I admit is pretty pitiful in the Pennington rankings, but at least nudges me above the relegation zone where the What Would Jesus Do? squad are destined to squander the rest of their high school days. My paramours were, in strict chronological order:

1. Brett Meyer the Third (not even joking), under the bleachers on a Massachusetts baseball diamond aged eleven. And if you think that sounds *My Girl* dreamy, you can stop right now because his braces got caught in mine and the school nurse had to untangle us with a pair of pliers. So it was kind of a no-brainer when Brett dumped me the next day for Rachida Stone who had perfect molars and a pair of C cups already on the way.

2. Ollie Pitt-Weston, inside Lexy's airing cupboard, on her thirteenth birthday, during her 'seven minutes in heaven' phase, inspired by whatever teen movie was her crack that week. But unless heaven means getting

your tonsils probed by eels, then that was five minutes of pure Lenor-scented hell.

3. Jonty Pitt-Weston, in Lexy's bathroom on her fourteenth birthday. Yes, he is Ollie's twin brother. Yes, he is similarly possessed of the aquatic tongue. And no, I am not proud of that one.

So when Lucas came along, with no orthodontic apparatus and an apparently normal tongue, is it any surprise I let him kiss me again? And again. Only by then I was sixteen and he moved on to second base so quickly, and then third, that the kissing got kind of forgotten. And even when we did, it was never like I was just kissing Lucas. I was kissing his football position, his SATS scores, the A & F jacket that marked him out as someone. I was kissing what he did and where he ranked. But with Matthew – god, Matthew; even thinking his name makes me jolt with it – with Matthew, there was no history to kiss. It was just about him, and me and that moment.

Only I don't even know who 'him' is.

Which is crazy. I mean, I just don't do this kind of thing – kiss a total stranger, let alone in public, in a frick-fracking hospital canteen. Not like Lexy, who kisses frogs on a regular basis – Millwall Dino outside McDonald's; some carpet fitter's assistant called Lee who came, literally, when her mum was getting lipo; the emo kid behind the counter in HMV – in the hope one of them turns out to be Prince Charming, which they never do, just another Buttons or, worse, some villain with a pocketful of barely legal highs instead of a moustache to twirl. Not that Matthew's one of them. Or even a frog, Jesus. The point is, I don't do this. I don't take risks. I don't even exceed the stated dose of Vitamin C.

'What if there's no tomorrow?' Lexy always says. What if there is? I think. Because the scans say there will be, and a day after that and a day after that, so why take a chance on five minutes of fumbling and disappointment.

Only today I closed my eyes. Literally. I jumped. I could have pushed him off, I could have slapped him, but I didn't. Because for some reason – hormones, desperation, or a butterfly flapping in the rainforest if Lexy had her way – today it felt like my one chance. Like, what if those three seconds were my freaking Disney True Love's Kiss? What if he is my frog prince after all?

The bus hits a pothole and jerks me back to planet earth. I stare through the scratched and smeared window at the redbrick rows and the last of the shoppers dragging Primark bags across pavements that are paved with dog shit, not gold. This is the north of England, I think. We can't even get a week of decent sunshine and I'm looking for an all-American Disney happy ending.

Not that there's much chance of that anyway because I DIDN'T GIVE HIM MY NUMBER.

What the frick-frack was that about? It's not like I've OD'd on Sherlock or Bond, or go geocaching on Sundays or any other mathlete crap. I mean, how many permutations are there? Ten? A hundred? A thousand? And what are the chances of him trying even one of them? How hard would it have been to write the truth?

Will would say I was deliberately sabotaging my own happiness because my damaged ego is telling me I don't deserve any better, which is basically down to my mother's perpetual disappointment (everything comes down to our mothers, according to Will). Lexy would say, 'Oh. My. God. This is so *Cinderella*. Because if he works it out it's like he rode the whole kingdom to find you.'

Which it so isn't.

Only maybe she has a point, the Lexy in my head. I mean, maybe that's why I did it. Some kind of warped mind game? To see if he thinks I'm really (cue L'Oréal hair toss) worth it? To make sure he wasn't pulling some pathetic spotl billy stunt and doing it for a bet or a pity fuck or a joke?

In which case Dr Gupta got it way wrong and my head really is screwed up after all. But that thought doesn't stop me checking my phone with a level of nausea that has been known to bring up my entire stomach contents in less than three seconds.

Shit. Two missed calls, both from Mom. And three messages from Lexy:

CALL ME, BEEYATCH

SERIOUSLY CALL ME

Y U NOT ANSRING? BAD???

I can't help thinking those question marks stand for hope.

I deal with Mom first. She picks up before the first bar of 'Build Me Up Buttercup' (don't even go there) has played out. 'What did he say?'

Hey, hi, Soph, how are you? I think. 'I'm fine. It's still static,' I say.

'Good. That's good. No, great.' I can hear the 'oh, thank god, no more chemo vomit for another six months' that underpins every word. 'Are you done? I can come pick you up. Thom's asleep but—'

'I'm already on the bus,' I interrupt.

Silence as she pictures the potential diseases or foul language or accents I might be picking up.

'Did you take your meds this morning?'

Well, if I hadn't, the chances are I'd be writhing on the gum-spattered floor of this single decker, wouldn't I? I hear Will's voice in my head and wish I had the balls, even his post-cancer not entirely functioning ones, to say it out loud. Instead of the 'Of course, Mom,' I do manage. Because I don't do drama. I hate it. This thing in my head. And now this . . . this dumbass game of whatever it is I appear to be playing in the pursuit of something I don't even believe in. This isn't me. It's Lexy. This is the kind of crap that Lexy lives for.

This IS the kind of crap that Lexy lives for.

'Listen, Mom. I'm going to be another hour or so,' I say.

'But—'

'Behomefordinnerloveyoubye.'

And I hang up before she can think up a ten-point list of why nots and text my own personal drama queen. Because for once, among all her OMGs and 'like, I KNOW's, Lexy might actually have an answer.

MATTHEW

Friday

I'd completely forgotten about Jango and Corky. Forgotten about that stupid plan. I tried to work out how long it had been since we'd gone our separate ways. Half an hour? An hour? A year?

I turned to see Jango loping towards me. When he's still you wouldn't know about the big shoe. Even at a walk there are times when you can hardly tell. But running makes it larger than life. And there's a tension to it, watching him, I mean. Coming downhill he seems totally out of control. You think he might career off into a tree or a car or just fall flat on his face.

I wondered sometimes if it was the big shoe that made me put up with all Jango's bullshit. His piss-taking, and brow-beating and general madness. And maybe there was something in that. An element of pity. But that was only a small part of it, the limp lettuce in the Big Mac. The meat was something else. The meat was need. Without Jango I was alone. OK, there was Corky, but he mainly lived inside his own head, and you can't have much of a friendship with someone who speaks like he's trying to cough up razor blades. So, yeah, there was a silence in my life, and Jango filled it up with noise. And there was boredom, and Jango is never boring. And to find yourself under the Jangoscope – that way he has of looking into your soul – is, in a weird way, flattering. It makes you seem . . . special.

But there was another part of it. Yeah, I needed Jango, but he needed me, too. And not just the way a cat needs a mouse, but in the way a cripple needs a stick. And when someone needs you, that's almost a stronger glue than you needing them.

Corky was there, too. Not running, just walking, falling further behind. It made him look as if he were shrinking right in front of me, as if he were being zapped with a shrinking ray.

But Jango, he was growing. He was a giant, an ogre chasing me down. The harp in the fairy story had cried out 'Master! Master!' and he was coming for me. And he wasn't slowing down. It was only at the last second I realised that he planned to just crash straight into me, and I braced myself. Even so, I fell heavily back on to the pavement with Jango on top of me. I was winded, and bruised, and it was lucky my head hadn't smashed back on to the pavement.

I'd feared that he was going to be mad, in one of his black moods, because I'd bailed. But Jango was grinning and panting in my face like a big dog.

'Should have been there, Matty boy. It was like some orgy from the last days of the Roman Empire, with all those hotties lying around. They had wine in the drips. They hooked us up – believe me, that is the only way to get wasted! And they fed me and the Corkster with grapes and cumquats and eff knows what else – that right, Corky?'

Corky had just reached us. He helped pull me to my feet, while Jango reassembled himself. We both know it's madness to try to help Jango with anything like that. It riles, no, *enrages* him. I looked at Corky, and he gave me a little shake of the head. There was a lot in it, that shake. And I knew that the mission had not been a success. And yet Jango was as light as helium. That can happen sometimes, with Jango. The things that ought to kick him in the guts tickle him under the chin. And other times, news that should lift him shoots him down.

'What's a cumquat?' I said, partly because I couldn't think of anything else neutral to say, and partly because I had no idea what it might be, and was actually quite interested.

'Little orange. You eat the whole damn thing, skin and all.'

'Yeah, sure,' I said. 'And I suppose the skin's the best bit.'

Jango pulled me round, so our faces were almost touching. His expression was now utterly serious, but I thought it was the seriousness of an actor playing a role.

'Matthew, Matthew,' he said, his voice low and sad and melodious, 'life is going to pass you by, and you are going to die never having tasted a cumquat.'

I still didn't know what a cumquat was, and part of me thought that it was probably a type of vole or something, or maybe a rude thing, but Jango was already striding down the street. It was lucky. If his face had still been in mine I would probably have told him that life wasn't passing me by, that I'd just gone up to a strange girl in the hospital canteen and kissed her in front of a hundred gasping strangers. But it would have been pathetic to jog along behind him, and say it to the back of his long black coat.

When I caught up with him I started to ask him about what had happened on the ward.

A long-fingered hand came up in my face. In fact, the fingers looked long enough to wrap right round my head, if he'd tried.

'Not a word shall I utter. Patient effing confidentiality.'

And such was the grave and sombre tone in which he uttered these words, and so serious was the face from which they came, that the only possible response was to laugh, but it was one of those laughs that begins slowly with a twitch from my eye, that's reflected by a twitch from his, and then moves back and forth between us, each move amplifying the one before it, until our faces explode in hilarity, and we double over, and then fall to our knees, with Corky joining in, but not to the point of hitting the floor.

Yeah, Jango, sometimes you just have to love him.

But I wasn't just laughing at what Jango had said. I was laughing at the whole enterprise, about its absurdity, and about the insane thing that had happened. And just as I had my own reasons for laughing, I guess that Jango might have had too, but only God and Jango knew what they were.

A few minutes later Jango peeled off towards his own street, not looking at us, but just lifting up his arm, and saying, 'Laters.'

Me and Corky carried on for a while.

'You better tell me what happened,' I said. 'I take it you didn't score?'

Corky shook his head. His stammer is never as bad when Jango isn't around. He doesn't get so stuck, endlessly repeating the hard sounds at the beginning, but it still takes him a long time to get each word out. I had to fight the impulse to help him. He doesn't like being helped any more than Jango does.

'W-we got in th-there. And there w-weren't r-really any t-teenagers there. J-just little kids.'

'So what did you do?' I was imagining Jango's scorn, his sneering contempt.

'I w-wanted to go, but Jango m-made m-me stay. Th-there was a k-kid there. M-most of the others had visitors. But he was on his own. Jango went and talked to him. Told him jokes and stuff. Did impressions. Some other kids – the ones who could get out of bed – came over. They were all laughing. I was laughing too. Then the nurse came and asked who we were, and Jango cheeked her off, and she got a n-nark on, so we l-legged it. That's it, really.'

I didn't know what to say to all that. It was surprising, but at the same time it wasn't. I could see it all in my head, despite Corky's trouble getting the story out. I imagined

Jango's routines, his way of making the kids feel special, focusing on each one for a moment or two, finding out the secret thing that could always make them smile. It made *me* smile, now. And then it was Corky's turn to angle away, and I went home.

I had some telephoning to do.

SOPHIA

Friday

You know those weird museums in small towns you get dragged to on Sundays – one part stuffed duck display to two parts Roman coins to four parts random crap? That's Lexy's bedroom. It's half honeytrap – all artfully arranged copies of Anaïs Nin and discarded bras – and half cabinet of wonder. A toy rabbit rides a Magic 8-Ball with a coterie of Bratz dolls and dismembered Barbies watching plastic-eyed and shaven-headed. Her bookshelves burst with everything from Blyton to de Beauvoir. And in the middle of it all sits Lexy at a backlit mirror like she's Marilyn freaking Monroe. And we've done the whole 'you're not dying this month?' scene so we're back on to her, natch.

'Do I look Jewish?' she asks, peering at her nose, actually willing it bigger. This is not the first time she's hoped to insinuate herself into another religion. In Year 8 she went Catholic for two weeks – all crossing herself and planned confessions, thinking guilt and incense would made her more interesting. It's like Will says – she needs drama, and acts like she's been short-changed by having parents who haven't done the decent thing and divorced, or passed on some hereditary disease. It's as if getting the short straw, the fluffy end of the lollipop, would be winning; that in the end only the one who gets dealt the bum hand can take it all. And at that point I wonder if the whole Matthew kiss thing might not be my short straw but the one that breaks the camel's back. I pick up the Magic 8-Ball. Should I tell her? I ask silently in my head, and shake it. 'Outlook doubtful' it tells me.

I put the ball down, and stick a plastic Harry Styles back on top. 'The Jews wouldn't have you,' I reply.

'Whatever.' She drops her hair back down and pouts, pleased with the effect despite the missing ethnicity or illness. Then checks out my dirty Chucks and distinct lack of lip liner. 'You are coming, right?'

'Huh? Where.'

'Er, Sarah Elle Weston's? You know, her seventeenth? Or did you forget?'

I try to remember if I ever knew. I must have done: parties are a hotter topic than possible pervert teachers or Diana Heston's probable implants, and invites as valuable in stock terms as a daddy with an open drinks cabinet or a big brother with a dealer.

'I don't think so. Coming, I mean.'

'Are you on glue? It's Friday night. You're alive. We have to celebrate. Besides, Lucas will be there.'

But Matthew won't, I think. And I'll still be alive tomorrow.

'I'm tired,' I say. The magic words.

'Oh. My. God.' She claps her hands to her mouth. 'I'm, like, so sorry. You should totally sleep. I mean, the stress of it. And you don't want to get worse, and stuff.'

No. But thanks for *that* sparkling thought.

'What should I tell Lucas?'

'Jesus, I don't know . . . I . . . Lexy?'

'What?'

And I almost do it. I almost tell her the whole crazy truth of it. The first feel of his eyes on me, the words, the kiss . . . Jesus, the kiss. Only the way she looks at me – radiating desperation and glee in equal measure – brings me up short.

'Nothing,' I say. 'Doesn't matter.'

'You are SO weird sometimes.'

'Yeah,' I reply. Weirder than you think, I don't add. Because I'm jonesing after a boy I met in a canteen for all of a few minutes, whose dad may or may not be a gangster, who thinks I look like a dolphin and who may turn out to have laid the whole kiss on me for a bet.

'Don't do anything I wouldn't do,' I say as she pushes her breasts up and pulls her top down into optimum eye-catching position.

'Yeah, right,' she says. 'Do I look like a virgin?'

'Hardly.'

She checks herself out in the mirror again. 'You're right,' she says, satisfied. 'God, even *I'd* fuck me.'

So, instead of watching Lexy slut-drop in some Year 10's puddle of puke on the cream shagpile; instead of taking bets as to which one of the first XI she's going to hook up with in the Jacuzzi; instead of watching her work Lucas for me like he's some kind of kid to be won over with the candy-coated promise that the chances of me fitting during sex are, oh, only, five per cent, I sit under a poster of Zepp and play six degrees of Kevin Bacon. I put the name Matthew into a Facebook search, figuring someone he knows must know someone I know. That somehow our mutual 'friends' will put paid to this whole X-marks-the-spot treasure hunt and I can just message him and say 'Hey.' But there are twenty-nine pages of Matthews with mutual friends. And not one of them is mine.

Mine?

Not even close.

'Shit,' I say, then add a silent sorry in case Thom is within earshot. Because that was supposed to be my golden ticket, my key to the treasure chest, my Enigma code. And it was as lame as his fake coins.

So it's all down to him now. And, as I realise that, I feel the flood of adrenalin and a lurch in my stomach because, somehow, despite me fighting it on every front – Lucas, love, life itself – a chink has opened up and hope has crept in. And when that bitch shows up, you know you're really screwed. And there she is, playing her game, starting on the what ifs. What if he works it out? What if he doesn't?

What if he doesn't even try?

MATTHEW

Friday

It was six when I got in. I heard the music of the news leaking through from the living room.

'That you, Matty?' shouted my dad from the sofa.

He lives on that sofa. He comes in from his round at about two, changes out of his postman uniform and into what he calls his 'lying down trousers', then sets himself at one end with his legs up. Mum says he looks like a Roman emperor, but he doesn't. He just looks like a man who's been working too hard. He gets up at four every morning. Sometimes I'll hear the kitchen door close when he's on his way out, and I'll see it's still dark, and the air will be so cold if you spat it would be a hailstone before it reached the floor, and I'll pull my nose under the duvet and be glad I'm not him.

Over the years, his end of the old sofa has been moulded to the shape of him, and if you sit there, you feel it is all wrong, that you're going out where you should go in and in where you go out. It smells like him too. Not a bad smell. Just a dad smell. Sometimes I lie on the sofa late at night watching a film by myself, and realise that I'm breathing him in. Musty.

But with a bit of mint in it, from the Polos he always has in his pocket.

'Yeah, it's me, Dad.'

Usually when he says that I make some kind of unfunny joke about it not being me, but a burglar, or the queen, or whatever, but my mind was on other things.

Mum opened the door into the kitchen.

'Hello, love. Just in time to go to the chip shop.' She held out a twenty-pound note.

We always have fish and chips on a Friday night, and as long as I can remember it has been my job to go and get them on my bike.

My mum is a teaching assistant at my old junior school. She used to like to embarrass me by hugging me at break times. She took the chance to hug me now, as I reached for the money.

'When did you get so big?' she said.

Funny, because I was thinking that she had suddenly become tiny. I could rest my chin on her head.

I shrugged and went straight back out. 'You can get yourself a special, if you want,' she called after me. A special is a bigger fish. It costs an extra two quid.

After tea I went up to my room. I usually watch telly with them on a Friday night, because I know they like it, the three of us sitting there. The telly's never off in our house but it isn't always watched. During the day my dad reads books, with the telly on in the background, the sound maybe turned down a bit, but still there, like the noise of birds in the woods, or traffic on the roads. But in the evening you pay it attention, like it's a kid you're suddenly conscious of neglecting.

But I wasn't in the mood for telly. All the way through tea I'd been shrugging off my parents' questions about school, about everything. They were just being nice. They *are* nice. That's the thing about them. Everyone else at school slags their parents off for not letting them do stuff they want to do, or making them do stuff they don't. But my mum and dad, well, they just love each other, and love me, and want me to be OK. And, yeah, having someone wanting you to be happy is a sort of pressure, a responsibility. But it's not like getting the belt for coming in late, like some kids talk about. Or like Jango and his mum.

So we just sort of ate without talking much, but it was all right. It wasn't one of those silences where you know people really hate each other, with a clock ticking like a bomb about to go off.

Anyway, all I could think about was the girl in the hospital. The feel of her lips. The taste of her. And I kept thinking how with nearly all the things in the world, there was something either a bit or a lot like them. A zebra is a bit like a horse. A pie is a bit like a pudding. A stool is a bit like a chair.

But there's nothing that's a bit like a kiss.

'He's not really with us tonight, is he?' said my mum, smiling, after I'd forgotten to answer one of her questions. And then she and Dad looked at each other and smiled some more, as if they knew what was going on inside my head. And I suppose they sort of did, for once.

Up in my room I got my phone out and put it on the bed next to the piece of paper with the number on it. I just looked at them both for a few minutes, reliving the whole thing from first seeing her sitting there with that faraway look in her eyes, to the end of the kiss. I didn't want to go past that part, because up until then it had been sort of perfect, but after that came the clattering trek through the canteen.

No, the part before that hadn't actually been perfect. Because I'd kept saying stupid things, or saying nothing. But it had those little peaks of perfection, like the tops of mountains sticking up over the clouds of dross. The look of her. The fact she didn't stab me in the eye with a fork. The kiss.

And now I had time to think about it properly, here on my own, I could make the kiss last for as long as I wanted. I could stretch it out into infinity. I could live my whole life in the kiss. And I wanted to do that, but if I spent my whole life just kissing her, then there would be no time to do other things, talking to her, being with her ... And that was no good. I wanted to be always kissing her, and always everything else with her as well, and that was wanting two incompatible things. And that was unsatisfying.

And then I thought about something we'd done in maths. Sets. How the set of whole numbers – 1, 2, 3, 4, 5, etc. – is infinite, and so is the set of odd numbers – 1, 3, 5, 7, etc. – but the set of odd numbers must be half the size of the set of whole numbers, so how can they both be infinite? But the point is that you can fit the infinite set of the kiss inside the infinite set of the everything else. And I knew that there was probably a flaw in my logic, but I didn't care. It was enough to get the problem off my back, so I could enjoy the kiss again, and stretch it out for ever.

And I was probably, if truth be told, putting off the work. I mean the work of having to phone her. Going through all those numbers. And then having to speak to her, to think of something to say that wasn't stupid. I thought about writing something out. I even started to, typing it out on the shitty laptop that my dad found in a skip on his round. There's something wrong with the hard drive and it crashes every time someone flushes the toilet or slams a door.

But it was impossible. I couldn't get past 'Hello.'

So I gritted my teeth and started dialling, thinking that I could wing it, and if I couldn't, if I failed, it wouldn't be so bad. I'd gone fifteen years without seeing her before. I'd probably never see her again. I could just quietly put the phone down. Then kill myself.

So, my system was this: for the first X, I started by putting in a 0, and for the second, first a 0, then 1, then 2 and so on. Then, when I'd gone up to 9, I'd put a 1 in place of the first X, and go through it again. That way, I'd be sure to reach her, in the end.

The first two went straight through to answerphones, with voices I knew weren't hers. Then I got some bloke, and I just said, 'Sorry, wrong number.' And then a girl, but I knew straightaway it wasn't her – she just didn't sound beautiful enough. And it went on like that for a while, with me marking off the dud numbers on the back page of my English lit exercise book. A couple of the answerphone messages just had the standard voice you get if you don't record your own greeting, so I had no way of knowing if it was her. I didn't leave a message with those, but wrote down the numbers to come back to later.

After half an hour there was a knock at the door. I'd got nowhere.

'Want a cup of tea, Matty?'

'No, Dad. Thanks.'

I got back to work.

Most people I spoke to were quite nice, and only a couple got annoyed. But it was still a bit soul destroying. Each failure added to the feeling I had that the whole thing was a sham, that Sophia (if that was even her real name) was just playing some sort of joke on me. Yeah, that had to be it. She'd seen what a doofus I was and worked out a way of twisting my gourd. It was genius really. If she'd just made up a number, then one call and I'd have been out of my misery. But this way kept me dangling, kept me hoping, stretching the torture out, like one of those guys you read about who could peel off all your skin and still leave you alive for long enough to look at yourself in the mirror with the insides of you right there, on the outside, and everything red except for the whites of your eyes, huge as eggs.

But still I kept dialling.

And finally a girl answered.

Oh jeez. Oh sweet jeez.

SOPHIA

Friday

Proverbs are bull. A watched pot never boils, right? Well my pot rings three frick-fracking heart-stopping stomach-flipping times in a row.

Caller number one is Lexy, natch.

'Babe?'

'No,' I say. 'It's Hot Housewives R Us. You're being charged ten pounds a minute for your pleasure.'

'In that case, I'll have a hand job, and can you wank my ego while you're at it and tell me I'm bigger than Justin Henson?'

'Jesus. That's a new one. Who was that? Kyle?'

'Flinty. And if it's true then this is one sad day for Lulu Baxter.'

'Huh?'

'Black bob? Big tits? Shagging Henson and his mini penis?'

I try to picture it. Then try to stop. Then thankfully Lexy gets to her point.

'So, Dawse is here. And she's already had Josh Porter's hand down her cheap La Perla rip-offs.'

'Classy.'

'I *know*. Sarah Elle found them in her mum's bedroom and told Lucas and now he's shut himself in the den and he's playing guitar. Which, like, is so achingly sad I can hardly bloody breathe.'

'Poor Lucas,' I say, hoping she can hear the sarcasm dripping like syrup even with some ironic chart shit raging in the background. But Lexy misses the point and gets back to her own.

'I know. It's tragic. He's like this injured puppy, like a Labrador something, all floppy blond hair and eyes. That's why you should be here, babe. He's totally vulnerable. It's so like eighties brat pack.'

It so is not. If anything it's a TV remake of *Marley and Me*. Dubbed. In Mexican. 'I'm sure he'll find someone to pet him.'

'Seriously? You don't want him back? Not even if he begged forgiveness and pledged everlasting troth or whatever the frick-frack it is?'

I am so not rising to this. 'Troth is an A-star word. I should use that more.'

'Jeez, Soph. Not even to prove you can then?'

Do I? I think. Did I? Maybe, for a day – a week, even. Back in my Smiths-soundtracked pity party for one I was throwing. But now? After Matthew? *Before* him even?

Not for a New York minute.

'Are you even listening?'

'Yes. Look, Lex, all it would prove is that I'm a sucker.'

'You, babe, are one hard-hearted woman.'

'Titanium,' I say. 'Look, I have to go.' Because what if he's calling? What if it turns out he's king of the freaking mathletes and is hitting the engaged tone while Lexy is comparing my ex to Lassie? 'Laters, yeah?'

'Laters, beeyatch.'

Lucky caller number two is Will. There are no hellos, no ceremony. He gets straight to the important stuff.

'Who'd you rather – Abe Lincoln or Roosevelt?'

I don't need even need to think about it. 'Roosevelt. The no moustache thing doesn't work for me.'

'*Ding ding*. Right answer,' he calls.

I hear shrieks of dissension in the background that sound suspiciously like he's been playing his own game of ex-chase.

'Is that . . . ?'

'If I told you I'd have to kill you.'

Caleb, definitely. The boy who broke his heart. Then stamped on it with his custom Docs and a boy called Brian.

'GTG, doll.'

Caller number three is Lexy. Again.

'You seriously don't want him? Because, like, I can talk to him if you want— Hang on . . . Fuck OFF, Kyle. Jesus. It's a fucking car crash here. I think Ollie just threw up in Harper Weston's mouth. Sorry . . . shit . . . so, really? You're done?'

'I'm done,' I say. 'I have never been done er. Can I be excused now?'

'I think—'

But the line cuts out. And I'm so busy thanking my lucky stars and the warped-minded fairy godmother who occasionally deigns to pay me some attention that when the phone rings two seconds later I don't even check the caller ID, just pick up and let her have it: 'Lexy, seriously, I am done with him. I don't care if he's playing his six-string like he's freaking Dylan. I don't care if he's cuter than the Andrex puppy. I don't even care if he decides to dish up sloppy seconds to Dawse again. She can have him. Sarah Elle can have him. Jesus, you can have him if he's that desperate . . .' I stop. Because I've gone too far. I don't mean it. Or maybe I do. But she wouldn't. And I don't want to argue with her. I just don't want to talk to her right now.

Which, when you think about it, is kind of ironic. Because it turns out I'm not.

I've pressed pause long enough for the caller to get a word in. And the word is definitely not one of Lexy's.

'Sophia?'

Sweet baby Jesus. He hit the jackpot.

'Matthew?'

He doesn't answer at first. And I swear I will kill Lexy. Then Lucas. Then myself. I will turn this whole sorry mess into the seventeenth frick-fracking *Saw* movie. But before I let loose with the slash fest, before he hangs up on the crazy chick with the messed-up head and the tendency to word vomit, he pulls another rabbit out of the hat.

'You used to go out with someone who looked like a golden retriever?'

'I . . .'And I realise this is that moment. The one when you're standing on the edge of the woods, staring at the fading paint of the 'Danger, Keep Out' sign nailed to the tree. And you could walk away, stick to the path, play it safe. Or you could just brave the dark and you might find treasure. It could go either way. I could stammer out a lame apology, or a pack of lies. I could say it's a bad time; that it's always going to be a bad time.

Or I could swallow the cake that says 'Eat me' and see where it takes me.

'Labrador. Subtle difference.' I pause. Then, 'Which would you rather: a Labrador with bad breath or an incontinent cat?'

He's quiet. Thinking. Please, I say to myself. Please don't mess this up.

'Cat,' he says finally. 'But I'd make it wear pants.'

Right answer, I think.

'Cats in Pants would be a truly terrible name for a band,' he adds.

And so it begins. And we're talking round band names from Velvet Elvis to Glass Jar of Moles. We're jamming on whether Marmite beats marmalade. Then segueing into school bullies and heroes and the kid most likely to. We're talking nothing, and everything. Because every word – even the small ones, the strange ones, the ones like 'sandwich' and 'scuba suit' and 'Johnny Thunders' – count.

So when he asks if we can meet again soon, there can only be one answer: a single word. 'Yes.'

'Tomorrow?'

'Sure . . . wait, no. I can't. I have this thing.' Well, what I have is to go round Lexy's to hold out a bucket, refuel her with McMuffins and OJ, and dissect whatever's gone down at Jules's. But that is a thing. A big thing in Lexy Land.

'Sunday?' I offer. 'Afternoon.' Because the meds zone me out in the mornings sometimes and I don't want to risk him seeing flaky Sophia; the one who looks and acts like she's been hanging with the stoners and space cadets.

'Sunday afternoon,' he says. 'Where?'

'You pick,' I say. 'Somewhere I don't know. Or would never guess. Somewhere that matters.'

'Do you always turn stuff into a game?' he asks.

And I realise he's on to something. 'When it counts,' I say. 'Only the serious stuff.'

I swear I can hear him smile in that moment. Then, 'Game on,' he says. 'I'll text you.'

And I want to ask him: when? When will you text? When will I see you? When will I touch you again? Will you kiss me when you see me? Or just hold my hand? God, I wanna hold your hand. I want to blurt it all out. Ask him for the truth. But this is a game, isn't it? And I picked dare. So instead I just say, 'See you, Matthew.'

'Not if I see you first,' he says.

Right answer.

MATTHEW

Friday

If I'd thought it was really going to happen, that I was actually going to find her, call her, talk to her, well, I don't think I could have gone through with it. I could only do it because it was impossible. Is that ironic or is it a paradox? Either way, it's the kind of thing Jango loves. But I might as well have stabbed myself in the guts with a samurai sword as told Jango about any of this . . .

And maybe I should have stabbed myself in the guts rather than coming out with all that crap. I mean, 'Not if I see you first.' What the hell was that? Why couldn't I have said something smart or flirty or bloody *anything*? I spent a little bit of time rolling around on the floor, my head in my hands, my body in a kind of foetal position, going over all the stupid things I'd said.

But I was also . . . happy. No, better than happy. There was something in my life, something that wasn't just the fear of exams around the corner, or working out how to get through another day without dying of boredom, or trying to keep Jango under some kind of control. No, now I had a thing, a real *thing*. A thing in my head and a thing in my heart.

I went downstairs after I'd stopped rolling around and groaning. I wanted some tea and some digestives, and I was going to dunk the latter in the former, the way I used to when I was a kid and feeling happy.

'What you smiling at?' said my dad, when he came into the kitchen.

I didn't even know I had been smiling.

'Nothing.'

Dad looked at me, strangely.

'What you been doing up there?'

I shrugged. 'Just listening to music. A new band. They're called Cats in Pants.'

I took my tea and biscuits back upstairs, leaving my dad shaking his head at the sorry state of modern popular music.

SOPHIA

Friday

This is what happens next:

1. I squeal, out loud, and no, I'm not proud of it.
2. I call Lexy, who, for possibly only the second time ever (the first time her excuse was she had her tongue in some kid off *Emmerdale*'s mouth and you never interrupt an actor at work) doesn't pick up.
3. I bite the figurative bullet and decide I'm going to Sarah Elle's after all. Because the whole Matthew thing is burning a hole in my pocket and, even if Lexy is snogging someone right now, that story sure as hell isn't going to beat mine.
4. I negotiate a costume change into an original (not copy) New York Dolls tee, sequinned hot pants, and black Lycra tights. And the faux fur. Carefully calculated to give enough coverage to get past the mother ship without dissection and detention, if not detection. Plus it's March not May, and this is Leeds. I need my layers.
5. There is a brief argument with Mom over the hot pants, whether or not I should be going out at 'this time', and

what 'being careful' means. I point out sheer hundreds of deniers in my tights that suck the evil out of the short shorts, and that I'm hardly likely to get pregnant, given my eggs have been truly fried by chemo, so that's one thing she can cross off her 'potential shame' list.

6. Dad drops me at Sarah Elle's with the gift of a line: 'Don't do anything I wouldn't do.' The reply is obviously, for a formerly exiled *Fawlty Towers* fan, 'Just a little breathing, surely.'

7. I walk into a scene straight out of Mom's Teen Hell Playbook, ask where Lexy is, and navigate semi-naked bodies and the worst kind of dirty dancing to some kid sister's bedroom on the top floor.

And it's not until I walk in that I get why Sarah Elle gave me that look. The one that says, 'I shouldn't let you do this but the fallout is going to be so freaking *Eastenders* I'm going to do it anyway.' Because there, on a Hello Kitty duvet cover, being gawped at by a menagerie of glass-eyed muppets and My Little Ponies is one glassy-eyed Lexy, who is hard at work.

Only it's not some B-lister this time. Or Flinty. Or even Millwall Dino.

It's not a frog.

It's the leading man. Or best supporting at worst.

It's Lucas.

And I could make a scene. I could play this like the soap opera she's living out and start some catfight that will notch up a few thousand YouTube hits before dawn and make a few Year 11 wannabe gossip-girl blogs by tomorrow's hangover wake-up call.

Or I could back out before she sees me, slip into the wet room and pull out my phone.

'Change of plan,' I text. 'What are you doing right now?'

MATTHEW

Friday

I was thinking about slurping the digestive slop at the bottom of the mug when I heard a ping. I looked for my phone, and found it half under the bed. I stared at the screen.

That thing people say about their heart stopping. Obviously, it's bullshit. If your heart stops, it's because you're dead. And I wasn't dead. I was the most alive, in those seconds, that I've ever been.

It wasn't even my breathing that had stopped, because it was still there – oxygen in, CO_2 out, just like we did in biology. But something stopped, and it wasn't just me, I mean in me – it was out there; it was the world; it was everything.

Fingers trembling as I texted back.

'Nothing.'

No, that was no good. It made me sound like a retard. I backspaced its ass.

'I'm reading your text.'

No, even shittier. Another one of those things that people say that looks a bit like a joke, I mean that have the shape of a joke, even the sound of a joke, but when you think about them, it turns out there's zero actual humour in them.

No, it was time for something else. For another strategy altogether. The cunning old truth ploy.

'I'm thinking of you.'

SOPHIA

Friday

Heart flips, stomach contracts, lungs forget to take a breath. Your basic internal organs failing to concentrate on their primary task moment.

In other words, right answer. Again.

I resist the temptation to send back a smiley, or a heart, or some kitten on a skateboard, because I'm not thirteen, or Lexy. But it doesn't stop me praying in the name of all that's unholy that he says yes when I text, 'Can you get out?'

'Depends on what's on offer.'

Cool. Very cool.

'Me. Let's meet somewhere.'

'Where?'

'You choose.'

Another one of my tests, maybe. I don't know. I want to see what he'll come up with. And I can hear him thinking, trying to get it right.

'You know the Porter? Off George Street? Up past the uni?'

I do. It's a regular hangout for Penn kids. The barman's called Danny Wright, the big brother of one of Lexy's exes. In an endless stream of bands that are never quite the Next Big

Thing. Hence the bar job. Hence half of Penn drinking down there only, bingo, not tonight.

'Yeah, I know it. And the staff, so you won't get carded.'

'Do you have any downsides?'

I smile (but don't LOL). 'I'm allergic to cats. I don't like dogs. And I never help old ladies across the road.'

Oh, and I have a partially defused tumour time bomb inside my head that may start counting down any minute, but, hey, the dog thing is pretty contentious.

'Not even Labradors?'

He remembered. 'Especially not Labradors.'

'See you at ten.'

And I don't text back. Because I'm not thirteen or Lexy.

And because I only have half an hour to get the hell out of the suburbs and into Sin City.

MATTHEW

Friday

This was insane. Five minutes ago I was staring into the sludge at the bottom of my mug, and contemplating going downstairs to watch the telly with Mum and Dad. Now suddenly this was happening.

A something instead of a nothing.

I'd had a panic attack when she'd asked me to suggest somewhere. The Porter came into my head, because I'd been there a couple of times with Jango. Because it's a student hangout, they're a bit sloppy about ID, and you can usually get a drink there without hassle.

I looked in my wardrobe, and felt a ripple of nausea. I'd never cared much about clothes. My main ambition in life had been to avoid looking stupid. But now, just not looking stupid wasn't enough. For a mad second I wondered if looking stupid was, in fact, the way to go. A clown outfit, or a cowboy hat, or my old *Lion King* pyjamas I knew Mum had stored away in the loft.

But no. There's never a time for stupid.

I found my black jeans. Mum had ironed a crease in them you could slice a tomato with. I didn't know much, but I knew that that wouldn't do. I scrunched and twisted them till they almost looked like jeans again. T-shirt? It seemed the obvious choice. But she'd seen me in a T-shirt already today. She'd think I couldn't be bothered making an effort. I had an OK white shirt. The only good thing you could say for it was that it wasn't hateful. I threw it on. Ironed so crisply I could hear it crackle. But it felt kind of good.

I checked out my look in the mirror. Jesus. Boring. The white and black made it look like school uniform. Too late, I thought. If I faffed any longer I might as well forget the whole thing. I spent five minutes in the bathroom brushing my teeth and trying out a couple of stunts on my hair with some gel that had dried in the cap-less tube to a sort of rubber, so when I flicked a ball of it at the mirror it bounced back.

And all through this, even though I was feeling a kind of despair at how shit I was going to look, the despair was lost in the excitement. It really felt as though something was happening at long last in my life. I wasn't just mooching around at home, or slinking along behind Jango while he did and said crazy things. This time it was me being crazy. Except no, not crazy. It was just a boy going to meet a girl. The sort of thing that happened a billion times every night. But not to me. This was the normal I'd been missing out on.

I was ready. And maybe it was ready the way a cow is ready, when they dump it off the truck and into the slaughterhouse on the way to meet the man with a bolt gun, but that was all the ready I was ever going to be.

I didn't want to explain the situation to Mum and Dad, but nor did I want to sneak out and leave them worried about where I was ... So I yelled some nonsense words from the hallway, ending in, 'See you later,' and got out of there before they had the chance to give me a grilling. I think I sort of knew that they wouldn't mind me going off to see a girl like this. In fact I guessed they'd love it. But that wasn't the point. You don't want your parents nosing in on this sort of stuff, even if their noses are happy noses, noses that only want the best for you.

The Porter's about a forty-five-minute walk from home. Twenty minutes on the bus, if I was lucky. And I'm never lucky with buses. Except now. Yes, on this glorious night, there was a number 166, laid on for me as if there really was a God. I smiled into the grey face of the driver and rattled two quid into the shute. I walked on and the driver yelled, 'Ticket', and I said, 'Keep it,' but then an old lady who got on after me came along and put it in my hand.

'You don't want to get in trouble with the inspector,' she said, and I felt a little bit of love for her and the driver and the inspector, wherever he was in this wide world.

And I loved those twenty minutes. Traffic lights changed for us, miraculously, just as we approached. The streets, it seemed, weren't illuminated by the sick orange neon of the lights, but by the shivering silver of moon and stars. And rather than mangy pigeons waiting for someone to shit on, the trees were full of singing nightingales. Not that

I'd know a nightingale if it came up and pecked me in the nuts.

I tried again to think of some stuff to say to Sophia, but it wasn't like the panicky emptiness of before. Because now I knew that she liked me – maybe just a bit, maybe more than a bit – and that meant there was a chance she'd like *whatever* crap I said, just because it was me saying it. But that didn't mean I could just say, I don't know, Nelson Mandela sucked elephants' dicks, or grunt like an ape, or whatever. No, I'd have to make an effort, but the pressure was off. It was like a race I knew I could win. And you still have to run those kinds of races, and if you don't turn up, you get nothing. But here I was turning up.

Halfway there I felt my phone buzz in my pocket. I snatched it out, thinking it was her. She'd changed her mind; decided I was a jerk. Or it had been a joke from the start. But then I saw 'JANGO' on the screen. Screw that. I squeezed the power button till he went away.

I was early. That was perfect. I didn't want her there already, watching me fall off the bus. She'd be all cool, and I'd be like some bum, tripping over my feet.

No, this way I could prepare myself. Think about how to stand. Get my face right. I could go for deep, my eyes dark and brooding, as if great thoughts and terrible events were scrolling through my brain. Or I could just look friendly, and glad to see her. Or I could caper around, drooling and grinning, which was kind of what I felt like doing.

But the way I got off that bus . . . well, now I wish she *had* been there to see it. A swing, a glide, a little leap. Like ballet.

No!

Jesus, what am I saying? Not ballet. Like, I don't know, Spider-Man. Yeah, ready to squirt my sticky web at you . . . Oh, no, that's . . . Just don't use that line on her. Ever.

I had my hands in my pockets and I found the bit of paper with her number on it, and my scribbles. I'd doodled something stupid on there – just a pair of tits with eyeballs instead of nipples. The kind of thing your hand does when you're not paying attention to it. I felt like an idiot, then. What if she'd seen that? I imagined the look of contempt on her face, mixed with relief that she'd found out what I was like before it was too late. In my head I saw her turn as she walked away, giving me the finger.

Well, that was one pair of tits I didn't need. The number was in my phone, safe as sex with two condoms. I balled the paper and flicked it into a bin, neat as you like. Truly everything was going as smoothly as hot buttered silk.

So I was there. The shops and bars glittered like Christmas. The Porter was full of people, talking, laughing, gliding through and around each other. They looked young and old at the same time. Young, because they weren't like the people in the pub where my dad goes. I've sat in there with him, and had a Coke and crisps while he has a pint of skid-mark-brown bitter, and everyone else is a hundred and fifty years old. So they were young – studenty, kinda, along with other people just starting out in jobs, still thought the world was OK, and that they were going to be happy. Or maybe because it was a Friday night, they were thinking, Hey, life is shit, and I hate my job, so let's party like it's the last day of the dying earth.

That Friday lot can sometimes be a bit edgy, but the students softened that. Students never go out looking for a fight. Not against the locals, anyway. That'd be like trying to hammer in a nail with a cabbage.

So, young, but old, too, because they were all older than me. And one of the weird things about me is that I look exactly as old as I am: sixteen.

Anyway, I was looking through the big window, when I caught the eye of a girl. Not my girl – not Sophia. A student, I guess. I mean, she had that look – sort of scruffy, but still with lipstick on, pretty enough to know that she didn't have to make a big effort. And she sort of smiled at me. For a second I thought, Hey, she fancies me, and I never think that. But I definitely didn't imagine it, because she looked away, and then back at me again, and smiled again.

Later on, after it all turned to shit, I thought back to that girl and her smile, and I realised that she was just smiling because there I was, some kid, in his uncool best clothes, the ironed creases still showing through the wrinkles despite my best efforts, waiting here for his date. It wasn't an unkind smile. The opposite. But it wasn't an I'd-like-to-snog-your-face-off smile either.

Anyway, I suddenly got a bit paranoid, wondering what Sophia would think if she came along and saw me ogling some random girl, when here we were, just about to have our first date. So I was just in the act of looking away, when:

OOOOOOOOHHHHHHFFFFFF!

It was on my back. Hands pushing down on my shoulders. Kids from the rough estate after my shitty mobile. Knife in the guts. Lying on the street, blood flowing in thick red streams to the gutter. My eyes go milky. And then she appears. Takes my hand. Goodbye. I loved you . . .

And then the words, spoken softly into my ear by the monster on my still unstabbed back.

'All dressed up in your Sunday best, lover boy. Now, if I didn't know any better, I'd say you'd found yourself a sweet little girly-wirly for an ickle bit of kissy-wissy.'

And then Jango shoved his tongue in my ear so far I thought it was going to come out through my effing nose.

I bucked and twisted, but couldn't shake him off. One long leg, with the giant shoe at the end of it, was swinging around like some kind of weapon from the days of knights in armour. I sensed faces in the bar looking, laughing. It must have been pretty funny.

Even at the best of times, having an effing nutter like Jango on my back, sticking his tongue in my ear, was not a good thing. But right now I was terrified Sophia was about to turn up. How the hell do you explain someone like Jango to a girl like that? 'Hello, meet Jango, my best mate, the kid with a giant shoe and a face like Count Dracula, and a stream of filth coming out of his mouth like a flushing toilet.'

And then I realised that explaining Jango was the least of my problems. If she came along now, Jango would say something about the St Michael's Hospital raid. About why I was in the damn place. About getting off with dying girls. It was a shit sandwich with a side order of shit. I had to get Jango out of here, and quick.

'Get off, you jerk,' I yelled back, finally, about a minute too late. 'What are you doing here anyway?'

'I was out and about in town, and thought we should have a bit of a chat, work out some strategies. Next stage in our conquest of the World of Girl. No answer from your phone, so I called your sweet little mumsy, who told me you'd just gone out. And that set the sirens ringing, cos there are stiffs in the effing graveyard, just decaying bags of pulp and bone, that go out more often than you do. Was about to give up on you when what should I see but your sweet little visage. So that's me. What the sod are you doing out on the mean streets all by your lonesome self, eh?'

'Nothing. I just wanted to get out of the house,' I said, a bit lamely. I finally managed to free myself by jamming Jango up against the jutting corner of the Porter, and scraping him off, the way you'd scrape shit from a shoe.

But then, before I could enjoy the whole not-having-Jango-on-my-back thing, I realised why he'd stuck his filthy tongue in my ear. It was a classic distraction manoeuvre, and in that long-fingered hand of his he held my phone.

'Don't need no Sherlock to find out what you're up to when this little beauty – and when I say *little beauty*, what I mean, of course, is this *tech OBSCENITY*, this slab of excrement in the form of a phone, this iSore, this—'

'Give it here, Jango,' I said, trying to control my rising anger. If I showed too much emotion it would just egg him on. I needed to make him think it was all a big bore. But for that, I needed to be a better actor.

'*OOOOOOOOOOOOOhhhhhhhh*, since when did you ever care who looks at your phone? I mean, why would you? The only person who's ever texted you is your mum, to bring home more chips.'

'Shut up, Jango.'

'Make me,' he said, in a mincing little-girl voice. And then he was off down the street, jabbing at the screen. I made a grab for the phone, but he snatched it away at the last second, leaving my hand to close around dead air. And then he held it up out of my reach. I had a hideous vision of me running and jumping around him like a little kid trying to get a bar of chocolate from his dad, while he tempted me by dipping it lower. Not cool. Anyway, the rage was burning in me now. I think I might have hit him – I mean really hit him, hard, in the face. But then I caught sight of something – of someone – across the street.

I knew her the second I saw her, even though it was just a glimpse, in the dark and light of the street, and she was fifty metres away, and I had my attention on something else. But it *was* her. Totally and utterly her. She was crossing the road, her eyes going this way and then that, looking for a gap in the traffic. And the miracle was that even though I'd seen her, I could tell that she hadn't clocked me. Her eyes didn't even flicker towards me.

But, my, she looked fine. The same as at the hospital, but totally different. She was wearing black leggings or skinnies or tights. Whatever, they were tight. And they worked. And then these hot pants that glittered, like she'd reached up and pulled a strip of the Milky Way around her thighs. She looked trashy and classy at the same time, like an *X-Factor* Greek myth. Yeah, that was it – Aphrodite in hot pants.

I took all this in in a nanosecond. And I knew I had to get away from here, from her. A sort of plan formed itself in my head. Get Jango out of there, retrieve my phone, text her that I'd be ten minutes late, double back, everything OK.

And the first bit was working. Jango was skipping off down the street, taking himself out of the danger zone. I followed him, close enough for him to think I was going to make another snatch for my phone, so he kept on moving. He thought he was leading me, but I was shepherding him.

He cut down a side street. That was good. Out of her sight. Hardly even a street, really – just a link between two busy roads. I yelled some words at him, just to keep him moving. I could see from the screen that he was in my texts, but he couldn't read them while he was jinking back and forth, and with the crazy running caused by his big shoe, so he bounded ahead again, trying to get himself enough space for a good look.

And then I saw shapes looming, the shadows mixing together with the solid forms, like black flames. Jango wasn't looking where he was going. Still holding the phone high; still running, spinning, laughing. I yelled out a 'Watch it!' but too late. And so Jango crashed into the group of kids, sending them tumbling and rolling away from him, like pins after a strike.

This wasn't good.

Grunts and curses came from the pale faces, rage-distorted in the dim light of the side street. They were kids, but not from our school. Hard kids, too. You could tell by the way . . . well, just by how they were. One-two-three-four-five of them. I darted through the gap carved by Jango, and stood next to him. We were both panting, breathless. The kids regrouped and faced us.

'You should watch where you're effing going,' said one, the first to get his composure back. He was shorter than the others, his hair shaved close to his scalp like a mental patient, and the bones of his face seemed to slice out from his skull, the way a shark's fin cuts the water. He was the first, but the others were with him now. Their fists were already clenched, and I could see gold signet rings, as good for pulping a face as a knuckleduster. And something worse. I saw the glint of silvery metal. A knife. Just one. But one would do. Not the sharp-boned kid, but another – a fat kid with a face like wet dough, and frightened eyes. Yeah, I saw it: he carried the knife because the others thought he was soft. He was going to show them.

Jango had staggered back against a wall, winded by the unexpected collision, but now he was himself again, and that was bad. I sensed that he was up for this, up for some mayhem. Well, I wasn't. Not five on two. Not with the knife in the hand of the frightened fat kid.

Not with Sophia, waiting . . .

'Leg it,' I said, getting all the urgency I could into my voice, and at the same moment I yanked his arm, and began to drag him away. He resisted for a second, and I thought he'd shrug me loose, but I held on, and turned him, and then we were off.

Maybe it was a mistake. Maybe if we'd fronted up, the other kids would have skulked off, or made do with a bit of eyeballing. Or maybe they'd have stabbed us and left us to bleed to death in the side street.

Anyway, *us* running set *them* chasing. And something about the act of running, even when there are sound reasons, turns you into a coward. I felt it in me. I felt it in Jango – and Jango has more guts; crazy guts, but guts still – than any other nutter I've ever met or probably ever will.

So we were running like mad things, with them right on our arses, and Jango was panicking just enough to make his limp worse, so he was slow, too slow. He'd lost that loping, uneven, galloping stride that covers more ground than you can imagine. He was more staggering, like he was drunk. Behind us I heard the kids start to laugh, and yell out, 'Cripple!' and, 'Spaz!' and worse. We were near the end of the side street, now, and I thought we were going to be safe, maybe – when we got out into the busy road there, Great George Street, where the normal people were. These kids weren't insane enough to kill us right there in front of people, were they?

SOPHIA

Friday

It's messed up what nightfall does to a city. Messed up *good* though. Just a few hours ago these streets were litter-strewn Lowrys: matchstick men in baseball caps instead of bowlers. Now the Headrow could be Broadway in all its billboard glory, and I walk through the Friday night crowds in my CBGBs-meets-Studio-54 outfit, as high on possibility as they are on pound-a-shot Jägers. I scan their neon- and sodium-lit faces in case one of them is his, but it's hopeless. I only have snapshots of memory, a jigsaw puzzle of Kodak moments. The way his hair falls over one eye. SNAP. The curve of his lips when he smiles. SNAP. The feel of his mouth on mine. SNAP. Oh god. That mouth.

Alone they're unique, unmistakeable. Yet I can't form them into a seamless picture, a solid being, at least not one on Great George Street. As I turn the corner to cross to the Porter, I think I see him, this boy in black and white, like a waiter or a schoolkid. But it is just some schoolkid, must be, because he turns away when he sees me, goes back to fooling around with his mate, play-fighting until they're dots in the distance. I'll recognise him, I think, when he shows up.

Because our eyes will meet and violins will play and the earth will move, right?

Danny's all high fives when I walk in and comping me a Sourz but I play it safe and order peppermint tea, because my meds and alcohol don't mix that great and the last thing I want to do is fall asleep or pull an Ollie Pitt-Weston. I'll tell him I'm a recovering alcoholic. Or maybe he'll order one too and say his favourite novel is *Gatsby* and then we'll know we're soulmates.

Sweet baby Jeebus, what the frick-frack is wrong with me? I sound like a Disney special. Or Lex.

The camera in my head pulls focus on her with her skinny legs wrapped round Lucas's scrum-half thighs and I have to fight the urge to tear up. Even though the number of effs I have to give is a fat zero. It's not like I want him back. Just that ... him and Lex? Though it makes sense, I guess. He's her wet dream of a love interest. Getting all torn up inside because he dumped his ex when she needed him the most. Getting wasted every Friday. Getting benched for Charley Hoy because he can't cut it on the field on a Saturday. It's like they were made for each other.

I check my phone. Nothing from her. Not that I give a shit, like I say. What I do, however, give more than a shit about is that it's gone quarter past now, which means he's late.

I text Will for want of something to do. 'Your superpower is invisibility; do you use it for good or evil?' But his texting fingers are otherwise engaged because ten minutes and a cold cup of toothpaste-tasting tea later I still don't know if he's Superman or Lex Luthor and, worse, there's still no sign of my own comic-book hero.

MATTHEW

Friday

We were nearly out there, in the relative safety of Great George Street, when Jango swivelled on his good leg, and this time it was him who grabbed me, and pulled me where he wanted me to go. It was an alley just behind the shops, the fronts of which lined the main road.

I didn't get it. The main street was salvation, but this alley was a death trap. I wasn't even sure there was a way out of it – there was no sign of light at the other end. It could have been blocked with bins or a wall or anything. I looked back, and the other kids were there, now, at the alley entrance. It was darker here, and they were just silhouettes, shadow puppets.

'We've got to get out of here,' I said to Jango. And then I looked at him. There was just enough light seeping into the alley for me to see that he was grinning. He had a big face and big teeth, and it was a big grin, but there was death in it, too.

The kids saw that we'd stopped and came towards us more carefully. Maybe they thought that, just like them, we were tooled up.

And it turned out, weirdly, that we were.

The alley was full of bins, overflowing with the slop and crap from the shops and fast-food joints on the high street. Now, with a great clanging, like Quasimodo at his bells, Jango kicked one of the big bins over, emptying the filth on the alleyway ground.

This baffled the other kids. It baffled me. I thought for a second he was just laying down a sort of moat, made of rotten kebab scraps, and chicken bones, and other, sloppier, garbage. And then maybe the plan was to use the delay to run for it down the other end of the alley. Yep, that had to be it. Maybe there was a way out down there, and he was just winning us enough time to get away without having to rely on the Friday-night crowds to save our arses.

But that wasn't his plan. Wasn't his plan at all. Because then with a sort of a war whoop Jango waded into the slops, scooped up a handful, and hurled it at our attackers.

They yelled and hollered in appalled disgust, and stepped back. Jango scooped another double handful – amid the unidentifiable gunk, I could see what looked like coils of intestine in there, though maybe it was just a string of rancid sausages – and flung it in a splattering, face-level arc.

'Hah! Eat pig bollocks; eat cow anus, you shit-lickers,' Jango screamed. And then, to me, 'C'mon, glory awaits.'

And by now I was caught up in the filthy majesty of it, and I stepped beside him. I put my hands into the rubbish, sliding them right down till they reached the cobbles of this ancient track. The stench of it was truly unbearable – the worst smells you've ever come across – piss and blood and crap, and the concentrated hot-sweet smell of a tramp, and above all that a melted rubbish smell that only an unemptied bin can generate.

But I didn't care. We were warriors in the heat of battle, and we were invincible. I chucked my dripping handful of garbage. Most splattered against the alley wall, but a good smear of it hit the fat kid – the one with the knife – right in the face. Then Jango hurled two more, his hands like buckets, and I dipped in again, this time putting my arms into the now sideways bin. There was something solid and furry in there. I pulled it out. It was a dead cat, rigor mortis making it as hard and dense as a log of wood, and that almost made me spew, but all I did was throw it at the gang. This time it hit the skinhead leader, bouncing off the top of his shaven skull. They were pulling away now, terrified of the monsters, the filth monsters, before them.

And then, a flashing blue and white and a quick blast from a siren.

'Police!' hissed one of the kids, and that was enough. In fact I reckon they were glad of the excuse, because no one likes having shit thrown at them. Anyway, they fled back the way they had come, skittering away like roaches before the police could pen them, although no police arrived, and perhaps the lights and the siren had been for someone else.

And now that they were gone, Jango's battle-lust left him, and he began to laugh, and I laughed with him, until we fell down in the slime of the alley, with animal crap, and food waste, and the filth that humans make and leave. And then we pulled each other up and ran from the alley. It was only when we were out in the light of the street that we saw the mess we were in. Slimed and smeared all the colours of the shit rainbow, from tarry black to dark yellow.

And it was then that I remembered Sophia, and the reason I'd come into town, and the laughter died in me with a splat, like a fat beetle hitting the windscreen of your car on the motorway.

Of course there was no way I could see Sophia, not looking and smelling like this. But at least I could call her . . . make up some kind of excuse. Beg her forgiveness.

'Give me the phone, Jango,' I said, serious again.

Jango was still grinning. There was a streak of something orangey-brown across his face. It might have been egg, but it could have been fermented cat shit.

'Phone?'

His grin came down a couple of notches, but it was still a smile.

He looked at his hand, as if he expected to see it there. Then he patted his pockets.

'Ah, sorry, Matty lad. Must have, er . . . It was a shit phone anyway. I'll buy you a new one – I can spare a tenner.'

My face was now rigid with fury. 'I needed that phone, you dickhead.'

'Chill, man, it's only a thing; a toy; a fistful of plastic.'

I knew I was going to hit him if I stayed. I stomped back into the stinking alleyway, hoping I'd find it there. Jango came behind me and put his hand on my shoulder. I shook it off, and spat a curse at him, with more hatred in it than Jango deserved, maybe.

That was enough for Jango. It was the closest thing to a real gesture of friendship he'd ever given me, and nobody likes to be rebuffed.

'Please yourself,' he said, and I knew he wasn't there any more.

I searched the alley for ten minutes, kicking through the litter and sludge. Then I traced the way we'd come. There was nothing. People avoided me, even before the stench of me hit them. My mind was churning and gurning and I gave off waves of hate even more intense than the smell.

I couldn't get a bus. The driver would never have let me on. I walked the long way back home, avoiding the main roads. It was only then, trudging through the street drizzle, that I realised the crowning glory on all this. The number – Sophia's number. I'd chucked it away. And now my phone was gone. I tried to remember what the number was, tried to recall the gaps and the substitutions, but there was nothing except white noise in my head.

It was ten-thirty by the time I got in. Mum and Dad were watching the telly. I went straight upstairs without saying a word and showered for half an hour. When I was done, I double-bagged my clothes, right down to the socks and boxers, and chucked the whole lot in the bin.

I went to bed hating Jango, hating me, hating the world. Maybe even hating Sophia for making me feel like this.

No, not that. Not that.

SOPHIA

Friday

The clock tick-tocks on, measuring out my embarrassment in faked sips from a stone-cold teacup and flicks through my iPhone messages. Or lack of.

10.22: Nothing.

10.23: Nothing.

10.24: I go against every how-to rule and text him. 'Is this a test?'

10.31: Nothing.

If it *is* a test, then I've failed. But so has he. Because I'm standing at a bar packed with students and suits in my best Kylie meets Chrissie Hynde, with no date, and a bitter taste in my mouth that could be the dregs of my sad-sack drink or defeat and I don't want any more of either. What I want is a shot of happy. A shot of truth. A shot of him running into the bar, his hair ruffled, his eye black, his phone lost because he's been in a fight.

What I get is a shot of JD slammed down by Danny, who's read my troubled teenage underage mind and is lining them up for a stag party and what's one more on their bill when they're already so far gone on Jägerbombs they can't count to ten? The alcohol trails heat down my throat and hits my stomach like a fever. I push some coins across the bar for a refill.

Fuck him, I think, as the second shot floods my bloodstream: warm anaesthetic.

Fuck him and fuck Lucas and Lexy for being walking clichés.

Fuck all of them at Pennington with their pity and their contempt.

Fuck Mom and her airless quest for perfection.

Fuck—

Oh fuck.

Because so on a roll of fucking the world am I that when my phone vibrates in my hand with incoming, I almost curse it for interrupting.

I flick the screen open, JD churning in my stomach, sending butterflies skittering.

At first I don't get it. Because it's not him. Just a random number I don't recognise. But it *is* him. It has to be him. Because what it says is, 'You still in the Porter, Sophia?'

What I want to say is no. What I want is to be numb. To ignore him. To say that four letter word that rolled off my tongue so easily just a few seconds ago. But what I say instead, all I can say is, 'Yes.'

'Meet me outside the Lamb on Wellington in ten minutes.'

Wellington Street? That's a mile at least. That's halfway home to the suburbs. Only very definitely on the wrong side of the tracks. This is where Lexy goes scouting out. This is where my mother refuses to even drive in case someone looks at the Beemer funny.

Fuck. This is where he lives.

And then I get it. The different phone. The wait. This isn't a stand-up, I think. It's a game. He's playing a game. Just like Will would do. Or me, if I hadn't been so pathetically romcommed up. And my stupid heart soars. My fickle, feckless heart.

'On my way,' I say. 'I'll be the one in the red carnation.'

And I am so on my way. I'm pushing through the bare-legged, high-heeled club crowd, grateful I'm still in my high-tops. I skirt the queues for Underground and Circo, and dodge the catcalls from the lads in logos and labels. 'Run, Lola, run!' someone shouts and I flick the finger, but I do as they tell me anyway, not looking where I'm treading, not caring that when I get there I'm going to be red-faced, bourbon-sweaty, out of breath. Because there'll be him. And me. And a kiss. Oh, frick-frack, let there be a kiss.

The Lamb's on the edge of the city centre, where the glass and chrome gives way to the first of the tangled rows of terraces and ginnels. The crowds thin out here too, just stragglers staggering home late from office drinks, and I slow down as I turn off Holloway Street on to Wellington. The Lamb's halfway down, the M missing on the lettering and an I and A added in spray paint on the end. Oh, ha ha. A locals' pub, I think, one I only know from the days of Millwall Dino, who drank in here with his dad. One I came to once with Lex, ate peanuts and played pool, putting on accents like we're not the silver-spooned, silver-tongued private schoolgirls we are. I wonder, now, if Matthew was there that night, if he lives round here, and I feel embarrassment creep over me, a blush deepening my already pantomime-dame cheeks.

But I can't see him. So he can't see me. Not yet. I walk past the pub; peer in. It's half empty, so unless he's put on four stone and the rest of his wardrobe is what can best be described as sportswear for the terminally unfit then he's not here. I check my phone. I'm late. So where is he?

It's one thing being stood up in packed bar in town where the barman knows your name and there's a bus stop round the corner. But it's a whole other world of hell being stood up in the middle of Hicksville where I fully expect tumbleweed to roll across the dog-shit-decorated cobbles any frick-fracking minute. There's an edge here. And not just in my Ken-Loach-boxset-filled head. A smell too, of bust drains or blocked sewers. I check my shoes to see if I've stepped in something other than bad luck. Nada. But I swear it's getting stronger by the second. On cue, I hear the rattle of a bottle being kicked down a back alley and I cross my fingers and turn, hoping to see him silhouetted in the street light.

There is someone there. But, even without seeing his face clearly, I know it's not him. This boy is taller, thinner. His hair's longer and there's a glint of an earring in one ear. And he has white trainers on. Which, don't even. Or at least, they used to be white. Now they're wearing the same patina of filth the rest of him is, right up to his hair. And they're not even his; one of them's at least three sizes bigger than the other.

Homeless kid, I think. Poor fecker. But I'm not in the mood for handouts. I'm not in the mood for this. I've had enough. It's too late for games. And he plays too rough. This isn't Pleasantville; the estate's a few hundred metres away.

I turn back, head down, and start walking.

A voice, that boy's voice, shouts after me, 'Oi!'

But I stick my headphones in, flick to the Mountain Goats and start running. 'I am going to make it through this year if it kills me,' I sing in my head. The sound of indie guitars and laments about lame mothers and loser stepdads drowns out any footsteps that might be following me. But not the smell. I must have missed it when I checked, I must have trodden in the biggest, oiliest pile of shit ever to have broken a bylaw because I swear it's getting stronger by the second and so as I finally hit the home straight on Arlington Road, see the picket fence and porch swing my mum has somehow managed to graft on to an Edwardian five-bed, I feel like I'm going to choke on it.

And then the song ends.

And then it happens.

And then I realise where the smell has been coming from.

A hand pulls my shoulder and I wheel round, my fingers flying automatically to the travel can of hairspray in my pocket that Lexy makes me carry in lieu of mace. 'I've seen it on TV,' she swore. 'It totally blinds them for, like, ten seconds, so you have time to run, or nunchuck him, or whatever.'

When I see the face of the boy, the last thing I want to do is nunchuck him, even if I had nunchucks. His gaunt face is contorted, his eyes bulging like he's got myxomatosis. He is out of my league. Even before the brain tumour and the meds and the two shots of forty per cent proof.

'I've got a twenty,' I say. 'That's all. You can have it.'

I reach into my bag with my other hand, distracting him, then with my right, pull out the can and press down on the button, sending a shower of Cheryl Cole's favourite right into his eyes.

'You effing cow,' he shrieks. 'Effing rich bitch. Ow, effing ow.'

And I should run. This is my window of opportunity, while he's doubled up, rubbing his eyes with hands so dirty with slurry that I'm pretty sure he's going to end up blind even without the Elnett. Only now, having run round after Matthew on his wild frick-fracking goose chase half the night, I can't move my size 5s.

'Effing typical,' he rants on. 'What makes you think I want your money? Clueless bint. I might've been going to do you a favour.'

And then it hits me. This night; this life in its pathetic total-ity: Matthew, Lexy, Lucas and what they've done. Me and what I've got.

'Really. A favour? Because what favour could you possibly do me? Stop me getting played on the set of *Holby* freaking *City*? Stop my slut of a best friend getting it on with the once love of my life? Stop me listening to the jerks who tell you to live for the moment in case there's no tomorrow? Invent a cure for freaking cancer? Favour? Well, screw you.'

And then I find my feet. And I walk, don't run, because I will have dignity if it's all I can get, down the few remaining metres of the street to my house. And I'm just saying, 'And, scene,' in my head when it turns out that Judd Apatow, or someone with an actual sense of humour, is directing my life after all because there, leaning on the gate, with a look like he stole the family silver, is Lucas.

I shake my head. 'You have got to be kidding me.'

'Soph . . .' he begins.

'No,' I say. 'No.' And I push past him. But then something in my oh-so-messed-up head occurs to me. That everything today is leading up to this moment. That maybe Matthew wasn't the point. That perhaps, just perhaps, my fairy godmother – by which I do not mean Will in a wig with his *Harry Potter* wand – has been watching over me after all, and it's all been some giant screwball comedy setup so that I do the obvious thing after all and kiss Lucas.

And so I do. I kiss Lucas. I kiss him like Lexy kissed him. Like Matthew kissed me. With meaning. With determination. With tongues, and my fingers tangled in the hair on the nape of his neck.

Violins do not play. The earth does not move. I don't feel those three seconds of perfection I thought I had this morning. I don't feel anything at all.

Nope. No one is directing my life but me. And I just called another bum shot.

As if to confirm this epiphany, my phone vibrates in its own hallelujah chorus. And this time I do know the number.

It's Matthew. Or part of him, at least.

I double take to check I'm really seeing what I'm seeing.

Yup. It is exactly what I think it is. There, in glorious, grainy technicolour, is the cherry on top of my swirling dog turd of a day. It's a photo of a penis. His, I assume. 'Suck my dick,' says the Hallmark message accompanying it.

'Fuck it,' I say. 'Fuck you all.'

And I do what I should have done hours ago: I block both numbers – Matt's and the one that lured me to the Lamb, and I switch the phone off. Then I open the front door and slam it behind me, leaving Lucas and the crazy-dancing, shit-smelling, homeless mugger to each other, and the world to itself.

Living like today's your last can go suck dick, I think.

And for the first time in a long time, I almost, almost hope that that is it. That there really is no tomorrow.

MATTHEW

Saturday

The morning light seeped through my curtains, yellow, weak and messed-up, like me. It took me a few seconds to work out why I felt so crap, so down. I was used to waking up feeling neutral. I'd got used to not expecting anything amazingly good to happen in my life – not expecting any zing, any thrill. That was just the absence of joy. But this . . . this was a presence – an orc sitting on my chest and punching my face with fists made of shit.

At least there was no school today. I couldn't have faced the mayhem, the yelling, the clatter, the teachers' rage or indifference, the cabbage smell of the corridors, the corridor smell of the cabbage.

No, today I'd embrace my gloom alone, in bed.

Wrong.

SOPHIA

Saturday

Things I do not do on The Day The World Does Not End:

1. Turn on my mobile.
2. Take the three phone calls (Lexy, Lexy and 'a boy') that manage to outwit Thom's desire to use the landline as a weapon of mass destruction.

Things I do do on TDTWDNE:

1. Lie in bed until my legs scream to be used, reading Plath and wondering if it's possible to commit suicide by induction hob.
2. Eat the best part of a litre tub of Rocky Road and decide it's definitely possible to commit suicide by Ben & Jerry's.
3. Google the distance of the nearest cooperative dolphins.
4. Slouch into Thom's room still wrapped in a duvet and build us a fortress of thousand-thread-count sheets and feather pillows; a Selfridges-bought castle in which we eat sneaky marshmallows and discuss the finer points of being dead – Thom's latest, unsurprising, obsession.

'When I'm dead, will my eyes be shut?' he asks.

'Yes,' I say truthfully.

'But what if I need a drink of water?'

'When you're dead you don't need anything.'

'Not even a duvet?'

'Nope. Not a duvet. Not Lego. Not even Pom-Bears.'

'Being dead is boring.'

'I guess so.'

'Do chickens need duvets?'

And so the questions continue, and I continue to answer. And not once do I lie, because with Thom I don't need to; there's nothing to hide. By rights I should resent him. And maybe at times I do: when he's wailing the house down because he's lost his straggly, sour-smelling monkey; when he's using the remote as a mobile and refusing to hand over the goods; or when he's stuck raisins in the DVD player again. But mainly he's just this pale, soft, miniature boy, all wide-eyed wonder at the world. And so I sit with him for as long as I can in the hope that just a sliver of it rubs off on cynical me.

MATTHEW

Saturday

I heard the doorbell go, and then, a couple of seconds later, my mum called out, 'Matthew . . .'

I threw on my jeans. Jango was at the front door, looking like some kind of deposed Eastern European count, down on his luck, with his pale face and his long coat and his long hair, and his lost look. He was holding out his hand. There was a phone in it. For a couple of seconds I thought it was mine, and my heart leaped at the chance of redemption. I could call her, sort it out, make things whole again.

But it wasn't mine. It was new. In this, at least, Jango had been true to his word.

'Peace offering,' he said. And then, before I had the chance to reply, to tell him to go screw himself, 'I was a dick last night. Lost the plot. Off the leash. Out of it.' He made a rough circling gesture. 'Head stuff. Mum stuff.'

Jango's mum. There's a story. Not that Jango likes to tell it. Crazy lady. I've met her maybe three or four times. Each time she was crazy in a different way. Sometimes flirty, sometimes dirty, sometimes batshit.

So, yeah, 'Mum stuff' wasn't a bad excuse for Jango being a crazy fucker himself.

'Anyway,' he said, putting the new phone in my hand, closing my fingers round it, like he was a Mafia crime boss, giving me my first gun, 'at least you've got an upgrade out of it.'

I looked at the phone. It was OK. Not an iPhone or anything, but not a polished camel turd, either.

'It's not the point,' I said, trying not to sound like a sulking schoolkid, which is basically what I was. 'It's what was on it . . .'

You could see the thoughts going through Jango's head. It's funny – usually you never know what's going on in that brain of his, but there are times when he's as easy to read as one of those *Magic Key* books, with Chip and Biff.

'That girl you were texting . . . did you not have her number written down somewhere? You didn't, did you? Dickhead.'

Typical, that, the way I was the dickhead in this.

I sighed. I realised I was going to have to tell him. And the truth is, a part of me wanted to talk about her, because that was all I had now: words.

But I was conscious of my mum bustling around. She likes Jango – he usually turns on the charm for her, and she feels sorry for his bad leg and his big shoe. She'd probably have joined us for a chat, if I'd let her.

'Come on,' I said to Jango, in a voice that sounded a lot like a continuation of the sigh, which it was, in a way. 'Let's hit Starbucks. You can buy me a bucket of coffee.'

'I'll throw in a blue-bollock muffin if you take the arse off your face,' said Jango, and a bit of me smiled, maybe an eyelash or something.

SOPHIA

Saturday

Of course, then I spend the next hour wondering whether the 'boy' was Lucas, Will or he of the overexposed genitals. Which, like, what is that about? Do boys really think that I'm going to get down and dirty over a #nofilter random body part? 'Oh, a blurry picture of a bellend. I'm so hot!' said no one, ever. Give me some Nin, some Miller. Christ, give me Judy frick-fracking Blume. (Though seriously, Judy, 'Ralph'? Who calls their penis Ralph? Who calls their penis anything?)

And then I spend the next half hour naming the penis from a shortlist of Dennis, Nigel and Monty.

And that's what does it. A penis called Monty. That's what has me reaching for the iStalk, clicking the button and waiting for it to flicker into mind-fecking life.

It takes two minutes for the missed calls and texts and emails and PMs to end their 'I told you so' vibrations. And of course not one of them is from Matt. But whatever hell that thing in my head has brought me, right now it seems to be dishing up a pair of balls to go with the dick, because I swipe and delete them all. Bar the dick shot. I'm keeping that for Will's amusement. And he sure as shiz needs some because there are eighteen texts, four missed calls and a selfie of him superimposed outside Number 10 holding up a 'Free Sophia' sign.

'Which would you rather: Nigel or Monty?'

It takes him forty-three seconds to reply. And, given his fat thumbs, I know how hard this is for him. 'She's alive! Crank up the Miley CD and crack out the Jammie Dodgers. So, what gives?'

But I don't want to get into that. Not yet. I've got more important fish to fry.

'Seriously, Nigel or Monty. Which would you rather?'

'As a dog name?'

'As a cock name.'

'Interesting twist. Personally, I like to call mine Mark-Francis.'

'Classy.'

'Always. What's with the naming ceremony?'

I have to tell someone. And that someone is so not going to be Lexy right now.

'You want the wiki plot or the director's cut?'

'Wiki – I need my dirt fast.'

'So, yesterday a stranger kissed me in the morgue café, stood me up, twice, and then sent me a photo of his penis.'

'What did he look like?'

'Can't really remember,' I say. 'Tallish. Darkish. Normcore.'

Good lips, I think. Those I can still see, and feel, and while my head tries to swipe and delete, my telltale heart beats a fraction harder.

'I meant the penis.'

I smile, forward the mugshot.

'Totally average,' comes back the verdict. 'No embellishments or distinguishing features. Definitely a Nigel.'

'That's what I thought.'

'Where did it score on Lex's scale of zero to Jordan Manning?'

'I wouldn't know. She was too busy boning Lucas to give it her attention.'

'WTAF?'

And at that point he clearly decides this is way too *Eastenders* for print media, that he needs the live-on-the-sofa interview, because my phone starts ringing.

'Hey, what's up, buttercup?' I answer.

'What. The. Actual. Fuck?'

'Yeah. I know. But it's no biggie.'

'I thought we were done with the penis talk.'

'Oh god, I think my sides just split laughing,' I deadpan.

'Come on, Soph,' he insists. 'This is huge. No penis pun intended.'

It should be huge, I think. It should be heart-breaking, earth-shattering, game-changing huge. Maybe it would have been a few weeks ago, a few days ago. But now, it just seems kind of inevitable. The obvious storyline.

'Really, I'll live,' I say. 'Well, probably.'

'What's *his* penis like, then? Does it have a name? Oh. My. God. Do you think she went down on him? Do you think he went down on her? Do you think he's comparing you at this very moment?'

'Jesus, Will!'

But he's probably right. And it's pretty clear who'd take the prize given that Lexy's made it her mission in life to give the perfect blow job. She has, I am not kidding, studied every how-to guide from *Cosmo* to phone porn, and when Millwall Dino told her she was the best he'd had, I swear she couldn't have been happier if she'd won a frick-fracking Oscar.

'Sorry, doll.'

'Whatever. I'm sure she's giving little Lucas the ride of his life.'

I don't tell him that Lucas came round after. I don't tell him I kissed him.

And I don't tell him either that I thought Matthew was the one. The One. My Heathcliff. My trip to frick-fracking Disneyland. Only he turned out to be a spin on the waltzer down the Goose Fair and I threw up afterwards on too much sugar.

Instead I ask him what he's been dying to tell me all day anyway and for the next hour we're riffing on Caleb's ex's Brian's tattoo of a glow-in-the-dark Jesus key ring, the statistical probability of him cheating with the guy who works the Saturday shift at Burger King, and the merits and demerits of them getting a miniature pinscher called Susy Q.

'Got to go, doll,' he says, eventually. 'Incoming hot naked guy on Skype.'

'Sure thing,' I reply. And I'm about to tell him I'll talk to him on the flipside when a thought occurs to me. 'Will, if you were straight, would you kiss me?'

'Babe, if I were straight, I'd marry you. And you could call my dick Mabel for all I cared.'

And that's why I love him. Because he gets it. He gets the need for games, for smart talk, for disguise. He gets me.

I thought Matthew did too.

Which only goes to show that Dr Gupta is wrong and that thing really has fucked with my head after all.

MATTHEW

Saturday

'That's a crazy fucking story.'

'Jango, you tried to get off with some girl – any girl – dying of cancer, and you say it's crazy because I met someone there just visiting?'

Jango smiled, and it was the sort of smile you'd get from a normal person, for once.

'I suppose you got me. But the way you just snogged her . . . never guessed you had it in you.'

'Me either. But it makes no difference. You lost my phone. I binned the number. I'm dead as a jellyfish on the beach.'

'Don't sweat it. She's not worth it anyway,' said Jango, with a sort of careful carelessness.

'How the hell would you know?'

Jango looked up from his espresso, met my eyes for a second, then out of the dirty window at the drizzle, and the hunched figures moving through it.

He shrugged. 'Her texts. Lame. Lamer than me.'

I was suddenly mad again.

'Jango, you make me sick. All you ever think about is yourself, and your own fucking tragedy. Well yesterday you stunk

133

up the one bit of my life that didn't already stink. Were you just trying to drag me down into the crap with you? Have you ever wondered why you've got no friends? You think it's because you've got a big shoe? It's not your foot that's crippled, it's the rest of you.'

The second it was out, I felt a jolt of horror. And another change came over Jango's face. The feelings that had been blowing across it were gone. Now his face was as impassive as a bar of soap.

'Fine,' he said. 'If it means that much to you, I'll get you her address.'

Another jolt. Not horror this time, but hope.

'What? How?'

'Piece of piss, really. You've got her name?'

'Yeah, Soph . . . Sophia.'

'And you know what school she goes to?'

'What? No, how could I?'

'Don't be a dick. She's posh, yeah?'

'I don't know . . . yeah. I guess.'

There was no guessing. She was posh.

'So that means she either goes to St Mary's or Penn. Did she sound Catholic to you?'

'Huh? Don't even know what Catholic is supposed to sound like.'

'Like the pope shitting in the woods.'

'That isn't even funny.'

'Guess.'

'OK, *no*. She didn't seem very Catholic.'

'Right, that means Penn. And she's same as us, Year 11?

'She didn't . . .' Although there was something older about Sophia, it wasn't exactly an age thing, a time thing. She was just, I don't know, she'd seen more, done more. 'Yeah, maybe. Or maybe lower sixth.'

'It'll take me twenty minutes to find out who she is, and where she lives.'

'How?'

'Google. A couple of apps. A monster brain.'

'Yeah, like Frankenstein.'

It was a sort of joke, and Jango sort of laughed. Or at least he made a noise that might have been a laugh.

And then he was looking at me in a new way.

'But I'm telling you, don't do this. The hospital thing was a big mistake. Nothing good can come of it. You put your hands in a bucket of shit, what do you think you're going to come out with? A wedding ring?'

I shrugged. I didn't have anything to say back to that. I hadn't done anything wrong at the hospital. Jango was bouncing his guilt on to me. Or something.

'Anyway,' he added, in a vaguely scraping-the-barrel sort of way, 'how do you know what she was doing there?'

'Huh?'

'At Mickey's. You said just visiting. How do you know she wasn't going to the clap clinic, or getting her verrucas burnt off?'

JOANNA NADIN and ANTHONY MCGOWAN

It was an interesting question. Hadn't she said something about it . . .? I couldn't remember. But if she really was sick, then she'd have told me. And, in another way, what either of us was doing at Mickey's was the last thing I wanted to bring up.

'Nah, she was just hanging out in the canteen. Waiting for someone. She told me. Some flaky friend of hers.'

Jango opened his mouth, then closed it again, and a few minutes later I watched him go stumping off down the street. He usually stands up tall, but he seemed kind of hunched. I guessed it was because he was going back to psycho-mum, her hair blue, maybe, this time. Her mood in the clouds or drilling down into the molten core of the earth. I realised that I hadn't even asked him about her and what was going on.

But, truth is, I didn't much care. Jango usually does what he says. He was going to get me Sophia's address, and I was going to make everything well again.

SOPHIA

Monday

Mornings are the worst. Laziness, youth and cynicism make me a bitch. The meds make me a drunk one. It takes all the will and coffee in the world to get me out the door and walking in a straight line. And the knowledge that first up on the agenda is two hours on the dissolution of the monasteries with a man who has the urine taint of sad-sack bachelor, of washing that's dried too slowly – possibly the most pathetic smell of all time – is taking up the other five per cent of my squashed-in brain. So there's just not that much room in there to devote to worrying about Lex. Besides, her embarrassment, her mortification at what her latest sexcapade may have done to me in my fragile state, lasts all of – time them – seven minutes.

The thing about Lexy is, whatever you've done, whatever's been done to you, she's always done it bigger, or had it done harder. Bar the brain thing, which wigs her out on a daily basis – the goddamn unfairness of it – she can trump pretty much any story you have to tell. It's not that she doesn't listen, just that she hears you, sees you, and then raises you like a pro.

That's why I can bear it – the Monday morning walk down the green-tiled mile to Penn's sixth form common room, past the gaping mouths and snickers of the Barbie dolls, the nudges of the mudheads on the first XI – because I know that she lives for this shit. That, to her, the whole Lucas thing is twenty-one-carat best-actress gold. She's going to cry, sure. But only because she doesn't miss an opportunity for a Cecil B. close-up shot of tears welling in those baby blues. And do I hate her for this? I should. I should scorn her. Pity her, even. But somehow, on her, it makes sense. Besides, she's made for the spotlight, and I'm at best the kooky sidekick, at worst a backstage grunt. Everyone knew it. Lucas knew it. But now he's got the leading lady, so everyone's happy, right?

'Oh my god, Soph.'

She's gone for full-on penitent. Black from her roll-neck down to her button-up faux Victorian boots. Christ, even her hair is doing some kind of *Sound of Music* come milkmaid arrangement.

But I'm playing it like she's the whore of Babylon, for now anyway. Because that's what she wants, after all.

'Hey, Lex. So, did you have fun screwing my ex?'

She claps her hand over her mouth; knits her eyebrows together so I can see she's trying to force up the saltwater. 'Oh, god. We so have to talk. Come into my office.' And she takes me by the hand and pulls me into the restrooms.

'You have to understand,' she pleads, 'I was drunk.'

'You're always drunk, but you never did this before.'

'I know. But so was he. And he was . . . upset. We both were.'

'Why? Did he get benched again?'

'No! Soph, come on.' She's indignant now. 'Over you. We were upset over you.'

'Right, so, when you think about it, it's all my fault.'

'Shit. I didn't mean it like that.'

She's actually crying now and I'm beginning to doubt the tears are pure crocodile.

'It's OK.' I hand her a wad of toilet roll.

She dabs at her industrial-strength mascara. 'Really.'

'I was joking. Well, not joking. Just, it doesn't matter. I said I didn't want him and I meant it.' My mind flips back to the kiss and I feel a stab of guilt. But he didn't kiss me, I kissed him. And it was an experiment, that's all. One that proved the theorem, because not even my fickle hormones could be bothered to flicker into life.

'Who told you anyway? Was it Dawse?'

Might as well give her the gift she's been waiting for. 'Er, no. You kind of did. I walked in.'

'No!'

'Yup.'

'Oh god. When?'

'Well, I didn't check my Swatch but I'd guess around half nine.'

'I didn't mean . . .'

'I know what you meant. You weren't . . . you know. Not yet, anyway.'

She pauses. And now I know this is genuine upset because she pulls a face she hasn't checked in the mirror for effect. 'Not at all. He totally bottled it. Like, he had some kind of panic or . . . or epiphany and said he couldn't do that to you.'

'Oh . . .'

'I know! It's, like, so *Casablanca* or *Brief Encounter*. He's such a martyr.'

He's not, and it's not. It really, really is not.

'I don't even know where he went,' she adds and, I am not even joking, she has her hand on her heart.

'Home?'

'You'd think, but no, because I totally went there to tell him that he's right, and we shouldn't do it to you, not until we've talked to you and explained that it's, you know, fated and everything. But only his dad was in – I swear he totally checked me out, which, like, not that gross – and, anyway, he said he hadn't seen him since he left with Jonty at six, so, where was he? I think he has some secret place, like the cathedral, or that temple in the park, where he goes when he has to find himself, or whatever.'

I have to choke back a laugh. As if Lucas would have to look very far. He's got 'jock' stamped across his forehead and Jack Wills sewn into all his clothes. Only then I remember where he did go. And what I did.

'You're right,' I say. 'He's probably torn up. But, listen, I'm not. And you can tell him that.'

'Forshiz?'

'Forshiz.'

'Take care of you,' she says, hugging me and dishing up the *Pretty Woman* like we're improbable prostitutes. But, hey, that's her number one *Cinderella* story, so who am I to argue? Especially when I already know the line.

'Take care of you,' I reply.

'So shall I come over after school? We could, like, voodoo him, or something.'

'Sure. Why not.' Because in the absence of alcohol, Lexy is the perfect pill to take the edge off the mom situation, which has been fairly brutal since my weekend pity party.

So, when the bell rings, summoning me to the nasal assault that is history and Lex to actual drama instead of her own perpetual one, we come out of the toilets hand in hand, lezzing out the Year 7s and pissing off Flick Cameron who was clearly hoping for a full-on bitch fight.

'Laters, babe,' she says, air-kissing me. 'Truth conquers all, see.'

Truth couldn't fight its way out of paper bag, I think. Not with all the lies and convenient omissions I'm serving up. But I'll tell her. About Matthew. Even Lucas, if I have to. Just not yet. Give it a week or so. I'll pick my moment.

'Laters,' I say, and thank the goddess of timetabling that is Miss Pritchard that Lucas isn't in a single one of my classes until Thursday.

I only wish that Miss Pritchard were in charge of the rest of my diary. Because seven hours later as we round the corner to

Arlington Road, as I see a figure so strange yet so frick-fracking familiar that it jolts me like being slapped awake from sleep, as the jumble of images from Friday plays out like a bad teen movie montage, I realise the moment's been picked for me.

I stop dead, yanking Lexy back so she doesn't get to him first.

'What the—?'

'Lex, I need to tell you something.'

'Oh my GOD. Are you—?'

'No. Whatever you think I am, no.'

'Then . . .'

I have to work fast. Right now he's looking over at the Hilditches' X5, which seems to slaughter polar bears even when it's just sitting smugly on their gravel, but any second he's going to turn and see us. See me.

'The thing is, I met this boy at the hospital three days ago and somehow, I don't frick-fracking know how, we kissed and then we were going to meet only we didn't because he stood me up once at the Porter and once at the Lamb and then he texted me a photo of his cock.'

'Like, ready to rumble?'

'Fully.'

'And you didn't tell me.'

'I know. I'm sorry.'

'And you're telling me now because?'

'He's standing outside my house.'

And as if I've called out, 'Cue, dickhead,' he turns and clocks us.

'Soph?' he says.

For which there is only one reply.

'Fuck you.'

MATTHEW

Monday

It turns out you can cram quite a lot of thoughts and feelings into one second. Even giving them an order can be difficult. But maybe I'll try, because feelings might come tossed and mixed together like clouds or stars or piss in the pub urinals, but words have to happen one at a time.

First I thought – no, not *thought*, this was a feeling one – I *felt* a surge of happiness flowing through me, reaching every part, like a teabag turning the hot water golden, and I thought my face was going to crack into a huge grin, but I knew that was wrong, knew that she was going to be hating me, a bit or a lot, and so I fought it back, but it came out anyway as a something else, I don't know, maybe a *gawp*. And this was all because even though my mind had been forming and reforming my memories – just scraps, really – of her in different ways, each one more perfect than that last, the real her – the true presence – was even more astounding. And I thought again how totally wrong the word 'pretty' was for her. Not that there's anything wrong with pretty. Pretty is damn good. But calling her pretty, or not pretty, because she wasn't, would be like criticising a peacock for not being fast, or good at table

144

tennis. There was too much of it, too much beauty, like an overfilled glass, and like when you overfill a glass and put your lips to it, I wanted to put my lips to her to lap up the excess.

And then I saw that she wasn't alone, and that sucked out a lot of the joy from the plain old seeing her part. I hadn't thought for a second that she'd have a friend with her. Every imaginary conversation I'd had with her, every opening gambit, assumed she'd be alone.

And then I focused a bit more on the person – the girl – she was with. And if I hadn't already been so smitten with Sophia, so buried that only the tip of my quiff was showing, I think it would have been bloody hard to look at anything else. She was dressed in black, but not like a goth, more like it was some sort of costume or disguise, because she didn't give off a black vibe. And the second I clocked her she reached up to her hair, which had been tied up somehow, and she unleashed this golden wave, and gave it the full head toss, so it caught the last of the afternoon light. And looking at her I thought of, I don't know, some kind of flipping elf or something, like Galadriel in *The Lord of the Rings*, except there was something else, too. Jango used to have this thing that he did when he went past a girl who was hot, and he'd say under his breath, 'She does,' and what he meant was, obviously, that she'd do it, she really would, maybe not with you, but with someone, because she had the look of someone who liked doing it. And I don't think Jango meant it in a bad way, as another way of

JOANNA NADIN and ANTHONY MCGOWAN

saying 'Slag,' or whatever, just that he was picking up on (or, I guess, plain imagining), some deep pit of sensuality, or desperation or yearning in the person that meant that yeah, they liked doing it, and wanted to do it whenever they could.

Well, what I thought when I saw this friend of Sophia's was, She does, and that sort of undercut the whole Galadriel elf-princess business. And then I felt a little bit grubby for thinking these thoughts – even at the speed of light, and without any choice on the matter – while Sophia was right there. And so I thought about her some more, half closing my eyes the way you do when you're in front of a fire, to feel it all intensely, but somehow I'd ruined it, and suddenly the wrongness of this, being here, the whole thing, struck me like a hard kick in the knackers.

How could I have missed it, the dumbness of what I was doing? Turning up at her door like this, out of the blue, after failing to show the other night? Why hadn't I sent a letter or an effing pigeon or . . . Anyway, I just knew that I shouldn't have loomed up like a stalker or a psycho.

Jango. I couldn't really blame him. He'd taken his time over it. First time I'd called him he'd said that it was harder than he'd thought, and there were ten thousand effing Sophias in the school – that, in fact, every single girl in Penn was an effing Sophia, except for a couple of Zoës, and a Clytemnestra.

But for once it was me doing the pestering, not him, and I wouldn't let it lie. I made it clear that the stakes were big. For me; for him. And so on Sunday night he came through. Just the address.

'I don't think you should do it,' he'd said, once I'd prized the street off him. 'Seriously, buddy, this is bad shit. The karma off it stinks like a monkey's finger.'

I wasn't really listening, but I couldn't let that one go.

'A what?'

'You know, that YouTube clip. The monkey sticks its finger up its hole, then sniffs it, then falls off the fucking bush.'

'Jango, I don't know what you're talking about. But thanks for this. We're quits on the phone. Just . . . just try not being such a dick for the next few weeks.'

And then I hit 'End call' on my new phone, which wasn't, actually, that shit.

My plan was to skip English on Monday afternoon, get home, change into something that didn't stink of school, then wait for her and tell her everything. But things got messed up. As I was slipping out of the school gates I bumped right into Mrs Peel slipping in. Mrs Peel is OK for a teacher. She is good at it – the teaching bit – and she sees that I quite like English, and don't suck at it, so we get on pretty well. And she's relaxed about the stuff that doesn't matter, and she has a joke with you in class. But that's why I couldn't let her see me, and then not be in the lesson.

She raised an eyebrow at me, and I said, 'Just getting some chips, miss,' so that's what I did.

Anyway, it meant that I was still in my school clothes when I reached Sophia's house. It's in one of those streets where all the houses are different – some really old-looking ones with little diamond shapes in the windows and fake turrets and shit sticking out of them, and some ultra-modern ones, either plain glass boxes, with nothing but blinds stopping you from seeing the people in there making their tea or having a crap, and some in weird concrete shapes looking like a piano or a waterfall or a nuclear fallout bunker. None of them looked like the houses in my street. And the gardens were full of trees with pink and white blossom, and complicated bushes and bird tables and swings and hammocks – the sort of gear that would get nicked in ten seconds flat if anyone was stupid enough to leave it in any of the gardens near us.

And I waited, feeling like an idiot, not knowing whether to sit on the garden wall or lean against a lamp post, and so I kept switching between the two options, until finally she was there, with her friend, and I felt like I'd found her and lost her at the same moment.

I meant to say something, get my words in first, but I don't think I even managed to get her name out before . . .

'Fuck you.'

And I think maybe that 'fuck you' was my salvation. 'You work a little fast for me. Any chance of a coffee first?'

OK, so it wasn't exactly Oscar Wilde, but then I never claimed to be a genius. The important thing was what I did with my face, and whatever it was that happened there, it seemed to work, or at least not totally blow chunks.

The girl with Sophia giggled. Sophia wasn't so easily amused, but some of the hardness went out of her. Then I sensed her toughen up again, like a time-lapse of a river freezing. She was angry, which I'd expected, but there was something more than that, and I wasn't sure what it was, or what I'd done to cause it.

'Proud of it then, are you?' she said, her voice ugly with sarcasm.

'What?'

'You know what, though?'

'What?'

'You shouldn't be?'

'What?'

OK, that was three 'whats', which was enough to last a whole conversation.

'Because, really, I've seen better.'

Now I was completely confused. I wanted to say 'What?' again, but swallowed it. I tried to reboot. 'I'm so sorry I . . . the other night. My mate, he's a nutter—'

'Cock.'

That was the other girl. I looked at her. Had she really said that? It seemed a bit harsh.

And then Sophia had her phone in her hand, and she shoved it in my face, so close I had to take a step back. There was a photo on the screen. I didn't recognise it at first – it was blurry and could have been almost anything.

But then I worked it out.

'I don't get it,' said Sophia, and she pronounced each word with incredible precision, so you could feel the beginning and end of each one enter you, like the twin cutting edges of a knife. 'If you couldn't make it, or didn't want to, you could have texted me. Or, if you really are just a jerk, you could have left it at standing me up. But no, you have to ice the fucking cupcake with your proverbial penis. And then turn up here . . . What did you think I was going to do? Beg you to get it out?'

'I—'

'Wrong. I'm going to call the police, you pathetic perv. You can explain it to them.'

Until she said the word 'police' I'd been in a sort of trance, with none of this sinking in. But suddenly I saw it, and understood it all.

'Whoa!' I said, or rather yelped. 'Let me explain it to you first. I get what's happened. It's not what you . . . I mean, it's the absolute opposite of what you think. I was there, almost, I mean right at the bar. And this mate of mine, Jango, he turned up, and snatched my phone, fooling around, as you do, and he wanted to know who I was texting, and then we bumped into this gang of . . .' And then I told the rest of the story, as straight as I could, right down to the shit fight in the alley, and me throwing the dead cat at the kid.

And at the end it was in the balance, and I didn't know which way it was going to go. I didn't think Sophia was still going to call the police – actually, I never really thought she'd do that – but she could easily have tossed her beautiful head and walked right past me into her house, and I'd have never seen her again.

'*Sooort* of fits,' said the girl – the other one, the one with the blonde hair, the one who *would* – and I felt a little bit of love for her. 'Sounds like it shouldn't, but it works. Like salted caramel. Or Cathy and Heathcliff.'

And then Sophia shook her head, and her hair moved lazily, like it was some kind of heavy liquid – mercury or lava.

'He could be making it all up. Lies, just to cover it up.' She angled the screen of her phone at me. 'A little mankini of lies to cover up his . . . *Monty*.'

'HIS WHAT?'

I think the other girl and I said this at the same time, and I realised at that moment that things were going to be OK, because I saw a twitch at the corner of that big mouth of hers, I mean Sophia's, and I don't mean big *bad* but big *good*. And for the first time ever she sounded a bit flustered.

'I . . . It doesn't matter what it is . . . I mean what you call it. There's no way I can know for sure that this isn't you. I mean . . .' she flapped her hand in the rough direction of my trousers . . . 'yours.'

And then the other girl gave her eyes a cute roll, and said, 'Well, there kind of is . . .'

And that was when I said what I suppose I should have said ages ago.

'That can't be mine.'

'Not got one?' said Sophia, and the girl laughed – snorted, really.

'Not one like that.'

A couple of beats of silence, the girls looking at me, baffled.

'I mean, well, the thing is, I'm not, you know, *Jewish*.'

Sophia looked at me, and then at her screen. And then she said, in a half-hearted kind of way, 'You don't have to be Jewish to, er, get it.'

'I know, I know, but, well, I haven't had it done. I guess I could prove it. Take a selfie. But that's sort of how we got here in the first place . . . .'

Sophia's face was still perplexed, puzzled, sceptical. But I could see that the smile was trying to break through. And then the other one pushed Sophia's hair away from her ear in a move that was incredibly intimate and, I've got to say, a bit of a turn-on, and she whispered some words, and while she was whispering she cast her big blue eyes over me. And then she pulled away and put her hand in her little bag and took out her phone and said in a kind of girly girl voice, 'Oh, look, I've got a text calling me away on *urgent* business,' and it was a neat performance. 'But listen, party at mine on Saturday, yeah. Kind of pre-Easter, end-of-freedom-before-exam-term thing. For you, anyway. What are you, Year 11?'

I nod. 'But, like, my birthday's September, so I'm old for my year.'

Saying that made me feel even younger, like some little kid making a big deal out of being six and a half, not six. Even my voice sounded squeaky, like Micky effing Mouse.

'Cute. Soph's the baby of the lower sixth – August the tenth You're practically the same age ... anyway, toy boy, bring someone. Or ones.' And then she gave Sophia's hand a little squeeze, and she was away, and after a few steps she turned around and gave me a wave, just her fingertips, unseen behind Sophia's back.

And that left Sophia and me standing there alone in the street, and her gaze was on me, heavy as osmium.

I had literally no idea what to say next.

SOPHIA

Monday

I shoot voodoo pins into Lex's back as it disappears round the corner, knowing the only reason she's ducked out of the drama now is to escalate it and then get the skinny later on. Though it's been ten seconds since she left and neither of us has said a word so unless she's up for a silent film re-enactment she's going to be disappointed.

Fifteen seconds. It's beyond awkward now. The kind of silence you could cut with a blunt frick-fracking mallet let alone a knife.

I have to say something. I open my mouth. But before I can even squeak out an 'I', another voice slices the void with its cut-glass sharpness and barely disguised disgust.

'Sophia?'

Mom.

And then it's a choice. Either I piss him off, or her. So I go for gold.

I turn to Matthew. 'Coming in?' I ask.

He gives me a look like I've asked him into the Halloween house or Narnia and he can't decide which it is or which is preferable. 'Er . . .'

I don't wait for an actual word to follow, just turn and walk; the sound of his endearingly fake Converse shuffling after me is all the yes I need to score a perfect ten against the mother ship, whose lips are pulled so tight she's looking like a candidate for collagen.

'Hey, Thom,' I say first, sweeping up Little Lord Fauntleroy, kissing him, and planting him back down at his Lego in one practised move. Then I turn to the lady of the house. 'This is Matthew,' I say. 'We'll be in my room.'

Because, for all the pissing off I want to do to both of them, there is no way I'm subjecting him to her Spanish Inquisition, or her to our whole awkward cock aftermath thing.

'Would you like some tea?' she asks.

'Nope,' I say. Seriously, someone should tell her and the entire adult world that we all know tea isn't tea but some big fat excuse to burst in and check we're not semi-naked or smoking or both. How dumb do you think we are?

And I drop my bag in the hallway and walk on up the stairs with Matthew still shuffling silently behind me.

My room's not like Lexy's. There's no Magic 8-Ball or teddy bears or conveniently placed underwear. Partly because I have a mom whose tidying OCD extends to sock separators, and partly because setting honeytraps hasn't exactly been high on my to-do list.

What it does have is: a pharmacy of pills, half of which are set out into a days-of-the-week flip-top box (guess which OCD-tastic relative couldn't wait to get her hands on that one), and half of which are scattered in their original telltale packaging all over the dressing table, and all of which I sweep into a drawer hoping that Matthew is still in his 'what the ...?' stupor; a dead lady's wardrobe of weird; and records. Lots of records. A whole rack of the things, sorted by genre and then alphabetised for good measure (don't judge me, I was off school for three months; it was that or take up needlepoint). Records – or music – make everything right. They fill silence with their crackle and hum; they change the way you see stuff; they make the world spin slower or faster – at 33 or 45 rpm. And right now I need to slow things down, so I pull out some Nina (stored between Simon & Garfunkel and The Smiths, in defiance of iTunes' first name filing, and taste) and kneel by the turntable.

I don't believe in any God, but putting a record on is a religious thing, and something my dad taught me. The pulling out of the inner sleeve, the careful slide of vinyl on to the flat of your fingertips, the careful dropping of the needle into the groove. It's reverence to these rulers of messed-up emotions. And Nina is a queen of that. Three drumbeats, then guitar, then her voice like honey sliding through bitter coffee sounds out, filling the room with melancholy, and promise. And then neither of us needs to say anything. I sit on the floor, back to the stack and my legs stretched out over the carpet, toes almost touching his. He slides down opposite me so our legs top to tail. And we listen.

And then, when the song ends, he finds his voice.

'I never heard that before.'

'Seriously?'

'Seriously.' He looks sheepish, apologetic.

'Nina Simone,' I say.

'Nina.' He tries the word out. 'But she sounds like a man.'

I want to roll my eyes, but something about his tone, incredulous rather than dismissive, means instead I feel my mouth crease up into a smile.

'Loads of people think that,' I say. 'But when you've listened to her once you'll never mistake her voice again. It's . . .'

'Butter,' he finishes for me, then reddens. 'Like, I mean, some voices are bland like margarine. Or that fake olive oil spread stuff. But hers is, I don't know, the real thing.'

I laugh. 'Butter,' I agree. Then, 'You heard any Patti Smith?'

He shakes his head.

'The perils of comprehensive schooling,' I say, doing my best mom bitch impression. 'You need educating.' And I put on *Horses*. Then I drop some Faces – my dad's mint copy of 'Tin Soldier'– followed by pre-Las-Vegas Elvis, which it turns out is pretty much the only thing he's heard of.

'Sorry,' he says. 'I just . . . I don't know a lot about . . . this stuff.'

'Doesn't matter,' I say. 'I don't buy it anyway, that liking the same music makes you soulmates or whatever.'

'Do you even believe in soulmates?' he asks.

Our legs are touching now, my toes against thigh, his against my hip.

'Lexy does,' I say for want of a better answer.

'Lexy?'

I stumble then, because for the first time someone knows me and not her. Because even with Will, it was her who homed in on him in the support group when she came with me that first day, who found him on Facebook, who got his number. 'Lexy,' I repeat. 'That girl who was here before. She believes in all that shit. Soulmates. And Prince Charming and white weddings and that fate is a baby with wings and a bow and arrow.'

Only that's not good enough.

'What about you though?' he asks.

'I . . .' But I don't have an answer on the tip of my tongue. I have to think about it. I used to believe in it, like I believed in Santa and the tooth fairy and Tinkerbell. Only they all turned out to be hokum, despite the whole footprints-in-the-flour charade my mom insisted on until I was way too old to buy into it; the same one she's now cranking out for Thom.

'I think there are moments,' I say eventually, 'of . . . seren-dipity, or something less fricking cheese-ball. When you know that you have something with someone. And it might not be for ever, or even for more than a few months, but it's something . . . tangible.'

And something about the way he's looking at me now makes me realise he's thinking this is one of those moments. And I should laugh or play-kick him out of it or get up to pee. But something about the closeness of our legs – like there's a current slip-sliding between us – makes me think, despite the whole phone cock-up, despite being stood up, despite the fact my mom probably has a glass to the ceiling right now to check that this low-rent kid isn't besmirching her porcelain doll of a daughter, or maybe because of them, that this is one of those moments too. And this time I do it. Clumsily, inelegantly, but determinedly, I pull my legs round and lean forward on my hands. So our heads are close. So I can feel his breath on my forehead; see the 'what the . . .?' in his eyes. And then I lift my face up ever so slightly, thank goodness I chewed some Wrigley's on the way home, and kiss him.

MATTHEW

Monday

None of this was happening.

Or not to me.

It was some other kid. He looked like me, probably smelled like me, but couldn't be me. Because things like this didn't happened to me.

He was following Sophia through the door, into her hall, past her mum. This other kid looked at the mum, not in her eyes but maybe somewhere around the chin area, and he nodded, and maybe mumbled something, and maybe there was a quick inappropriate thought about her being quite hot for a mum. And there was a little boy there, a brother, and the kid that was me and not me at the same time ruffled his hair, like this was the kind of thing that happened all the time. And he was taking in the fact that this house wasn't like his house. Everything in it was . . . big. You could swing a cat in the hallway – except they wouldn't have a cat, they'd have a leopard or a tiger. No, not a tiger, kind of tacky, a tiger. A panther. Maybe panthers are tacky, too. Is there a kind of big cat that isn't tacky? An ocelot, maybe. But this kid thought that an ocelot might only be the same size as a normal cat, so that was no use. So, yeah, leave out the cats. All cats are tacky.

And this wasn't a tacky kind of place. There were pictures on the wall. Real paintings, not of things, animals or people or whatever, but paintings of nothing, just shapes and colours, like the inside of a crazy person's head. And then there was a drawing, a drawing of actual people. And this kid, he stopped and looked at it. It was in charcoal – he'd done enough art to know it was charcoal. It was of a lady and a little girl, and the lady was naked, except for a sheet draped around her bottom half, and the little girl was next to her, and even though they were almost touching, the fact that there was a tiny bit of white paper separating them made them look like they were on different planets. And then he realised who the people were in the drawing.

And at that moment Sophia reached out and took his hand, and before he followed her up the stairs he glanced down and saw the mum looking up, her face impossible to read, but not happy, definitely not that.

And then he was in her room, on the floor, sitting opposite her, their legs touching. And he thought of a joke that some-one had told him, about watching a load of videos back-to-back, but luckily he was the one facing the telly, and he might even have said that to her, and she might have laughed, but mainly she was fussing with music, and not MP3s on her iPhone, or even CDs, but records, actual vinyl records like his dad had.

And then something about the music brought the *him* and the *me* back together again.

'Nina Simone,' she said, and it didn't mean much to me. But I loved the faint crackle of the record. Loved even more her clever fingers doing the things you have to do: taking the record out of the sleeve; giving it a spin with her thumb, so it turned over on to the side she wanted; lifting the arm of the record player; putting it down gently, but not so gently there wasn't a little bump, which made your heart bump with it.

And I could tell that she was enjoying doing it all. It was a dance, a performance, not like shuffling through the tracks on your phone.

And then there was some talk. Something about soulmates, but it was hard to follow, because the music was a bit too loud, and I was worried that I'd say the wrong thing, and she'd think me an idiot, and uncool. And all the time our legs were touching, and it was the most amazing feeling I'd ever had.

I thought about telling her the joke again in case she hadn't heard it, but I stopped myself because it would have been just so fantastically lame. So I said, 'Your voice . . . it's funny.'

And she said right back, before I'd had the chance to say what I meant, 'So's your face. And I can change my accent, but you're kinda stuck with that.'

And there was bite in it, as well as a smile.

'I only meant . . .'

She laughed then.

'I know. American mom, British dad. Fucked-up me.'

'Everyone's fucked up. It's the human condition. In fact, you have to be weird not to be fucked up.'

I was quite pleased I'd managed to say something like that. Not that it was exactly profound or anything, and Jango would have ripped it to shreds like a kitten with bog roll, but it was better than drooling and grunting.

And drooling and grunting was what I felt like doing. Somehow, more of us was touching now. It had just been our legs up to our knees, but now it was pretty well the whole leg, which meant that our hips were close, and her face was there, right in front of me. And that face, well it was something I could have looked at for ever. Those huge eyes . . . they were just so complicated, all the colours somehow distinct, and unblended, like some mineral, some volcanic glass. That makes it sound hard and stony, but these were alive, and I wanted to put my lips right against them. But that sounds crazy, like I wanted to suck her eyeballs out or something. Anyway, it wasn't just the eyes, it was that whole face, and I felt like I could spend for ever looking at every part of it, the eyelids and the long lashes, like burnt golden feathers, and the corners of her wide mouth, and her ears that – unlike the rest of her face, where the beauty had a boldness to it and a confidence – were made delicately, as if someone had spent years on them, making sure they were just right, and forgetting about the rest of the world, and in the light from the anglepoise lamp that was behind her, I could see the fine golden fuzz on her ears – I don't mean, like, you know, hairy ears, like a troll or something, I just mean the human down that you can't even feel – and I traced it over her ears and on to her neck, beneath the heavy hair, hair that weighs so much that if it was on top of you it would kill you for sure.

And now somehow we'd got even closer, and I could smell her hair again, like in the hospital, and feel her breath on my face. And then she put her hand on my cheek, and it was only then I knew for sure that we were going to kiss, even though it would have been obvious to any normal person from the moment she had touched my hand on the stairs. And then we were kissing, and it didn't matter that I hadn't done much of it before, because, it turns out, it really isn't that hard, and all the time she had her hand on my face, so I did the same, my right hand on her left cheek, her right hand on mine, so it was almost like a soft vice, holding us together.

But I didn't know what to do with my other arm, and the hand stuck at the end of it. I was sort of leaning on it, but that seemed like a waste of a perfectly good hand, so I moved it towards her, but that meant that I overbalanced, and fell towards her, and I was worried she was going to think I was a clumsy oaf, but instead she made a sound, a little sigh, and I thought that maybe she thought that I'd done it on purpose, I mean that it wasn't a fall but a move, a move on her, and now we were holding each other, our hands moving every-where, and my main worry now was to not touch her breasts, I mean touching her breasts with my hands, because I thought she might slap my face or stab me with the sharp end of the metal comb I'd seen on her dressing table.

And the thing about Sophia is that you can sense the strength in her. I don't mean like she's the She Hulk, or anything, just that she isn't one of those girls made out of tissue paper and spider silk. She has this physical reality to her, fills it with her flesh and her muscles and her bones and her teeth. And the thing is that while I was trying not to touch her breasts with my hands, it was sort of ironic, because, well, the top half of me was touching them all the time, my chest on hers.

And then there was the other issue, which was way more urgent and way more serious than the hands, because, well, you can kind of tell your hands what to do, but *down there* something was going on over which I had absolutely zero control, and I thought, Oh god, she's going to notice it any second and then she's going to call her mum and dad, and that threat to get me arrested will finally come good, and how am I going to explain that to *my* mum and dad?

And then I realised, and I guess it was obvious, really, that she knew it was there all along, and that she didn't mind. In fact, maybe she was kind of pleased about it.

And I put my fingertips on her cheek, and I felt the shock of the touch go through her, and sensed a change in her skin, a moment of heat, and tiny pulses of excitement, and afterwards, after everything, that's the thing I remember the most, the energy, and I'm trying not to say 'electricity' because as well as being a massive cliché, it makes you think of blue light, and if there had been a light, then it wouldn't have been the cold blue of electricity, but a golden light, like the sun at the end of the day when at last you can look at it.

And then I thought, Is this it? Are we going to do it, here, on her bedroom floor? And I felt two waves that flowed together, so they were kind of one wave. There was a wave of panic – panic because I didn't really know how to do *it*, the thing that was about to happen here on the floor. And even that wave was quite complicated, because if she just thought I was an innocent virgin and wasn't expecting much, then that would be OK, but I had this feeling that she thought that I might know what I was doing, that I'd been here before, because I was poor and rough, and this was what poor and rough people did, instead of going to the effing opera or whatever. So she was going to be thinking that I had some . . . moves. But the truth about that whole wave was that I didn't but, jeez, she bloody definitely did.

And right after it, no, now surging through it, now past it, now washing over me, the wave that *really really really really really* wanted to do it. I mean more than I've ever wanted to do anything before in my shitty life that had been made up mainly of stuff I wanted to do, but would never be able to.

Well now I could, and I would, and we were so close, so close . . .

And then, and I think this is mainly because I was so hyper-aware, so here, so jangling with the joy and terror of being alive in this moment, some bit of my brain noticed something else, something silvery glinting on the white carpet, and I remembered how when we'd come in, Sophia had opened a drawer in her desk, and swept the stuff on the desktop into it, and I hadn't really thought about it, because I'd still been in a trance, but now I could see that it was a frayed strand of foil, torn from the top of a blister pack of some kind of tablets, and it only caught my eye because the room was so tidy, so weirdly neatly arranged, and because now I could see everything, down to the dust hanging in the air, down to the molecules, the atoms, the electrons.

And something made me want to reach out and pick it up, that silvery curl of foil, and put it in the bin, which was a stupid thing to want to do, given that I was wrapped up in the arms and, jeez, legs of the most beautiful girl I'd ever met.

When.

It.

Stops.

SOPHIA

Monday

That's when I feel it, that part of him pushing into me. And part of me is feeling it right back, all Lexy-pleased with itself, and part of me is scared and wondering what the frick-frack my next move is, when that picture pings into my head. And, even though I know it's not his, I can't stop thinking about it and about the whole indie weird-as-shit nature of our story so far. And maybe it's that, or maybe it's my shonky wiring, or my carefully cultivated scepticism, but this question starts bugging me, and what with that and the thing on my thigh, I pull away.

'Is this for a bet?' I say.

'Wh-what?' he half pants, half stammers.

'Me. This. Us. Is it all for some bet? You know – do it with the rich kid, then laugh about it with your mates later?'

'No,' he snaps. Then softer, 'No. It's . . . not like that. It's . . . I don't know what it is. I just—'

But whatever he 'just' is drowned out by the clarion call of my mom telling me supper's ready in five. I check the clock – five fifty-five. I sigh. 'You could run trains by that woman,' I say and haul myself up.

He follows, pushing his hand down on to his crotch to finish what the mother ship interruption started.

'So, that party on Saturday?' he says. 'Is that for real?'

I hadn't heard anything before Lexy's announcement, but I have no reason to doubt her determination to make like Gatsby. Only, a Penn house party is not the next scene I had in mind, or any scene with Matthew for that matter. I may be smitten but I'm not deluded. I know that town and gown don't mix. 'I guess,' I say, not wanting to make him think I'm barring him. 'But maybe we could meet before then.'

He nods. 'When?'

I don't know. Tomorrow's too soon. Wednesday I have lacrosse (I know, so shoot me). Thursday's too, I don't know, sad? 'Friday?'

'Yes,' he agrees quickly. 'Definitely.' Then, like he's checking his own enthusiasm, 'Sure, sure . . . I'll come over then? Here, I mean?'

But, for all that that would give me great pleasure to royally screw with my mom's suspicious mind, I don't think that's fair.

'No,' I say. 'You've seen mine, now show me yours.'

'Huh?' He feels his crotch automatically again. Seriously, what is it with boys and their balls? Their hands are wedged down there half permanently; if they're not scratching them, they're checking they still exist.

'Oh, as if,' I say. 'Your house. I'll come over, I mean. You know. Check out your world.'

'Oh, right. No. Yeah.'

I can't tell if the one-word sentences are because the blood hasn't returned to his head yet or if he's thinking this is the worst idea in the history of shit ideas.

'So which is it? No or yeah?'

'Yeah. I think.'

'You think?'

'No. I know. Just. Yeah. Cool.'

'So you better tell me where then?'

'Right, the address.'

'Bingo.'

'I'll . . .' He feels his pockets, pulls out a phone. A new one. Not the one the cock came from. 'Give me your number. I'll text you.'

And so I do. We do. We swap numbers and addresses and some more saliva for good measure before heading down-stairs. And then, my mom firing daggers at his giveaway year-younger several-income-brackets-lower school blazer, I close the door and, oh yes, here it comes, the involuntary sigh.

'So do you want to tell me about him?' asks Mom.

I scoop up Thom; focus on the Playmobil cowboy he's trying to make ride a crocodile.

'Not especially,' I say. And for once, it's not a lie.

MATTHEW

Tuesday

I was expecting a piss storm of messages from Jango on the new phone. I mean, the whole time we'd known each other I'd never had a girlfriend, and then, in what were pretty weird circumstances, I suddenly had one.

So, you'd have thought he'd have asked . . .

But that was way down my agenda that evening. I lay on my bed and looked at the stars. The fact that there was my bedroom ceiling, and then the loft full of bulging black bin liners, and then the roof of the house, and then clouds thick enough to gel your hair in between me and those stars didn't matter much. I could see them, and they were beautiful.

I didn't even let myself think about Sophia coming round on Friday. Being embarrassed about your family and your home is a double-decker shit sandwich. First you get the thing itself – the cringing fear that people are going to take you for a loser just because you live in a crap house and your parents aren't cool or rich. Then you get the knowledge that feeling like this is a kind of moral failing, a sign that you've got a, I don't know, small soul. Because you know you should be bigger and better than that. So I was dealing with it by not thinking about it which is the worst way of solving a problem, but better than not solving it at all. And usually, with me, the small bad things take over in my head, but that night there was no room for the small bad things, because everything was Sophia, and the smell of her and the feel of her and the taste of her. And the stars.

The next day, I was thinking Jango would be all over this, and part of me really wanted to tell him. He'd take the piss, but he'd understand. Because we both know that underneath that crust of bullshit and darkness there's a kind of poet, and a heart full of thwarted love.

But I didn't see him all morning. We were supposed to be in maths together, and he wasn't there. And nor did I see him stalking through the corridors, like a black T. rex – a black T. rex in a giant shoe.

And then at break I clocked him. He was in the schoolyard, alone, as he usually is when me and Corky aren't with him. Alone, but not alone. He was beaming out some sort of dark energy, and it was sucking in attention. Other kids in the yard were staring at him, nudging each other, laughing nervously. Something was going to happen, you knew it.

I followed the line of his gaze, and it struck, like a crossbow bolt, the great, flabby, animated form of Fernando Ribero.

Fernando is a freak – a fat, pink flamingo that has flapped down in a grey duck pond. He's half Portuguese, and that's probably why his parents didn't realise that you can't send a kid like him to a school like ours and expect him to survive. You see there are some schools – Penn is one – where gay kids do OK. No one seems to care. Or it's maybe just another interesting thing about you, like having a sticky-out belly button, or the latest iPhone.

But at my school it is different. Any kid who the mob think might be gay is dead-legged, spat on, slapped, kicked and punched by the hard kids, and pretty well ignored by everyone else, the non-hard kids fearing death by contamination.

So your one hope as a gay kid at my school is to un-gay yourself, to keep your head down and pray no one notices you.

But Fernando arrived, halfway through Year 9. Tall and fleshy and flamboyant and loud. He laughed and honked and joked and flirted in a way that was beyond camp. He wasn't just a queen – he was an empress. Sometimes he'd dye his hair green, sometimes pink. He wore diamanté earrings, and once came to school in ballet pumps stretched around his size 12 feet. The teachers usually come down pretty hard on any little infringements of the school uniform code – it's the pathetic way they think they're keeping control – but for some reason they let Fernando do what he wanted. Some teachers were mesmerised by him, some amused, some just baffled.

And Fernando had followers. Girls to begin with, then some of the quiet, hiding kids, and then almost everyone, except for the meatheads. And the brilliant thing about

Fernando was that the hard kids were scared of him. Something about the *out-ness*, his fearlessness, unnerved them. Sometimes they'd sneer, or call out the usual words, but then Fernando would turn on them, flirting, laughing, smiling, stroking, pirouetting around them, making *them* not *him* ridiculous. And rather than ganging up and beating him to death, they'd slink away like whipped dogs.

So, as I said, Fernando was a kind of hero in the school. The lowest of the low suddenly had a figurehead, a champion.

So why did Jango hate him? They should have been mates. They were on the same side, sort of. I mean against the jerks who like to spit in your ear and then punch it, and against the teachers who just want us to shut up so they can get through the day without doing any work, and against, well, the world.

But ever since the day he first appeared, Jango . . . well, I suppose the word is *despised*, yeah, Jango despised Fernando.

'What is it with you and Fernando?' I once said to him. 'You could be mates. He's all right. He's just a bit . . . over the top.'

'Huh, yeah,' he said. 'Jango and Fernando – we'd sound like a shit cabaret act on a cross-channel ferry. I do crappy magic tricks while she plays the effing Bontempi organ. Screw that.'

'Yeah, but that's not a reason to hate him the way you do.'

He never had a proper answer. All he did was shun him, scowling and moping while Fernando did his thing.

But I could tell that something different was going on now. It wasn't just the background dislike. I could sense . . . trouble. Blood.

'Come on, Jango,' I said, forcing lightness into my voice, like someone trying to blow up one of those balloons that doesn't want to get blown up.'Let's nip over the fence and get some chips.'

Jango didn't reply. He moved his head, and it could have been a no, or it could have been the thing you do when a mosquito buzzes in your ear. And he was moving towards Fernando. You could hardly notice it, because his eyes were so fixed, like a lion stalking an antelope. But, yeah, closer. We were both closer.

And now Fernando was looking over, smiling, laughing lightly, saying something to a big-boned girl called Rachel who's one of his regular handmaidens, one of the outcasts who'd found a safe place in the Court of Queen Fernando. She burst into extravagant giggles, the hand pressed to her mouth failing to conceal her enormous teeth.

And now Jango was moving more quickly, and I had to trot to keep up with his uneven lope. The line of his jaw was taut and hard, as if there was nothing under the skin except for the bone – no flesh, no blood. It looked like a flint axe head.

And now the whole schoolyard was focused on him, and whatever it was he was about to do.

Six metres away, he stopped. There were five of them with Fernando. Rachel, two other girls, and a couple of insignificant kids, the sort you could blow away like dust bunnies.

But Fernando you can't blow away. He'd stopped laughing now, though his mouth still looked like it was about to break into a smile. I thought he was going to speak to Jango, but Jango got in first.

'You've been saying things about me.'

So that was it. Some whisper had come back to Jango. Something Fernando had guessed, and then spoken.

Now Fernando did smile again.

'Of course I have. You're all we ever talk about. You're trending on Twitter. Hashtag Jangotangos.'

There was a titter that came both from Fernando's crew and the wider crowd that had now gathered. It was a typical Fernando line. It wasn't actually that funny or clever, in fact it didn't really mean anything at all. But it sounded as if it might, and that the fault for not getting it was yours. And it also carried that suggestion that it meant something . . . *dirty*. That a Jango tango was some obscene act he'd do for money.

Even then it might have been OK if Fernando had left it at that. The crowd were already thinking that nothing was going to come of this. Fernando's comment had baffled Jango, baffled us all. It was time for Jango to hurl some insult back, then for Fernando to laugh and pluck it out of the air, and eat it like a plum.

But what happened was that Fernando blew a kiss at Jango. A solid kiss that you could almost see as it curled its slow, heavy way towards Jango's mouth.

Before it reached there, Jango took the two, three long strides to Fernando and punched him.

It wasn't a real punch. Jango didn't draw his arm straight back and drive it into the middle of Fernando's face, the way

I know he can. That's a killing punch, a fight-ender, a nose-breaker, a face-destroyer. This punch was halfway to being a slap, his fist loose, no real energy or hate in it. And I knew that Jango had pulled it, that some time between the decision to punch and the punch landing, Jango had changed his mind. That Jango had realised that he was being a dick.

But then Fernando did something . . . *special*. Before Jango's loose fist had bounced off the skin, Fernando caught it in his own big pudgy hand. It was a lovely move. In fact he'd pulled it off so easily I thought he could have deflected the punch before it had landed. But he'd chosen to let Jango hit him. And now he held Jango's astonished fist to his cheek, and then moved it to his mouth, and kissed it.

Now the crowd were screaming with outraged joy. There were gay hate words, hurled like rocks, but then someone said, 'Get a room,' in a camp American voice, like something from a sitcom, and that set off a new surge. I found that even I was smiling.

And Fernando had dragged Jango closer, into something like an embrace, and I began to feel that he'd gone too far, and even in that moment I saw Jango's elbow come back, and heard him make a sound – an animal sound, part sob, part yowl – and I knew that this time the punch would not be pulled, that this time it would land on Fernando's face like that asteroid that wiped out the fucking dinosaurs.

And I also realised that I didn't want that to happen. Partly for Fernando, who didn't deserve to get punched, and partly for Jango, because I knew how much he'd hate himself for it later. And partly for me, because I didn't want to have to live with the knowledge that I'd done nothing, when I could have done something. So I stepped forward and caught Jango's arm before it began to accelerate into Fernando's nose.

I heard a groan from the crowd, who wanted, like all mobs, some blood, and didn't much care if it was Fernando's or Jango's.

And then Jango half turned his head so he could look at me, and I saw the rage and madness in his eyes, and I suppose I realised what this was all about. Fernando was Jango. And all the loathing Jango felt for himself, all the heaped humiliation of the years, the limping years, the years with the giant effing shoe, years when he was too little to make the fuckers fear him, years when he looked for comfort at home, and found only his flake of a mother, and a hole where his dad should have been. And he dragged himself clear of Fernando, and I thought for a second that he was going to come for me, and it would have been brutal, but instead he first staggered, and then walked, and then ran away from Fernando, from me, from the crowd, who hurled words after him, the way monkeys throw their shit.

But then some kid – I didn't even know who he was – stuck out a leg, and caught Jango as he ran, and my friend went down, arms and legs and giant shoe, flailing, so he looked like some monstrous black beetle. And that was it. The mob moved around him, hungry. The big beast was down, and it was time to feed.

I was frightened for Jango now. He didn't spring up, like I thought he would, but stayed down, curled into a ball. The first kick went into his kidneys, and he made an ooooof sound. I started to push my way towards him, pealing a couple of the little kids off the pack, the way you pick the flaking bits from the edge of a scab. But it was almost impossible to get through, and I really thought they might kick Jango to death. Well, maybe not to death, but right back to St Mickey's Hospital.

And then a great cry came from behind us.

'LEAVE HIM!'

And Fernando hit the mob like a tsunami, and he was through to the middle, and he hurled himself down over Jango, forming a protective shell, like a fat turtle, and the couple more kicks that came he just absorbed, and then the bell went for the end of break, and the crowd drifted away, like autumn swept up into a pile but then left for the wind to blow. And in the end it was just me and Fernando, and Jango. And Fernando stood up, and offered his hand to Jango, but Jango ignored it, and Fernando said, 'Please yourself,' and then he was gone, and I waited for Jango to say something to me, but he just got up and walked across the deserted schoolyard and out of the gates and into the world.

SOPHIA

Wednesday

I figured that, by Friday, I'd have worked up a convincing get-out clause, or at least persuaded Lex to ditch the party idea for something less carpet/reputation-ruining. But it's Wednesday morning and she's already set up a Facebook event and invited the entire sixth form, Matthew, and some friend of his called Jango whose avatar is a gif of a monkey blowing chunks, which, like, what the actual?

'How the hell did you find him?' I ask, checking out her iPhone on the common room sofa.

'I have my ways. And since you weren't forthcoming with the digits, I had to use other sources,' she said, trying to sound like she's either psychic or a spy.

'You mean you asked one of the tech freaks to hack the Corpus Christi register?'

'Oooh, no!' she says. 'Damn, now I wish I had. I just asked Tegan Titan.' (Actual name.) 'Her cousin goes there. They, like, used to own a factory but the whole China economy thing and the recession just, like, happened and they had to down-size and move school. It's tragic.'

'Totally,' I agree. 'I can almost hear the violins.'

'You are SUCH a beeyatch.'

'I thank you. And since when did you know so much about the Chinese economy?'

'Since Webber took over AS politics.'

'That figures.' Webber is officially number three on Penn's hottest teachers list, losing out to Hamner and rugby coach 'Abs' Murphy and his six-pack. If you like that sort of thing. Which, like, give me some credit.

'Anyway, I'm more interested in this Jango,' Lex says, going through his uploads to see if she can find one of his actual face.

'You're interested in a vomiting simian? You really do need therapy. Or more therapy.'

'Oh ha ha. But come on, he "likes" *The Godfather* and Jägerbombs, and he's so totally wrong side of the tracks. God, it's like someone wrote the script for us. Plus, like, such a good name, yeah? Do you think he's foreign? Or maybe his mum's a hippy. Or . . . a drug addict.'

'What happened to Lucas?' I throw in. 'I thought you two were fated.'

'We are.' She looks genuinely put out. 'Only he doesn't know it yet. And I've tried to tell him only he's, like, been avoiding me since Saturday when you totally burst our bubble. So, you know, what better than flirting with a Duckie to make Blane realise his destiny. And if not, I've got my backup sorted out and not only does he live on Halton Moor, he's Catholic, which is, like, double points.'

She is unbelievable.

'You are unbelievable.'

'Oh, what, you want to keep all the love across the divide for yourself? Come ON. Give me something. You have the whole medical shiz going on, and Matthew gallantly over-coming that and stuff.' (She actually says 'gallantly'.)

Silence. Which, in this case, says it all.

'Oh. My. GOD. You haven't told him!'

I think back to that afternoon, to what I did say, and didn't. 'Just visiting,' I hear myself tell him. And it's not a lie. Not like I'm on a ward for an overnight stay. And besides, that's what Dr Gupta calls us: the lucky ones. Just visiting.

I shrug in nonchalant answer to Lexy's emphatic exclamation.

'But why not? It's pure frick-fracking gold.'

I've already wasted my daily 'you're unbelievable' allow-ance, so instead I try honesty. 'I just don't think he needs to know . . . everything. It's not like it defines me.'

Which is, of course, grade-A bullshit in Lexy's rose-tinted eyes, if not in actual factual truth.

'Oh, I know you're scared he'll be scared. That he'll . . .'

'Bottle it,' I finish for her. 'Like Lucas, you mean? Your wonderful perfect Lucas?'

'He didn't bottle . . . Well, he did. But he saw sense eventu-ally and anyway you're not meant to be together, it's obvious, not like you and Matthew.'

'What, even now you know it's not prime Jewish penis in his pants.'

'I know. Such a shame. It looked like a good one. Plus, you know, religion is so romantic.'

'Tell that to the Middle East.'

I know that, right now, Lexy is wondering who does, in fact, own said penis. Though it's a miracle she has to wonder given how many in this postcode she's already seen. And that's not something I want to ponder right now.

'I have to go.'

'Sure,' she says, turning back to the puking primate. 'Laters.'

'Laters.'

Only later I have other fish to fry. OK, so maybe I haven't told him what's literally going on in my head. But there are things he needs to know first. Other ways of him knowing me, and what I think, and how I feel about life, the universe and fricking everything, without knowing that. So I make like every clichéd, misunderstood, lovestruck teen from the Michael Cera mould and I make him a mix CD.

The thing about clichés is that they're clichés because they're true. And the thing about mix CDs is that they're a big fat clichéd window to the soul. It's not eyes, it's music that lets people into your world, your head. Trufax. And so, with my uploaded vinyl and my trusty friend iTunes, I make Matthew a diamond of a list.

There are classics on there that if he hasn't heard he hasn't lived. There's new stuff that if he has heard I will respect him for evermore. There are in-jokes about hospitals. There's even

'Touch Myself' in honour of the porn text. And there's even that song by Nina. (All together now: 'Ahhhh.')

And then I snaffle a Jiffy bag from Dad's office, sign it 'See you Friday' and catch the last collection at the post office on Park Avenue. So by the time he gets home from school tomorrow, he'll know everything he needs to about me.

Or at least, that's what I'm telling myself. And why would I lie?

MATTHEW

Thursday

'There's a package for you.'

I'd just come in from school, and was halfway up the stairs. I'd had a crap day. I wanted to be thinking about Sophia, but my head was full of Jango angst. He hadn't spoken to me – or anyone – since the face-off with Fernando. But other people had spoken to him. Or *at* him, rather. He'd lost his mojo; his aura: his power. No one was afraid of him now. Fernando was Delilah, and Jango was Samson, except his hair was his giant shoe. Not sure that makes sense . . . Anyway, because no one was afraid of him any more, it meant they could rip the piss. They copied his limp – even little Year 7 shitheads. And they said stuff.

I am Jango's friend. He is a massive tool, but we've been through things together, experienced stuff. And, yeah, I don't like him all the time, but friendship isn't to do with liking, not really. There are people you like who aren't your friends, so that isn't the key, the heart of it. Your friends are the ones you're . . . entwined with. The ones whose lives wind around yours, so that whatever happens to them happens to you. And so that's what I felt – that what was hurting Jango was hurting me. That day, I tried to get close to him, to stand by him while this was happening, but he stumped away from me every time, and so, in the end, I gave up. It would have been different, I suppose, if I hadn't had Soph to think about.

'A what?'

'Parcel – package. A thing,' said Dad.

'I thought you were a postman – shouldn't you know what it is?'

'Cheeky bugger.' My dad laughed. 'When's a package a parcel? How long's a piece of bloody string?'

He gave it to me. One of those padded envelopes. With extra tape around it.

'Waste of stamps,' said my dad. It was covered in them. Way more than it needed.

I think my dad wanted me to open it downstairs. I couldn't remember the last time I'd got a package. Or parcel. I'd bought some stuff off eBay. Apart from that, never.

I knew it was from her, though. So I took it to my room.

I was already ripping it open before I even got there. There was a note, written on heavy white card. It just said, 'See you Friday,' and a couple of Xs. Her handwriting was careful, beautiful – not like my scrawl. I wrote like Jango walked. I thought there'd be more, though. I mean writing, words. I looked on the back. Nothing. I sniffed it, thinking it might smell of her. I thought it did, but then realised I was just imagining it. So I did some more imagining, and rubbed it slowly across my lips, feeling the flat of it, and then the edge of it, almost enough to give me a paper cut.

Then I remembered that it was a package, not just a note. I emptied the padded envelope, and a CD fell out.

She'd done me a music mix. More of her writing, this time much smaller, squeezed into the lines on the paper lining of the case. It was kind of old fashioned. Kids usually share mixes on Spotify, or just email ripped-off MP3s.

I looked at the disk, moved it under the light bulb, so the rainbow colours shimmered. And then I thought, How the hell am I going to play this?

My parents have this ancient music centre from before the days of CDs. I used to have a ghetto blaster, but that had been nicked from the beach when we were on holiday, years ago. There was always the CD drive in the laptop. The trouble was, there was a CD stuck in there. You could hit eject for a week and all you'd get was a grinding sound, and then a little sigh of despair as it gave up.

I went and got my mum's eyebrow tweezers from the bathroom, and had a go with them. I remembered seeing some wildlife doc about a bird that uses a cactus spike to pierce and pull these fat white grubs out of holes and crevices in tree trunks. This was a bit like that. Eventually I managed to catch the edge of the disk with the tweezers, and dragged it out. I spun the old disk into the bin, and slipped in Sophia's. The second I did it, I realised that it was insane. What was to stop this one getting jammed in there as well, unplayable, lost?

But the laptop seemed happier with this CD. iTunes came up, and the CD began to play.

I was thinking that I could lie back and bathe in some beautiful sound and let Sophia wash around inside my head, like seaweed in a rock pool. But it wasn't happening. The speaker on the laptop was too shitty. It made everything sound like it was coming from a megaphone a mile away. I found an old pair of cheap earbuds, but the left ear had died like a dog on the motorway, so I went back to the crappy speaker. But even the music itself didn't ... I don't know, *reach* me. There was some kind of jazz song, and I've never got jazz. Then a couple of cheesy songs from like the '80s or something. I half recognised some of the tracks, but when I tried to read the titles on the case, I saw that she hadn't written the names of the songs, but random lines, some from the songs, some just, I guess, from her head. And I liked that – liked it more than the music, if I'm honest. But it all still left me feeling guilty, and fake and ignorant and a loser. And I don't know much, but I do know that part of the deal for getting a mix tape is that you have to give one back. Soph was going to be expecting a hotline into my soul, by means of music.

Pressure.

But that was just the music thing. The rest of it, the everything to do with her, the look and the smell and the feel of her, or rather the memory of the look and the smell and the feel of her ... well, that was something else.

SOPHIA

Thursday

If I give the impression we haven't been full-on eye-roll-and vomit-inducing IMing for the last four days then that, my friend, would be an act of serious omission. And if I haven't made it clear that I'm about to slap myself at the whole pathetic romcom scripting of this then that would be an even bigger one.

On Monday, the messages are your basic boy-meets-girl PG-rated innuendoes. There's his coy, 'Well that was . . . unexpected.' And my notch-it-up a-little, 'But not unpleasant. Or unrepeatable. Or several other "un" words, only my mind's a bit hazy right now.' (Oh, the irony. Or whatever.)

On Tuesday I tell him I don't do this kind of thing, and then I do it anyway and send him a snapshot of two beetles that land on my hand in an emerald embrace. And to my relief and joy, the Instamoment I get back is not bestial but the bark of a birch tree stripped off in a heart. And I do not even throw up.

Wednesday my phone's vibrating at such high frequency Webber asks me if there's some kind of medical emergency going on, and Lexy wants to know if I've been raiding Ann

Summers and if so, can she borrow the silver bullet when I'm done.

By Thursday the number of MBs we've uploaded, exchanged and, be-still-my-beating-heart, sighed over is threatening to take me over my more-than-generous monthly allowance, and way out of my cliché-free comfort zone. Though in my defence and his, not a single LOL, emoticon or overexposed body part, erect or otherwise, has passed between us.

So you'll forgive me if I say that, when I don't get a lengthy dissection of every track back, a waxing lyrical on how they speak to him, and at least one emphatic quoting of any of the lines of song seventeen, I am disappointed.

And then, disappointed at my own disappointment, I do what every girl does in a relationship crisis. I message my Gay Best Friend and hope he's not too busy watching *Buffy* repeats whilst simultaneously Skyping someone who claims to have a pair of Harry Styles's Calvins in his memento drawer (never knowingly under-clichéd).

'Say I made you a mix CD that featured side two, track one of *Blonde on Blonde*. What would your first and strongest reaction be?'

'I'd say a) classy, especially if you'd segued in from leftfield, maybe side one, track three of *Licensed to Ill*. I'd then assume b) you wanted sexual conquest within the next forty-eight hours, but that c) you'd forgotten you don't own the number one requirement for me to engage in that kind of debauchery.'

'A velvet jumpsuit?'

'In one, doll.'

Supreme though that image may be in the pantheon of strangeness Will concocts for me on an almost nightly basis, this is one time I need him to notch it down. 'Seriously, though.'

'*Seriously*? Shit, *seriously* is so not you. *Seriously* is serious. Are you in . . . lust?'

'Yesnomaybe,' I hedge.

'Well, Whisky Tango Foxtrot. That requires a number of exclamation marks I just am not prepared to indulge in.'

'I know, right.'

'And is this yesnomaybe requited?'

'You tell me.'

And then, like every girl in every town in every story, I break any implied code of privacy and send my sort-of-boyfriend's non-committal non-specific non-requited nice-ties to someone else for dissection.

'This, my friend, is nothing more than a case of straight boy.'

I feel the Wonderbra-tight grip on my ribs loosen. 'You think so?'

'I know so. Just because he's not quoting Joni back at you doesn't mean it's doomed. He likes you. More than, maybe.'

More than. I don't let those two little words flicker in my already electrified head for more than the nanosecond they deserve. Because that would be one mindfuck too far. Besides,

Will has a talent for distraction rivalled only by Lexy in falsies and a thong.

'So can I sleep over?' he asks.

Huh? 'Message does not compute.'

'S A T U R D A Y, after the P A R T Y.'

I am still *huh*. But now also a little *WTF?* 'Seriously?'

'God, we are all about the serious today. I have to persuade the father figure to lend me the fare, and drive me to the station, and buy me a litre of JD to pack in my spotted hand-kerchief but, yeah, seriously. Lex texted. And I think it would be FUN!!! See – I'm so excited I lost my senses and triple exclamationed you.'

My thoughts track off in several imaginative directions, most of them involving karaoke, one of them including cow tipping, but all of them ending in a kind of complicated Matthew-me-Lexy-Lucas-Will club sandwich and punch vomit. But *FUN!!!*? Yesnomaybe.

'Come on. When was the last time you danced to electro with a hot boy in a leotard?'

'Never.'

'Then this is a situation that needs to be rectified as a matter of emergency. Plus, Caleb isn't playing nice and I need LOVE!!! And AFFECTION!!! And someone to tell me I look devilishly handsome in a trilby.'

'What happened?' But I know the answer. He cheated. Again.

But that's not the version that Will wants to tell. 'We had a fight over the names of our children. He wanted Lulu and

Lemsip. I favoured Milk of Magnesia and Brian. So I am totally ☹. So ☹ that I am using ☹. Which, like, WTAF? And by way of blackmail, if you don't say yes with a cherry on top I will be ☹☹☹.'

I literally feel my skin crawl. And I know he's lying.'Enough with the text litter. The answer's yes. As long as the mother ship can be persuaded.'

'Tell Mrs G. I'll leave the fairy dust at home to save on hoovering. I know the glitter goes against her decor rules.'

'Everything goes against her rules. Me included.'

'GTG. I have wardrobe planning to do. We'll tackle yours when I get there. I am seeing Venus in a seashell. And also Ophelia drowning.'

'Are you trapped in a fourteen-year-old's bedroom?'

'I wish.'

'Too much information.'

'Never.'

'xxx'

'xxx. And may the odds be ever in your favour.'

'And in yours.'

And I minimise the chat box and the future conversation with Mom, and maximise my iTunes Dylan dilemma, clicking play on the list that I picture him mellowing out to now.

Will's right. Matt's a straight boy. And it doesn't mean he doesn't get me. It doesn't mean he doesn't want me. Or maybe more. It just means he can't tell me that. Not in so many words. And so, as Nina strikes up the band, I feel my stomach flip in a soup of fear and need and wonder at him, and at what we've said and what we've done, and what we'll do again.

And maybe more.

MATTHEW

Thursday

I was still feeling all . . . *wrong* about the CD when I had a brainwave. I went back through the texts we'd sent. That week I'd literally sent more than in the rest of my life put together. I'd had no idea I'd had so many words in me. But her words were better than mine. She was so clever. Maybe too clever, sometimes – you could see her trying hard to be smart, to impress me. But that just made me feel better. No one had ever tried to impress me before. Except maybe Jango. But that's different. That's more like a boss lion trying to put the shits up the whole fucking jungle with his roar.

I found the message I was looking for. A book. *The Great Gatsby*, though she'd just called it *Gatsby*, like it, or he, was a personal friend of hers. Of course I'd heard of it. Knew it was by F. Scott Fitzgerald. Even half knew what it was about – rich people doing rich stuff in America in the 1920s. I don't know, maybe I'd seen the film on the TV.

Anyway, Sophia said how she'd read it till the glue melted, and the book fell apart . . .

Well, I could fix that.

JOANNA NADIN and ANTHONY MCGOWAN

It was 6 p.m. now. Shit. But I had a funny feeling the book-shop up by the university was open late. I grabbed twenty quid from my money drawer, and sprinted out for the bus. When Mum called out from the sofa, 'Where . . .?' I had the satisfaction of startling her by saying, truthfully, 'Bookshop!'

I kind of liked it in the bookshop. It was bright and warm and smelled clean and it was full of students looking cool and brainy at the same time. I felt a bit out of place, though, and I had the feeling that the people there were checking me out to make sure I wasn't going to shoplift or piss in the corner or god knows what.

'Fiction' was on the ground floor, and it only took me a couple of minutes to find the Fitzgerald shelves. There was a lot of him – I guess he's the kind of author you study at uni, so they had everything he'd written. There were two different editions of *Gatsby*, and they both looked OK. But I was hoping I'd find something a bit more . . . *special* – a hardback, maybe.

And then I saw it. It was a heavy hardback. It looked seri-ous and important. It was called *Trimalchio*, and I wasn't even sure I knew how to say it. But the subtitle was: *An Early Version of The Great Gatsby*.

Pay dirt.

This would look like I'd made a real effort; dug out some-thing different. It was *The Great Gatsby*, and at the same time it wasn't. And it wasn't just some paperback she was going to give away to the charity shop in a year. She was going to keep this for ever.

Then I looked at the price on the back. I'd been thinking that I might not have much change from my twenty quid. Turned out I wouldn't have had any change if I'd brought fifty.

I felt sick. I put it back, and pulled out one of the paperbacks.

It was OK. She'd like it. Glance over its cover; say a quick thanks.

And then I felt a little surge of anger and annoyance. The way the shop staff had looked at me when I came in. And I thought, Screw you.

I hadn't shoplifted anything in a couple of years. I used to nick sweets and stuff, but I didn't ever want to have to face my mum and dad if I got caught, so I just quit it. Other kids thieve all the time. Not Jango – he sticks out too much and he'd never get away with it. But loads of others. Even little Corky. And there was no way the book was worth fifty quid. It was only paper and ink.

I could feel my heart beating faster. It was like it had already made the decision for me, and was getting ready for action.

The shelves covered me. I knew there'd be CCTV, but that didn't matter. All I had to do was make it to the door, and I'd be out of there, and no beardy bookshop nerd was going to catch me.

So I just held the book in my hand, as if I was going to buy it after I'd browsed a bit more. I tried not to look innocent, because you only look innocent when you're guilty. I didn't think my heart could pound any faster, but it kept on revving up, like a motorbike. I was scared and excited, the two feelings shaken up together and ready to explode like Coke from a can.

And then, a metre from the exit I realised that there was a security gate – a metal frame on either side of the door – and that meant I was going to set off the alarm.

Didn't matter.

Too late to turn back.

I just ran for it. Through the doors, out into the night.

I heard the alarm ring, but I was going faster than sound, and I left it behind me. Round the first corner, round another, pelting down one long street, not even breathing, the way a cheetah doesn't breathe when it's after a gazelle.

And I think I might have been laughing. Laughing at the joy of it, and the relief, because I was out of there and away and safe.

I was thinking I'd post the book, but it was too late now. My next plan was to go to her house and drop it off, secretly. But then I got into a thought-tangle, wondering what I'd say if I bumped into her, and maybe it would seem a bit too stalky, and if I did see her I'd have to put some effort into how I looked, and I felt kind of seedy and sweaty from tearing around town.

No, it was obvious, really. I'd give it to her tomorrow. Not before. Because that might seem like I was trying to, I don't know, bribe her or something. It would have to be after we'd, after she'd . . . I mean as a thank you. Not a thank you – that's crappy. Just a thing. And when she looked at it, she'd think of me.

I got lost in the thought of this, and then my mum was shouting me down for dinner.

I put the book under my bed.

'I've got a friend coming round tomorrow,' I said, sort of mumbling, with my mouth half full of shepherd's pie.

I don't know how they picked up on it, but somehow they did. Picked up, I mean, on the idea that this wasn't just Jango or Corky or some other kid. I suppose sometimes your parents see inside you. Or, more likely, what you thought was inside you is in truth written all over the outside. Or maybe it was just a lucky guess. Anyway, they looked at each other, and my mum did a little smile.

'Who's the friend?' said my dad, and I could see he was trying not to catch my mum's smile.

'Just, er, a friend.'

There was a pause.

'What time is she coming?'

'I didn't say it was a . . . a . . . She's just coming round to play music. She's into music.' I had a head on me like a tomato, and I reckon even my toes were blushing. 'About seven, I think.'

Another pause. Then my mum said, 'That's lucky, because me and your dad are going out tomorrow.'

Dad looked a bit startled at that. My mum and dad only went out about once a month.

'There's that film on,' she continued, a bit vaguely. 'At the pictures. And we were going to get a bite out, as well.'

'Aye, that's right,' said my dad, and he looked a bit rueful. I think he was working out what it might cost. But now I was grinning through my embarrassment.

'But we'll be there to say hello, later on,' said Mum.

'Great,' I said. But that wasn't quite what I was thinking. What I was thinking was, Shit.

SOPHIA

Friday

Things I have asked my mother for and been given the kind of death stare that could fell an orc:

1. A pony, on a four-times-a-day repeat from age five to the day I discovered Marc Bolan.
2. To have my eighth birthday at Chuck E. Cheese.
3. My own set of house keys.

So it's no big shakes that by the time I stumble back from school on Friday I still haven't mentioned the Matt thing or the Will thing or the Lexy thing or, basically, anything beyond my protest at her continued ban on drinking OJ from the carton.

I figure the only way to get my way is to carpet-bomb her. Throw it all in one sustained attack that temporarily stuns her into a vague nod that can be interpreted as a 'Hell, yes,' by my own troubled mind. I choose my moment carefully, when she is blinded by the smug glow of the Smeg (which, don't even) and occupied by one of life's most taxing conundrums.

'Salmon or chicken?' she asks no one in particular.

'Dairylea Dunkers,' I want to say, knowing Thom for one would back me up. (She thinks he doesn't know junk food exists, but I feel it's my job to alert him to the joys of this world. Someone has to.) But that won't win me this skirmish.

Instead I lock and load my most successful weapon: assuming it's a given. 'Neither, I'm going to Matthew's tonight, and then tomorrow there's this party at Lexy's and I said Will could stay the night.' And I reach into the fridge and take an apple just to sweeten the pill of the trans fats I know she's imagining I'm going to be mainlining at Matt's. The kind of grease-laden poison that she fears feeds the Gollum, the homunculus hunched in my head. I take a deliberately loud, large bite and shut the door, adding save-the-environment points to healthy eating.

'Polar bears, yeah?'

'Where are the bears?' demands Thom, opening the fridge immediately.

'Nowhere. The Arctic. Or Antarctic? Whichever. But if you don't shut the fridge and turn off the lights the ice caps will melt and the polar bears will all be sad.'

Thom slams the door, eliciting an automatic wince from the mother as jars of expensive jam clack against olives and dulce de leche. But right now ice caps are bottom of her 'to give a shit about' list.

'Matthew?'

Oh please. 'He was here Monday, remember?'

She pretends to ponder this. Then asks what she's really thinking. 'Where does he live?'

Because that's the million-dollar question. Because then she can figure out his income bracket, education and potential to be on crack, or worse be scoring below a C grade average.

'Preston Street. It's not far. I'll walk there and cab home. And I'll be back before midnight.' Like Cinder-fucking-ella.

Her jaw is set so rigid you could slice cheese off the bone structure, and I'm not talking Dairylea this time. 'And this Matthew, he's your . . .?'

'Friend, Mom.' Yeah, so I muddy the water a little, because it's easier on her that way, or at least that's what I'm telling myself because I haven't managed to choke the longer version out myself yet.

She's weakening now. 'Does he . . . does he know what to do if . . .?'

I feel my stomach slip. If . . . If I wig out on the sofa while we're drinking tea, or worse, in bed while we're doing something else entirely? No. No he doesn't know. Because that is one aspect of me that can't be conveyed in a song line or IM. That one requires an IRL show, and so I figured I'd lay that one on him later, alongside issuing the standard safety procedures and a hard hat. Which means I can get away with a deliberately vague 'Yu-huh,' now.

She nods. Satisfied. Or as satisfied as the perpetually paranoid can ever be. And I know the next line by heart, and know it means she's effectively throwing in the towel. 'I'll have to ask your father.'

And that's when I go for gold. 'And Will, that's cool, yeah. He's so looking forward to seeing you.' And it's not even a lie, because if there's one thing Will loves more than Elvis, and his orange suede shoes, it's winding the hell out of my mother.

'I . . . I'm sure that will be . . . fine.'

Bingo.

'Thanks, Mom.'

'Thanks, Sofa,' says Thom, making up for her selective mutism.

I laugh, unbidden, and as I turn to exit stage left I hear the audience cheer another Oscar-worthy performance from yours truly.

But as I count out the twenty-two treads to my vinyl-lined sanctuary, for once my mind's not on sweet victory or Saturday night. But on him. And on the promise and possibility of tomorrow. And as a thrill runs through me purer and more intoxicating than any shot of Stoli, I know it's not 'more, maybe'. It's definite. Real. A sure thing.

And so am I.

MATTHEW

Friday

Sometimes I think that if my brain was just, I don't know, ten per cent bigger, everything would be OK. I could fit everything in. I could have understood Jango and Sophia, as well as all the other school shit, the exams and the teachers and the world. But there was too much gravy for my plate, and it was all over the table and the floor and my trousers.

I went into school with my head full of her, and I was sort of floating through the school gates. And then suddenly there was Jango. And he was coming towards me with his black coat blowing behind him, and his big shoe like the prow of a ship, and I thought he was going to batter me, getting his warped revenge for whatever it was he thought I did or didn't do.

And, to be honest, I suddenly thought, Fuck this, I'm not going to put up with his bullshit any more, and I got ready to fight him, not exactly putting up my fists, because I knew that would look stupid, but clenching them in my jacket pockets, so I was ready.

But there wasn't a fight. Jango's face broke into one of his rare, goofy smiles, showing off his long teeth. He threw his arm around me – more around my head than my shoulders, and pulled me in towards him.

'Matt, Matty, Matthew. Loving that new look.'

He put his fist in my hair and scrunched it, drilling down into my scalp. It was a friendly way of beating me up.

And it's true – I'd gelled it, and spent more than my usual thirty seconds in front of the mirror. Even though I wasn't seeing Sophia till later, I still, I don't know, felt her around me, and wanted to look OK, for even her imaginary presence.

I managed to wriggle out of his grip.

'That's better,' he said, opening his hands either side of my face. 'That's my Matt back, looking like you've been dragged through a hedgehog backwards.'

'Screw you, Jango.'

He was mock serious now. 'No, screw *us*, Matty, screw *us*.'

And then a vulpine smile again, and we walked towards the school.

I wanted to ask him about Fernando, what the hell it was all about, but, well, as I said, my head wasn't up to it. I was just pleased that Jango seemed OK with me.

The rest of the school day was a vague woolly noise outside my head, and the coiled hot intensity of Sophia inside it. Except, well, she didn't stay inside my head, but infected the rest of me, moving through my blood and bones like a disease, but a disease you really want to get.

It came to a boil in maths, and I just had to stagger out, gasping, 'Not well, sir,' to Mr Mortlake, which made the rest of the class either jeer or make puking noises, and I guess I did look like I was going to hurl my guts into the stinking bog, but all I needed to do was splash cold water on my face.

But I wasn't just burning up with lust. There was also a lot of fear in the mix. I knew there was a good chance that tonight I was going to do *it* with Sophia. That maybe sounds like I was taking things for granted, but even though I was a know-nothing when it came to sex and girls, I knew that Sophia was into me, and that for her sex wasn't the sort of barrier it was for me, I mean, just because I *hadn't* and she *had*.

And that was just it. I didn't know what to do. I'd seen stuff. It was hard not to . . . but that hadn't related to me or my life. What I needed was a friend, someone who knew more than I did, and could reassure me, or just take the piss in a friendly way and diffuse it. But I don't have any friends like that. I have the Virgin Corky, and the Mad Virgin Jango.

Despite his attempt at being normal, I wasn't going to talk to Jango about this. That left Corky. I found him at lunch, a section of pizza before him. Like all school pizza, you couldn't see any individual elements, no separate cheese and tomato and peppers or whatever, but just a kind of orange sheen, like a Hazchem warning.

'Corky, that girl, the one I met . . .'

Corky was suddenly alert, though he kept on eating the pizza. If he ever has any kids they are going to be mutant fish.

'She's coming to my house tonight.'

'M-m-m-m . . .'

'Mum and Dad are off out.'

Corky grinned.

'The trouble is I-I . . .'

'V-v-v . . .'

'Yeah. I don't know what to . . . how to.'

'F-f-f.'

'Shut up, Corky. It's all . . .'

There was a minute or so of silence while Corky gummed the rubber orange discus. Then his expression changed.

'C-c-c-c . . .'

'What?'

'C-c-c-c . . .'

'I don't know what you're . . .'

At last, with an explosive effort, he got it out.

'CONDOMS!'

At least a hundred heads turned our way, and one of them was Jango's.

'What have I missed?'

'Oh, nothing. Corky let one rip.'

'And that's the follow-through?' he said, pointing at the orange slick on Corky's paper plate. 'That is Satan's shart. Must have burnt like lava on the way out.'

And so that was the end of my heart-to-heart with Corky.

For the rest of the day, time did its weird thing, stretching out every second like spider silk, till it reached around the planet, but then suddenly it was gone. As if you'd spent all day watching a kingfisher on its perch, and then in a smear of greeny-blue it dived.

I walked home alone. I had some embarrassing shopping to do . . .

SOPHIA

Friday

Nothing is viewed straight any more, for the first time. It's all filtered through a TV camera or an app's retro haze or, in this case, someone else's eyes. Because, as he leads me through the narrow hallway and up the staircase, I'm not seeing the tired wallpaper, the worn carpet, the china dogs on the crowded mantelpiece, I'm seeing him seeing it through my eyes. Seeing him imagining my disappointment, or, worse, a kind of perverse, patronising revelry, the kind I know Lexy indulges in on a regular basis through her Millwall Dinos and now, Jango. He is, she declared, 'totally minimum wage', in a tone that made clear that this was as slick a sexual lubricant as a minor role in *MiC* or a no-limits credit card. They've been texting in his breaks and her free periods. Not sexting, she insists. But she's probably playing coy with me, or playing up to her new part as the uptight uptown girl.

Maybe Matt thinks like that too. Maybe he imagines I'm living out some *Outsiders* fantasy, Cherry Valance to his Ponyboy. Just trying to piss off my mother and Lucas the soc. Yeah, so that's a useful side effect, but it's not why I'm here. This isn't some stage so I can throw out a well-timed 'Be cool,

Sodapop,' and ride off back to the right side of the tracks in my Mustang. This is where I want to be because it's where he is. And because it's something I don't have. And I hope that whatever he's seeing, he's taking in the green tinge of envy that taints me. Because here there are no glass tops to fear smearing, no vast surfaces to be afraid to clutter, no hard, sharp lines to cut your hip. Just scuffs and soft edges, signs of life, signs of love. Is that patronising? It's not meant to be. It's jealousy, pure and simple.

Oh, don't get me wrong, I frick-fracking love the size of my house for the fact that my bedroom is out of earshot of my parents' and Thom's is out of mine; I love that there are three bathrooms so that I don't have to pee in the sink if I'm desperate, which Lexy claims to have done round some Ken's she met down the fair; I love knowing I have the dollars to get the hell out of Dodge as soon as my A level results are in. But that's the thing. I want to get out. And I think maybe he doesn't, because he doesn't need to.

And I think something else. Something crazy: maybe he'd come with me.

MATTHEW

Friday

My mum and dad had gone out. The house felt weirdly quiet. I realised that I was hardly ever in it alone, even though there was just the three of us. I sometimes wonder why they never had any more kids, but I've never asked, and they've never told me. In families like ours we don't talk about things like that. What's the point? You can't fix things by talking about them.

I looked at my room. It was pretty embarrassing. Nearly everything in Sophia's house is white or cream, and everything seems to fit in with everything else, as if the whole house has been conceived together, as a unified *thing*. But our house is just random stuff that happens to be in the same place at the same time, for no good reason. The mantelpiece downstairs is full of pointless pottery ornaments and orphaned remote controls for gadgets that are broken or lost. Every room has different wallpaper, different carpet, bought when my dad found bin-end bargains. The carpet in my room is brown. I hadn't ever really noticed it before.

Brown.

Jeeeeeeez.

At least I didn't have the Spider-Man duvet cover and matching pillowcase on my bed. I mean, you couldn't really do *it*, could you, with Spider-Man looking on. It'd be wrong on at least three different levels. But the duvet my mum had put on in its place was . . . *busy*. Geometric patterns, and splodges of colour. I suddenly realised what it reminded me of: vomit. Yeah, that was it – it looked like I'd had a heavy night out on the lash with Jango, woken up, leaned forward, and spewed my guts all over the duvet. I briefly considered going back to the airing cupboard and getting out the Spider-Man, but then decided even the puke duvet was better than that.

I looked at the bookshelf on the wall over the little table I use as a desk. Most of the books have been there for ever. Kids' stuff about planes and animals. Dinosaurs. Tanks. Some classics and other books I like as well. I didn't mind that. It's like the archaeology of my head, the layers going back and down.

But now the bookshelf had something else in there as well. An unexpected artefact. Smaller than a book. Scarier than a T. rex.

I began shuffling the books to try to make sure she'd see what I wanted her to see. But it was like trying to cover up a zit. It never really works. You might as well just put up a sign with an arrow pointing to it, and the word 'UNCLEAN' written in pus. Sophia wasn't going to mistake me for an intellectual, just because I hid *The Guinness Book of Animal Facts and Feats* behind Dante's *Inferno*.

I opened the window wide, sprayed some Lynx around, then tried to waft it out, so it wouldn't be obvious, then sprayed some more in case I'd completely got rid of the Lynx, and left it smelling like it usually does, of me.

Don't know why I was bothering. She wasn't going to come. Of course she wasn't. Why would she? Why would anyone?

And I thought about hating Sophia. Hating her for being stuck up. Hating her for going to a school full of other stuck-up kids. Hating her for being clever. Hating her for being beautiful.

And then the doorbell went, that embarrassing *ding-dong,* like something you'd hear on the rerun of an old comedy, and I walked like a zombie to answer it.

SOPHIA

Friday

The bedroom's small and dark, and has that tang – sport socks and dirty hair and some kind of secret agent X that coalesces into 'teenage boy', which no amount of window opening or Febrezing or Diptyque candles can entirely eradicate (Lexy has tried both, believe me). Only somehow, when you add a stack of poetry to the mix, and a poster of that Keats film and the way his hair falls over his left eye, that smell is one huge frick-fracking turn-on.

I run a finger along the corrugation of his book spines: brindled charity-shop hardbacks and creased GCSE set texts, *Wuthering Heights* and *Romeo and Juliet* among them. It is the east, I think to myself, then push that thought down. I am so not that kind of girl. I don't need a Romeo or a Heathcliff. My world turns without men to spin the wheel.

Doesn't it?

'So, *Gatsby*,' I say quickly. 'Did you read it?'

He flicks a look away for a second, then comes back half smiling. 'Not yet,' he says quickly. 'I didn't have time, and I—'

'It's not like it's a requirement,' I interrupt. 'I just . . . I love it. The cynicism, you know?'

'I know.' He nods.

But this is just treading water, wasting time with small talk. The big stuff, the stuff we need to say, is dancing invisibly in our heads, held on the tips of our tongues by the knowledge of what we want to do.

And that's when I know how this will go. Or how to make it go. Music. Because a soundtrack changes everything; the songs saying what we can't. Even if it's just yes. I look round the room for a CD player but there's only his laptop, which, I'd rather stick needles in my thighs. So I dig out my iPhone and sideswipe to the 'Songs for Matt', scroll down to track thirteen.

'What are you—' he begins.

But I don't let him finish. 'Just listen,' I say, and hand him an earbud.

And then we're both being carried on the swell of Matt Berninger, then Morrissey. Their voices, their lyrics talking for me, for us. I know I have more to say to him – I want to tell him about the songs, about why I chose them, what they say. And about the stuff they don't. The stuff I'm supposed to have laid out and gained a signature of consent for just in case. But I've taken my meds and I haven't had a full-on freak-out for a month and I know that could mean I'm due one but it could also mean I'm over them. Or at least that's what I tell myself when I put my hand on his thigh and my lips on his.

MATTHEW

Saturday

I hadn't noticed that it was raining, and it barely was, really, just that fine stuff that hangs in the air. But it was enough to give her hair a soft sparkle, and coat her face with dew.

'Hey.'

'Hey.'

And she took a step towards me, and moved her face in to mine, and I wasn't sure what she was doing, until I remembered that people like her said hello by kissing, but I proved myself inept at this particular social manoeuvre by landing my lips not on her cheek, but on her ear, and I felt the kiss suck the air out of her ear, so she reeled away sharply.

'Ow!'

But then we were both laughing, and she was in the hall, and I was vaguely aware that my mum must have really tidied up the place, because it looked spotless, and there were flowers, daffodils, on the little table by the telephone, and I didn't even have time to remember how stupid it was to have an old-fashioned phone like that, out in the hall. Didn't have time, because Sophia was kissing me now, properly, on the lips, and I could taste the rain on her.

'Where?' she gasped, and I suppose it could have been 'Where are your parents?' or 'Where shall I put my coat?' or 'Where in the name of god exactly are the Maldives?' but we both knew it was 'Where shall we go?'

And then we were flowing upstairs, like a waterfall filmed backwards.

But then in my room the flow stopped. There was an awkward half stumble, and then I became hyperaware of my scuzzy room, and that brown carpet, and seeing Sophia in it was all wrong, like when you see a swan in the road, with its big black feet. And I thought she felt it too, the sudden disconnect, and even though she hadn't moved away from me physically, and if I'd just stuck out my finger I could have touched her again, she seemed far away, like through the wrong end of a telescope.

And then she was looking at the books, and I was really worried she was going to come across the packet of condoms I'd stashed there, and that would have been beyond terrible, and if she had, I don't know what I'd have done; maybe I'd have just walked out of there and downstairs and out of the house and taken a boat to South America or somewhere, and lived for ever in the Andes as a hermit, rather than have to face her again.

But it was OK. She looked at me and said, abruptly, 'Did you read that book, the one I told you about, *Gatsby*?'

And I had to hold in my grin. I tried to look nonchalant, and I said, 'No, but . . .' and I was going to get the book from under the bed, and produce it for her with a flourish. But I think she misunderstood what I was saying and doing, and she sat on the bed and reached into her bag, so I'd have had to put my hand through her legs, or awkwardly round the back of them, to get the book. And then she was pulling her iPhone out, which I just didn't understand at all.

'So you didn't love the mixtape,' she said, and I realised what was happening. I thought I'd better come clean.

'Yeah, I loved it.' OK, so that wasn't clean. That was dirty. 'But I didn't get to listen to it the way it, er, deserved. I mean all I had was my . . .' I waved my hand at the shitty laptop. 'And I was going to make you one back, but I . . .'

I was still standing up, like an idiot.

'Come here,' she said, and patted the bed next to her.

She unwound the headphones from around the iPhone, and then held out one of the earpieces to me. I was a bit freaked out. Which ear did I put it in? The ear next to her? Or the one on the far side? Both seemed right and wrong. She solved it by taking the thing back from me, and stretching round to put it in my left ear. It meant we had to get close, and I had to put my arm around her, with my hand resting behind her on the bed.

'Listen,' she said, and the music started to play. And within a few notes the awkwardness had gone. Our cheeks were so close I could feel the electric currents under her skin. And then there was no distance at all, and our cheeks were touching, and we stopped being two things and became one thing, breathing in time to the music. And when we drew together like that, our faces joined, it kind of blocked out the world, so the music came alive and pulsed and raced and soothed all at the same time.

And I *got* them, this time I really got them, though it was probably all because of the intensifier of having her skin on my skin, and the sweetness of her breath, murmuring, laughing, talking, teaching. Of course we only managed three or four tracks before we were kissing, and I think we did pretty well to last that long. The earpieces kept falling out, and for a while we tried putting them back in, but eventually we just let them tangle round us, with the *tsk tsk tsk* of the rhythm spilling out.

And it was incredible and terrifying all at the same time, because we were alone, and so *everything* was possible. But I was so happy (effing hell, that's an inadequate word) just to be kissing her that I'd have gladly (ditto) gone on doing that for ever.

But then I realised that she'd got her hand down *there*, which shocked me and frightened me a little, because it reminded me that she was better at . . . *this*. She had some sort of a top on, with buttons, and then she didn't. I touched her bra, fighting the urge to just grab . . . *everything*. And then my shirt was off, and I don't know if it was me or her pulling it, but I heard a button ping off the metal wastepaper bin. And there were parts of her that were so soft, softer than anything I'd ever touched before, and I wished that I could have my eyes open and closed at the same time, closed so I could concentrate on the feel of her, open so I could see her beautiful face. And in the same sort of way I knew we were going to do it, and I also knew that I didn't have a chance, because it was like an ape asking an angel. But still I asked.

'Do you want to?'

She looked up at me, and I could see the humour in her face, even though she was trying to be serious, and I realised that what she wanted to say was, 'Duh!' as in 'Of course I do – what the hell else do you think I'm doing here, doofus?'

'Have you got . . .?'

I nodded. And panicked. I'd forgotten about that. And there was something else I'd forgotten: to have a practice run. I'd never used one, obviously, but I'd meant to have a go, before, just so I didn't look like an idiot. I got up, trying to, well, hide what was going on, which was stupid, given what we were about to do. The condoms were between my school edition of *Of Mice and Men* and a book called *The Dodo, the Auk and the Oryx*, all about creatures that had become extinct, or were about to. Sort of appropriate, I was thinking.

Then Soph said, 'So, tell me an interesting animal fact,' and I looked back at her on my bed, with that terrible duvet, and she was on her side, her lovely head in her hand, and the hair flowing around her shoulders, and I felt my lips move without quite knowing what they were saying. But Soph's face changed, and it was good. And she said back to me what I'd said, but with her quizzical smile.

'Mermaid?'

'What?'

'You said,"Mermaid"...'

And yes, I realised that was what I'd said, and that it was true. I mean that it was true that I was thinking that she looked like a mermaid, lying there, on the soft rock of my bed. And I'd always had a secret thing about mermaids, something going way back and way deep, but this wasn't the time to explore that now, so I said,'I just meant, you look beautiful, so beautiful.' And then I saw her face change again, and I went over to her, with the thing, the condom, still in my hand and I lay beside her on the bed.

SOPHIA

Friday

Do I want to? That's easier than I thought it would be: yes.

Have I done it before? That's when it gets complicated, with a series of subclauses and trade-offs. If I say no, am I a prude? Or a prize that'll win him points in the virgin league I know for a fact the mudheads are trying to climb. If I say yes, am I slut? Or am I making this easier, so that neither of us is worrying about any cherry-popping blood on the sheets and we can concentrate on what actually matters. I don't get the virginity thing anyway. Holding on to it like it's some kind of sacred amulet, in the hope that when you do do *it*, it will be a night of tantric wonderment and you'll come in a chorus of angel song and frick-fracking unicorn dancing. As opposed to the five minutes of frantic fumbling and wet patch most of us are left with.

Because, if you hadn't worked it out, the answer is yes I have.

It was Lucas. Pre-diagnosis. When I knew something was wrong but I didn't know what and I thought I might die and, well, the obvious answer to that seemed to be to drink half a pint of vodka and shag.

It wasn't that bad. I said yes and meant it. It didn't hurt. He didn't gag at the fact I own pubic hair or try to re-enact *Alice in Wang-derland* or any other anal-obsessed tediosity that the Pitt-Westons flooded innocent inboxes with in Year 9.

It wasn't that good either though. It was sex. That's all. Fifteen minutes; three positions; he came; I left.

This will be different. It's already different. This isn't desperate; this isn't ticking something off a list before I die; this isn't an ending. This is the start of something. This is so full of possibility and the promise of time to practise and get it right, we can afford to take it slow.

Yeah, right. Come on, we're seventeen. Or I am. By the time I remember that I still haven't shown him my medi bracelet, camouflaged conveniently in a clatter of cheap Claire's Accessories, we are way past words. We are way past this being nudged back into PG territory thanks to every T-shirt we pull up, every low-rise we pull down, however many times the whole scene threatens to turn into farce as my sock gets stuck, as my hair gets tangled in the buckle of his belt. Because that's part of it. That's what makes it work. Means it isn't awkward. It doesn't stop us. It makes it easier, better. So that then, after we, half laughing, half heart-hammering, manage to work out what to do with the condom (practice cucumbers and penises are just not the same, no matter what Lexy insists), it can all go perfectly, filthily R18.

MATTHEW

Friday

We are folded together, and I really can't tell which bit is her and which bit is me, until I put my lips to it. But there are parts of her I can't reach – so tightly are we coiled – without uncoiling, and I'd rather be dead than uncoiled, right now. And so I'd never know if that line was her, or that curve me.

ME: I'm really sorry – that was terrible.

HER: Gee, thanks!

ME: NO! I mean, er, *I* was terrible. Not you. Not it. Well, sort of it, because of me. It, I mean, you – you were . . . amazing.

HER: You weren't terrible. You were . . . nice.

ME: Nice? That's the first time I've ever heard you use a normal word rather than one with a PhD.

HER: Stop playing the fool. You're smart. The stack of books says you are, whatever you claim.

ME: Smart enough to . . . to know I'm really into you.

HER: I kind of got that.

ME: But, well, er, the thing is, and I'm going back to the beginning, back to the terrible bit . . . it's because, and this is so lame, but I don't want you to think that I'm usually like that . . .

HER: I don't really know what you're getting at, but . . .

ME: No, hang on, I want to say this. I was going to fake it, but you're too brainy to con, and, anyway, I don't want to have stuff that isn't true, I mean as part of us, at the start.

HER: This is like listening to Albanian radio on the internet.

ME: No, look, the thing is, when I say that I'm not usually like that, I meant that—

HER: I know what you meant.

ME: No, I don't think you do. I meant that I'm not usually like that because there isn't a usually. In fact there's never been a . . . an . . . *it* before.

HER: Yeah, I got that.

ME: You got that? You mean, you could tell? I really was terrible, wasn't I?

HER: Yeah, you sucked. I mean, I'm not sure I could bear to go through that again, it was so bad. Unless, you know, you asked.

ME: Oh, well, I suppose I'd better ask, then.

HER: I'm waiting . . .

ME: Would you like to . . . you know. Again?

HER: Uh-huh.

SOPHIA

Friday

Books should prepare you for this.

I mean, I'll be totally savvy if I find myself the chosen one in a designer dystopia, or fall for a moody hot vampire, or even, which is actually possible, if not plausible, my secret-if-psychotic admirer tries to burn down the school and student body with it just to win my fucked-up, fractured heart. But has anyone primed me for the sheer gobsmacking lost-for-words-ness (see?) of good sex? Have they frick-frack. Unless I'm about to get pregnant, chlamydia or run over by a bus. Because consensual stuff between under-eighteens in which both participants get on and get off, and which doesn't then segue into death or disease? That can't happen in books.

Only, in real life, it just has.

I'll spare you the mechanics and bodily fluids but, sweet Jeebus, that is what it's meant to be. Or at least the second time was. The first was kind of like a test run; the experimental pancake you know is going to come out looking nothing like it should. And to be fair, it was one pretty fucked-up pancake what with it being his first time. But all first times are weird, surely. And a bit awkward. But like those pancakes, they're necessary to get to the good stuff. And it was. So freaking good. And so is the next bit, the aftermath. Because it is so devoid of any cliché or gone-before. He doesn't fall asleep. I don't pull the sheet round me in belated embarrassment at my nudity. Or exit stage left still shaking from the shock of it because I have literally nothing to say to him.

I have everything to say. And so does he. And the best bit? None of it is about *it*, it's about us.

'So who's your ICE?' I ask.

'ICE?'

'Yeah, you know. In Case of Emergency? On your phone? It's the first place the paramedics check if someone calls an ambulance.'

'I don't . . . My dad?' he guesses, laughing at how dumb, and sweet, this sounds.

'Not Jango?' I ask. Because my ICE is, of course, Lexy. Because she made me, on the grounds that she didn't want to miss a second of drama. And because, my mom? As if. Yeah, she cares, but there is caring and all-out end-of-civilisation panicking and that is so not what I need if I ever get blue-lighted.

He hesitates. 'Maybe. If the emergency was, I don't know, *Planet of the Apes* actually happening. Or if I needed to know the line-up for the 1987 United squad in a life-or-death hostage kind of situation.'

'What's going on with you and him?'

'Huh? Nothing.'

Which, using my freakish ability to translate standard girl-answer, I read as 'everything'.

'You want to talk about that "nothing"?'

He hesitates, then opens his mouth to speak, and for one second I think tonight – us – has unlocked his magic frick-fracking uptight straight-boy doors and he's going to 'fess up to at least something, but instead what comes out is, 'So what's tomorrow going to be like?'

I smile. 'So I know you haven't read it, but have you seen *Gatsby*? Not the good one – the new one?'

He shakes his head. 'Sorry.'

'Don't be. Anyway, it will be nothing like that.'

There will be no beautiful music. Or truly beautiful people. There will be no champagne. Well, not unless the Pitt-Westons have raided Daddy's cellar again. There will be Jäger and pills and shit R & B. Someone will puke in a punch bowl and someone else will drink it. Someone will pass out on laughing gas. Someone else will find that funny.

'It will be as far from fricking F. Scott as you can imagine.'

'Are you sure it's OK for me to come?'

'Don't you want to?' And part of me really hopes the answer to this is no, so we can both find an excuse to duck out of the Hieronymus hell that awaits. But part of me is so bursting with it, and him, and wanting the world to know it, that I actually do an internal 'Yay!' when he says, 'I do.'

Yeah, I sicken myself at times.

'Unless you don't want me to,' he clarifies.

'No. I do.' And inexplicably, irrationally – because why would I want to invite in the kind of fallout that this is so going to kick-start in my already teetering-on-purgatory Pennington world – I do. Even though I know Lexy is going to be all over him and us like the Jewish mother she wishes she has. Even though I know he's going to get stared out by the Hollister hounds or psyched out by their bitches. Even though Lucas is going to . . . actually I don't know what the frick-frack Lucas is going to do. Yesterday he could barely acknowledge my presence. Which, number of fucks? None. And I'm pretty sure this Jango being AWOL is not in any way a bad thing. At least not for my sanity. Although Lexy will sure as shoeshine see it in a different light, as in I've stolen her follow spot by taking the low-rent glory for myself.

And that's when I look at him again. Into him again. And hate myself for even letting her drip those words into my vocabulary when they're strictly her lexicon. Lexy con. And so I throw them out, discard them, along with my mother's thin lips and the pressed promises for me to text her before I leave 'just in case'; along with the imagined looks from Lucas and worse from Dawse. They count for one big frick-fracking zero and we, we are everything. That kid from Perks had it right, because with Matt beside me, inside me, I feel infinite.

And infinite is something I want more of.

MATTHEW

Friday

Maybe there would have been a third. In fact, maybe we'd have carried on doing it for ever, until we burnt away, and there was nothing left of us but ash, and maybe teeth, because the teeth always survive. If I could have pressed a button and made it so, I would have. But something more obvious and terrible happened.

My mum and dad came home.

I think I'd basically forgotten that mums and dads existed. It was just me and Soph and the vomit duvet. But then the doorbell rang, and then the sound of keys being rattled very loudly in the keyhole, and then the door opening and my dad saying, 'Why'd you ring the bloody bell?' And my mum shushing him, and the whole thing their way of being decent, and letting us know they were back.

I didn't think I'd ever see Soph looking uncool and flustered, but watching her speed-dress fixed that. Turns out that tights are just something you can't put on in a hurry without falling over. Or saying *fuckfuckfuckfuckfuckfuck*.

I was quicker. I thought that it was better to avoid obvious skulking around, so I put my head out of the door and shouted down, 'Hi, Mum. And Dad. We're just up, er, revising.' I don't know if I really went 'er'. But then Soph gave me a friendly punch in the kidneys.

'How do I look?' she hissed when she'd finally got most of her clothes on, along with a surprisingly neat smear of lipstick.

'Like you've just been to heaven twice, or maybe one and a half times . . .'

And then she smiled again, and ruined her lipstick by kissing me, and as I held her, it was as if she had no bones, because she just melted into me, like cream poured into coffee.

'Come on,' I said, 'we've got to go and say hello. Just don't expect them to talk about Shakespeare and stuff. But they're nice, they really are.'

'I know – I can tell,' said Soph, putting on more lipstick. Then she took a tissue out of her bag and wiped my lips.

'Don't want to give them the wrong idea . . .'

We went downstairs, and I was feeling about eight things. Elation, I guess you'd have to call it, about what we'd just done. And a layer of what I'm going to call love, and I don't care if it sounds stupid. Because, really that's the name for it. It wasn't fancying. It wasn't liking. It was loving. So that was the first part, the happy stuff. Then there was the fear about what Soph was going to make of Mum and Dad. Then the embarrassment about us knowing that Mum and Dad knew what we'd been up to. Because they must have done. I was sixteen. She was seventeen. We weren't up there playing

Monopoly. And then a lot of pride at being able to show off a girl like her to them. A girl out of our world.

And it was OK.

I introduced them all, and they shook hands, and my mum offered to make some food, and I said, 'Mum, it's half ten . . .' and Soph said she had to get back, and she had that app on her phone for getting a taxi, and my dad said I should go back with her to make sure she was safe, and Soph laughed and said she'd taken plenty of taxis, and when I thought about it I realised that I'd taken exactly three taxis in my entire life.

And then the taxi was there, and I went out to it with her, and we kissed again, but not like a massive snog or anything, just this perfect sweet kiss, which stayed maybe two seconds, and I wanted to say 'I love you,' but even I'm not stupid enough to have said it out loud, yet.

I lay in bed alone, and the bed was a sort of bath made of her, of the memory of her, but also the smell of her that was still there.

And then I remembered the book, still under the bed. It didn't matter. I could give it to her at the party. That would be better, in fact. So it wouldn't seem like a bribe to do it, or a stupid thank you for letting me do it, but just a gift. A love gift. So I lay there, and I began reading the book, and it was pretty good, and I fell asleep with it open on my chest.

And so that was how the best day of my life ended.

SOPHIA

Saturday, 2 p.m.

If this were any kind of film worth its ticket and extortionate popcorn price, I'd have fallen asleep in his arms, woken at five minutes to midnight, and then starred in my own, across-city escapade (set to 'Modern Love', natch) as I tried to get home before my mother's gold clock chimed twelve and her forefinger, poised provocatively on her iPhone, pressed the emergency button.

But this is life. And I'm not Lexy, I'm the good girl. The Sandra Dee. So I negotiate the parents – which, not even weird, but another layer of thrill because I can feel how big a deal it is for him and that he wants them to like me as much as he does, so, pleadingly, pathetically, I want them to like me too. And then I call in my curfew and call a cab and get carried back across town in the back seat of a Ford Moronic. And I don't even get the third degree when I get in, just a cup of cocoa and the combined hair-swish-and-sigh of perpetual disappointment that is more familiar than Bowie in the soundtrack of my youth.

But still I don't sleep. As the red digits on my retro alarm flick through the minutes from midnight to one a.m., then through two and three, my beats per minute outracing any tick-tocking going on, I picture us and I am stunned that it is me in that image. That I am capable of any of this. That I let this happen. This is so not what I had planned for this year, or ever, even. Not that I subscribe to my mother's fully scripted day-to-a-page diary plan, but I am supposed to be concentrating on, you know, being alive. Passing exams. Giving withering stares to anyone who claims to be in a 'maybe more' situation. Only no, this is me, and this is more than 'yesnomaybe more'. This is 'yes'. And so bewildered am I by this unsolicited made-over me that I've seen 4.56 click over on my bedside table and the first light filter round the edges of the blackout blind before I finally catch any Zs.

So when I do wake up, I've missed whatever sorry vegetables have turned into overpriced baby food for lunch, ten missed calls from Will, and his train pulling into platform two.

'Sorry,' I blurt as I pull a dress over yesterday's don't-even-think-about-the-stains underwear.

'What gives?'

'Sorry, sorry, sorry. Overslept. Didn't you call the landline?'

'Obviously. But no answer. I thought maybe you were all being held hostage by infidels or midgets.'

I plumb the messy depths of my mind to pull out a vague memory of my mom mentioning a trip to a garden centre for something unpronounceable, and a pirate party for one of Thom's similarly obsessed nursery inmates. Rock and roll.

'I'll call a cab,' I say. 'Come and get you.'

'Too late,' he replies.

'Where are you?'

'Look outside.'

I yank up the blind, and blink into the too-bright sunlight, and, as I finally manage to will my tired eyes into focusing, I see him, standing on the gravel like an outcast from a Tim Burton meets Baz Luhrmann movie. I hang up.

'It is the east,' he shouts up. 'And Sophia is my sun.'

I jolt as I'm taken back to that bookcase, to that bed, to last night; feel the ache in my limbs, and between my legs. But I force myself to snap back. Will is here. My gay best Romeo. And so I laugh and flick him the universal sign for fuck off, followed by a kiss, and some vague indication that I'm coming down.

'You smell of sex,' is the first thing he says, after I've refound some calories from a 2.34 a.m. Mars Bar binge and launched myself at him in a full-on limpet hug.

'Oh. God.' I drop to the floor, take his bag, think better of it because he seems to have his entire wardrobe packed inside, and lead him into the house instead. 'Really? Do I?' But I'm not embarrassed. I'm not grossed out. I'm secretly, dirtily, thrilled. Because secretly, dirtily, that is the first thing on my mind.

'And you didn't even try to deny it,' he says with the smug satisfaction of a TV cop.

'Am I that transparent?' I click on the coffee machine.

'No, you smell that badly of boy. Anyway, I'm just jealous.'

'Caleb?'

'Don't even say that name. He is as dead to me as last season's skinnies,' he declaims, in a manner that makes it clear Caleb is anything but.

'I'm sorry,' I say. Which I'm not. And he knows it.

'Pants on fire,' he says. 'Which brings me to ... Matt, I assume?'

'Never assume,' I say. 'Because someone will always trot out a cliché as the next line.'

'So sadly true.' He sighs.

'But yes, obviously Matt. I've not turned into Lexy in the last, what is it? Six months?'

'Thank the sweet baby Cheezus for that. So was he good?'

I feel my cheeks redden and lady-land turn electric again as I am teleported Spock-style back to that bed, and to him.

'I'll take that as a yes.'

I turn away; focus on conjuring up the caffeine hit I am so craving. 'You can take it any way you want to,' I say.

'So Cool Hand Lucas is totally out of the picture?'

'Shit.' My hand slips on the metal and I scald my finger. How frick-fracking appropriate. 'Yeah. Well, kind of.' And the teleporter takes me from my more-than-comfort-zone to total-horror-story on the doorstep a week ago when I stuck my tongue in Lucas's pleading mouth. But I make like Taylor and shake that one off swift. 'It's a long story,' I say. 'But, yes. It's done. Over. He is more history than Henry the Eighth.'

'Oh I like that.'

'Yeah, me too.'

He tips four, count them, sugars into his coffee, stirs, and takes a sip of the sweet stuff. 'So we're going to Lexy's fashionably late at, what?'

'I don't know. Eight?'

'And when does the mother ship dock?'

I shrug. 'Five, maybe.'

Will clicks on his phone and I know it's not the time he's checking. No missed texts. No calls. No, his sneaking, cheating ex does not love him. He clicks it off again. 'So that gives us three hours of retail therapy, at least an hour of pissing off Mrs G. and still plenty of time left over for hair and make-up.'

'You want to go to town?'

'When don't I?'

'I . . . OK, just let me shower first.'

'Let you? I'll scrub you down myself if I have to. I am not walking round smelling like the toilets at the Tavern.'

'Nice.'

'I thought so.'

And so I shower Matt off. Or part of him anyway. The other part, the better part, the part of him that's camped out in my head and heart, I can only try to ignore as I make the most of the one other person who gets me, and gets all of me, including the skulking sac of cells in my head, and the fact I don't need to talk about them, haven't even been able to with Matt. Not yet.

I have twenty-four hours with this boy, and I am not wasting one of them. I am Cinderella, at least in Lexy's eyes, and goddamn, I am going to the ball. And I am going to act like I belong, and act like Will and Matt and even Jango if he makes it belong. Hey, maybe me and Ponyboy will be the start of something big tonight, and it will be like Montagues and Capulets, or Sharks and Jets, all laying down their one-liners and weapons of choice and getting on and getting off like it's one big beautiful world.

Frick-fracking Jesus. I really am in love.

MATTHEW

Saturday, 2 p.m.

I know there are schools where kids go to house parties every weekend. You hear stories about them. Maybe a friend of a friend will know someone at my school, and the word will come back about it being some kind of amazing orgy with booze and drugs and hot girls just gagging for it, and maybe the police get called but it's all OK because Daddy's a solicitor, and it's all sorted out with a handshake, and maybe someone getting grounded for a week.

But those kinds of party just don't happen in our school. Or maybe they do, but it's, like, one a year, and I'd never been invited to one. True, you get a bunch of kids hanging out under a motorway bridge sniffing glue out of a plastic carrier bag, but I didn't suppose that was going to be the deal at Lexy's tonight. So I didn't even know what to expect, what to imagine. And, as usual, that made for a churned-up load of feelings, mixing up good and bad. As usual, I mean, since I'd met Sophia, in the hospital canteen, back a million years ago.

Nothing's been simple since then.

I remember in a geography lesson with poor old Mr Harker, we got shown some slides of different rock formations, and there were some where you could see these nice simple layers, like a cake, and I can't remember exactly what they were, but say one was a seabed, and the next was a forest, and then there was a desert – I don't know, something like that. And the lines were straight, and anyone could understand it. And then there was another slide, and the world had undergone some big seismic trauma, and the layers were mixed up, as if someone had taken a fucking hammer to it. So, that was what Sophia was to me. Earthquakes and volcanoes. A big fucking glorious hammer. Because who wants simple? Simple was what I had. Simple is when you're dead.

And it wasn't just the feelings side of this that was interestingly messed up. There was Jango. I'd sent twelve texts to him, but I was shouting in a cave with no echo. It might have been that it didn't mean anything. The world is made up of a billion billion things, and most of them don't mean anything. A lost balloon, a falling leaf, a car crash, a dog taking a shit, a song coming out of someone's bedroom window, a pain in your balls. Being human makes us want to see them as signs, but they're just stuff happening in the world.

Wait, that's making it sound like I was on a downer, you know: It's all meaningless; I hate everything. But I wasn't down. I was up. Because when I'd been finding meanings for things in the past, it was because everything seemed like it was designed to make my life shit. Well now I'd swept that away.

And if Jango wasn't replying to my texts, Sophia made up for it. She just seemed so full of words, and they were always the right ones. And she could make me snort with laughter or blush whenever she wanted to.

But there were practical things I had to do. I had forty quid in my bank account. I needed a shirt and a jacket and a haircut, and I was afraid it wouldn't be enough.

'Dad, can I borrow . . . twenty quid?'

My dad looked up from his newspaper, and put his cup of tea down. As I said, my dad is a nice man, but if he has a fault it is that spending money always hurts him. And I know it's because we don't have much, but I didn't have my caring-about-the-family-finances head on that morning.

'What's it for, son?'

'I'm going to a party. Er, with Sophia. I need some new gear.'

I thought I was going to have to work hard for this, but my dad sighed like he'd heard a bad football result on the telly and reached into his trouser pocket. He has a flabby leather wallet that's older than me, and him opening it up always feels like something from *Indiana Jones*. Then, to my amazement, he took out a fifty.

'This has been getting on my nerves for months,' he said. 'No bugger round here will change it. They all think it's a fake. You'll be all right with it down in town.'

'Thanks, Dad,' I said, and felt like hugging him. But that isn't our way.

And so I hit town with more money than I'd ever had on me in my life. And what I found out is that there's a sweet spot when it comes to money. If you're skint, you can't buy anything, and you feel shit. If you're a millionaire, you always want more and more expensive things – a bigger yacht, a hotter supermodel girlfriend – and whatever you have feels inadequate, and so you feel shit. But if you've got £90, and all you want is some clothes and a haircut, then you can do it. Just. Result: happiness.

The other thing money can get you is drunk. And so I picked up a half bottle of cheap, no-name vodka, which I could fit into my pocket as neatly as a hand.

'You look good, Matthew,' said Mum, as I was giving myself a last check in the hall mirror. The jacket wasn't hanging quite right, what with *Trimalchio* crammed in one pocket and the bottle in the other. But it was better than carrying it around in a Tesco bag. 'That young lady's lucky to have you.'

My dad loomed up behind Mum, and gave me a look. We both knew I'd pulled well above myself. Except not even that thought could get me down today, because I knew the answer: Sophia didn't think so.

I grinned back at my dad, and hugged my mum, and I was out of there, not so much walking as riding a hover-board. This party was going to be the best. The world was OK. And I was a kind of a god. A little one. A minor deity. No, I was one of those mortals who gets off with a goddess.

I tried to remember them, but the names wouldn't come, and then I decided to think about something else, because I had a funny feeling it doesn't always end very well, for the mortal . . .

SOPHIA

Saturday, 8 p.m.

Pennington house party prep according to me:

1. Haul on deliberately obtuse outfit preferably involving obscure 1970s tour T-shirt.
2. Line stomach.
3. Grit teeth.

Pennington house party prep according to Will:

1. Three hours of retail therapy spanning Harvey Nics to the thrift store by the canal, delivering one pair Black Milk leggings, one dead man's trilby, and a lipstick that screams Marilyn. Although I'm pretty sure the ensemble whispers crazy lady, whatever Will claims.
2. Two Snickers milkshakes, two salted-caramel brownies and four chilli-vodka shots, which, he asserts, cover all the food groups, ruling out any catering requirements later.
3. One play of Bowie, assuring us at full tinny volume that we can be heroes, and that Will isn't on the number 12

but in the back of a pickup truck on the tunnel approach to the Pittsburgh bridge.

So by the time we're home, costume-changed and ready to trip back out for round two, we're more than infinite – we're flying. And not even the highly trained sights of the mother ship can shoot us down.

'Have you—' she begins.

'Got clean underwear?' I interject. 'Check. And twenty for a cab. And a rape alarm. And yes, I took my meds.'

Or, rather, I probably took them. Because not once in the five hundred and whatever days of living with this fricking time bomb in my head have I forgotten to take the one thing that keeps it from going off. At least too often. Besides, I don't have time to go back to check the date-stamped boxes. And if Mom does it she'll only hit the panic button because, in an echo of my five-year-old determination to flout the laws imposed by days-of-the-week knickers, I have deliberately worked backwards, and this, my friend, at least in tablet terms, is Tuesday.

Besides, once isn't going to kill me, right? And I'm in the mood for daring. For living each day like it's my last. It got me Matt.

Mum looks at Dad for backup, but he's got his headphones on and I'm guessing Dylan turned up to eleven (and, frankly, I don't blame him). Then, as she opens her mouth to lodge an official complaint, my phone emits a convenient chirrup.

'Where the fuck RU?'

Lexy.

Will's phone beeps in swift suit with the same demand.

'We should hightail, Mrs G.,' he says (no, really, he actually says this, and gets away with it, and yet if I try to call her Carol, I get the silent treatment).

'No later than midnight,' she insists.

'One,' I try.

But she's not playing. 'Midnight. Or your father will be round.'

I flick a glance at Dad again, his face buried in Larkin, his head a hundred miles away. I'm pretty sure by midnight he'll be further gone but I shrug and say what she wants to hear – the magic password 'fine' – and then she opens the door and we're tumbling out, arm in arm, heading the three, long, privet-hedged blocks to Wonderland, to West Egg.

To Lexy's.

'Come on,' he urges, pulling me along the gum-stippled grey-brick pavement. 'There's fashionably late and then there's being left with the fat kid.'

'You are seriously overestimating the hotness of Pennington boys,' I warn.

'Hey, I've seen my fair share of Pennington boys across the hockey pitch, remember? Besides, I live in Leighton Buzzard now,' he laments. 'So indulge me, for fuck's sake.'

'Fine,' I echo.

'So, on a scale of one to Zac Efron, how hot?'

'*High School Musical* or *Paper Boy*?' I ask.

'The former. Obviously.'

'One, two, or three?'

'Do you really need to ask?'

'OK, three. In which case, five, at a push.'

'Well, I can always stick soft filter on,' he sighs. 'And besides, it's size that counts.'

'You are the last of the romantics.'

'And you know it.'

And it's my turn to pull him onwards, because I've remembered – how could I forget – that there's at least one ten-out-of-ten there, and for once, he's mine.

Lexy opens the front door channelling the improbable combination of Edie Sedgewick and cheerleader.

'You,' Will declares, having taken a step back to admire her concoction, 'are a heartbreaking work of staggering genius.'

Lexy squeals as he hits his cue, word-perfect, air-kisses him extravagantly, then takes his hand and wields him like some gay Lazarus trophy as she leads us to the engine room of tonight's orchestrations: the kitchen.

If they handed out Oscars for cramming the largest amount of irrelevant information into one sentence and a ten-metre-sprint then Lexy would take home gold. By the time we're downing our first V & Ts (not even Will has a big enough death-wish to risk the punch), I know that Dawse has been happy-snapped in the downstairs toilet giving one of the

Henderson twins head, and it wasn't the one she was shagging last week; Prue Weeks has given up being bi-curious long enough to comfort the other Henderson twin; and Lexy sexted Jango a picture of her in a La Perla balconette and he's gone quiet since and what the hell is that about.

'Wanking?' I suggest, telling her what she wants to hear.

'Gay,' retorts Will. 'Is he coming?'

She shrugs. 'He said yes but that was before the double Ds. How about Matt?'

Again I am transported back to last night: I see a flash of pale body over mine; feel a delicious quiver rippling out inside me; feel the flesh of my cheeks redden. 'Yeah, I ... he should be.' I click my home screen to check for messages. Nothing yet, which could mean he's on time and doesn't need to text. Or it could mean ... actually I don't want to think about what else that could mean. Not that Lexy is interested. She's moved on, or back.

'Ooh, talking of gay, there he is.'

'Jango?'

'No,' she sighs as if I'm retarded. 'That kid in Year 11 with the hat.'

Will and I follow her gaze across the Hogarth-by-way-of-Hollister scene of royally fucked-up bodies to see an overweight redhead in a panama.

I smirk at Will. 'You go, Glen Coco.'

Will looks at me, then the big kid, then back at me. 'I'm gay,' he says. 'Not blind. But that ...' he nods towards a figure negotiating the carnage in the far corner . . . 'that I would do in a New York minute.'

And I don't know if he's joking or poking, trying to get a rise, because the boy he's staring at, the one with the blond quiff and the studiedly lowered eyes and lazy smile, is Lucas.

And he's seen enough back-catalogue Instagram to know it.

'*So* the wrong tree,' Lexy drawls, saving me the bother.

'So whose tree is he?' asks Will.

Lexy and I look at each other. 'Not mine,' we chorus.

'Really?' I ask.

'Fuck knows.' She shrugs, then sticks a hand down her bra to answer the full-throttle vibrations of her mobile.

'Ooh, Jango,' she says to no one in particular, and slips slick as an eel in her metallic blue sheath through the crowd.

I check out the corner again and see Lucas squeezing his way towards us through the tangle of fake tan and fug of Chanel.

'I am off like a dirty sock,' I say. Then, to Will, 'Coming?'

He sighs, his eyes still focused on the prize that is my ex and Lexy's sloppy seconds. 'I guess.'

'He's straight,' I insist.

'I don't need his dick,' Will says. 'Just that pretty boy face next to mine, maybe with a touch of tilt shift and an ambiguous caption.'

'Insta revenge?'

'Served hot. The sweetest kind.'

'You, my friend, are a lost cause.'

'But don't I look cute while I'm drowning?'

'Super cute,' I say.

'So where's your lifeboat? Matt, I mean.'

'Like I need rescuing,' I drawl. 'I'm not freaking Sleeping Beauty.'

Which is the exact point at which, in a jacket that crackles with bought-today newness, and a second-hand smile borrowed straight from last night, my very much non-ex knight-in-shining-Topman swoops in with a kiss straight off the silver screen.

Cue fireworks and fairy freaking godmothers; I think John Hughes has finally accepted his directorship.

'Hey, Matt,' I manage. 'You made it.'

MATTHEW

Saturday, 9 p.m.

I heard the party long before I reached it. The house was even bigger than Sophia's. There was a wall with a gate in it, and a buzzer thing next to it. I hadn't seen this before – a doorbell even to get into the garden . . .

I pressed the buzzer, thinking up what to say. 'Hi, I'm a friend of Sophia's . . . Except it was her friend's party. My mind went blank for a second, then I remembered, Lexy. Yeah, I'd say, 'Hi, Lexy invited me . . .'

But no one said anything: the buzzer buzzed back at me, and the gate opened up. I crunched along some gravel, and then there was an open door, with the music blaring out of it, and kids sitting on the step, smoking, drinking out of bottles, laughing like the world's funniest ever joke had detonated among them.

A girl, half sitting, half lying, her long, straight hair falling wispily on her shoulders, looked at me and smiled.

'Hello,' I said, but then I realised that she wasn't looking at me, just away, for a moment, from the boy she was with, and then she faced him again, and my 'Hello,' fell dead like a shot bird. So I stepped over her and was in the house.

It wasn't completely rammed – you could move around without squeezing past people, but there were still kids everywhere, and I could have punched or kissed five of them in a couple of steps. They mostly had that Penn look – cool clothes, cool hair, cool souls, cool cash. Another time I'd have been hating them already, but I didn't hate them tonight. Tonight I was sort of loving them, because Sophia was one of them – was here, was waiting for me. The girl I'd been ... inside twenty-four hours ago.

But I was still pretty shy, and wanted very much to see a friendly face.

I didn't get one, yet, but I did get a face.

'Taste this,' a girl said, pirouetting away from a wall. She was small and dark and pretty. She had a mildly gothy look going on that wasn't quite the same as the others. Her face registered a moment of puzzlement – I think she'd thought I was someone else.

'What is it?' I peered into a glass – a proper glass, not a plastic one. It contained an orange liquid, viscous enough to coat the sides.

'Oh, it's the punch. It tasted like Lucozade Sport before. I added some more, er, *goodness*, and now it works.'

I had a swig. I could taste something bitter in it, like aniseed, cutting through the syrup.

'That's foul,' I said. 'What did you say you put in it?'

'Absinthe,' she said. 'You know, the stuff that makes the tart grow fonder.'

'What?' I said, but she was away, disappearing darkly into the heart of the party. I didn't mind. It was going to be one of those nights when nothing makes sense, and I decided I'd just go with it. I had another gulp of the punch, and followed the girl.

Noise. It sounded like there were two competing sound systems. Or maybe that was just the kind of music they liked. The room I was in now had three or four girls dancing in the middle of it, and lights swirling around them, and bunches of floppy-haired guys leaning against the walls. I scanned it for Sophia, but she wasn't there. I'd have known in a second, because you do, when you're really into someone. You can spot them from a shoe, from a finger, from an eyelash.

Another room. Rowdier, this one; mostly boys. Pushing and cuffing each other, as boys do, in play. Close-cropped hair, short-sleeved T-shirts, muscles. The sporty guys.

A couple of them noticed me, which no one in the last room had. A nudge, and another glanced up at me. Someone said something and they laughed. I didn't feel welcome here, but I didn't really care. I met their stares. At my school that would be enough to start a fight, but these weren't really fighting kids, despite the muscles. I raised my chin in acknowledgment, and moved on.

And I bumped into someone who was coming in as I was going out. She gave a little squeal, then, rather than bumping away from me, as people usually do when you collide with them, she clung on, almost as if we were dancing together.

Lexy.

And she was still holding me, and like the first time I saw her I was struck by the fact that she was formidably hot. Obvious hot, not subtly hot, like Sophia. But still hot. She was wearing a dress that seemed melted on, and she still had that look, and it wasn't in any single part of her – not in her eyes, I mean, or even her body, but in the everything about her, the look, I mean, of someone who doesn't really care about what's right or wrong, and I guess it was a sexy look, if that's what you like.

'Matt!' she said, sounding genuinely pleased to see me, which I kind of got anyway by the clinging-on bit. 'I've been waiting for you.'

'Nice house,' I said.

'Yeah, well, it turns out there is a point to Daddy after all. You're looking . . . neat.'

Neat. Was that a dig? Did I look like I'd tried too hard? She took her hands off my shoulders, but she was still very close. She was wearing perfume. I've no idea what kind, but it was . . . strong. I don't mean that it overpowered you or anything, just that underneath the flowers or whatever the hell perfume's supposed to smell of, there was something darker, that made the world go vague around her. Her lips were very red.

I focused.

'Sophia?'

'Oh, yeah, she's here. Through there.' She gestured with her thumb, dismissively. 'With . . . oh, some guy.'

A sly little look on her face. It was as if she was saying, 'I'm only pretending to try to make you jealous, and we both know that, but let's do it anyway.'

But now I knew where Sophia was, I had no interest in dangerous Lexy.

'Thanks,' I said, though I don't know what for. We were still in the doorway, taking all of it up, and I had to press against her to get through it. She made the smallest movement back to let me. It was the minimum to avoid having something close to simulated sex in a doorway.

I breathed a sigh of . . . relief, I guess, and passed into the next room, and there, against the far wall, half hidden behind more dancers, I saw Sophia, laughing.

She hadn't seen me. As Lexy said, she was talking to a guy. He was wearing a hat, not a beanie, but the sort of thing you see in old films, and even from here, with my junkshop gaydar registering nothing but static, I could see he was no threat.

But I didn't care about the cat in the hat. It was all about Sophia. She hadn't really dressed up the way Lexy had – just a simple T-shirt – but she gave off a light, except it wasn't one you could see, so it was more radiation; good radiation that gave you love, not cancer.

And I knew then what the right thing to do was – the thing that had made this happen in the first place, the one bright idea I'd ever had, even though it wasn't an idea, more a huge yell from my soul. And so I moved towards her, slipping to the right of another girl, and to the left of another boy, like a sea lion sliding between fronds of kelp, and I felt alive and excited and full of energy, and I reached her, and she looked up, her face full of happiness, and her lips began to part to say something – something, no doubt, clever and funny – but for once I stopped her words, by means of a kiss, that made a perfect landing, not too hard, not to soft, not too dry, not too wet, a perfect kiss, and my tongue touched hers, and my hand was on the small of her back, and I pushed her into me, and the world vanished, and again we were on my bed and inside each other, me in her body, she in my head.

'Well,' came a drawling voice – belonging, I realised, to the guy she'd been standing with – 'I'd say get a room, but this is too good. So how about popcorn and some tissues?'

And Sophia couldn't help but laugh, which kind of spoiled the kiss, but in the best way. And then she was looking at me, her eyes sparkling in the light of the party.

'You made it,' she said.

'I'd have walked through fire.'

I tried to make that sound ironic, but I meant it.

'What, and spoiled your nice new clothes?'

'Oh, shit, I was hoping you wouldn't notice.'

'Ahem,' said the kid next to us. 'Maybe an introduction might be polite?'

SOPHIA

Saturday, 9.30 p.m.

As introductions go, it's your standard: 'Will – meet Matthew, Matthew – meet Will.'

But the way my heart skips and my stomach slides belies its ease because this is so far from standard. This is serious; bigger than meeting the parents. Dad doesn't notice anyone unless they're dead and fictional, and who cares what the mother ship thinks? Let's face it, if she did give me the seal of approval I'd know I'd fucked up royally. And as for Lexy, if he's got a dick, he's passed the magic test. But Will? Will is my own Magic 8-Ball. He is the Simon Cowell steering my sex life, holding the power to say yay or nay or 'ask again later' with one raised eyebrow.

He looks Matt up and down, assessing the level of effort (and you'd better believe too much is worse than not enough), assigning a clique. But Matt doesn't fit any of the tribes Will knows and hates. He's . . . just Matt.

And that, it turns out, is the key to the kingdom.

'You,' Will says, 'are too adorable. Both of you.' He flings an arm around each of our shoulders. 'I'd say you're Cathy and Heathcliff, but that's Lexy's line.'

'Have you seen Lexy?' I ask Matt.

'Yeah. She was . . . huggy?'

'Just a hug?' Will faux-declaims. 'That's like a limp hand-shake to you and me. Now listen. You two have each other. Lexy has . . . fuck knows – everyone. I need someone. Come on. We are on a mission to get me some.' He pulls us, stagger-ing through the crowd.

'Some what?' asks Matt.

'Seriously?' Will stops in his tracks. 'Oh, I think I love you even more.' And he plants a kiss on the top of Matt's hair. Hair I know smells of Head & Shoulders, and, frick-frack, if that isn't the sexiest thought on the planet right now.

This is going like a dream, I think as we plough through the bodies, distinguished only by the colour of their Baby Lips and level of messed-up-ness; a fairy tale. I am at a Penn party, with my boyfriend and my best friend, and I am having a ball.

But it takes less than an hour for me to realise that John Hughes has left mid-shoot and some lame-ass who couldn't script his way out of a parking lot has taken over, because it turns out the fairy godmother hasn't delivered the one line she needed to: 'Watch out for the wolves, little girl.'

And, worse, these ones aren't hunting for vampires, or Little Red Riding Hood – they're just looking for trouble.

MATTHEW

Saturday, 10 p.m.

I kind of liked this Will kid. You could see that he was what
Fernando might have been if he'd gone to some other school
– a school like Penn. Going to our school meant he had to
invent himself as a kind of huge, camp monster. And because
he has a sort of genius for it, it works. But if there's a real
Fernando still alive in there, somewhere, then he is lost for
ever. With Will, it isn't that he is any more genuine than
Fernando, but the act is less destructive of his true self. The
fakeness seems real. So when he kissed me on the head I
thought, Yeah, why not?

And then we were trailing through the party, looking
for someone for Will to get off with. Or that was what he
said. Maybe it was just part of his act, and when push
came to shove he'd be as chickenshit with guys as I am
with girls.

'We can look for your friend,' said Sophia, her voice just
reaching me through the white noise.

I didn't know what she meant. Was it the girl I'd spoken to
earlier . . .? Was it a jokey bit of pretend jealousy? Or maybe I
misheard.

To be honest, things were starting to get a little fuzzy around the edges. Whatever the hell the aniseed stuff was in the punch, it was working. And when something works, you want more of it. Well, not *it* exactly. I saw the light of a kitchen, and yelled in Sophia's ear, 'I'm gonna find a drink. Get you one?'

'I'll come,' she said, and her fingers were touching mine. She tapped on Will's shoulder, and made a drinking sign, but he was already engaged in a giggling conversation with some other guy. The kitchen was dazzling after the flashing gloom of the rest of the party, and quiet enough to talk at a normal level. It gleamed with chrome and stainless steel, and everything that wasn't made of shiny metal was polished stone. There were glass doors at the back, opening out into the garden, and in the garden more lights like giant candles flickered.

There were plenty of other kids in the kitchen, and Sophia knew them all and said, 'Hi,' and, 'Hello,' and, 'How you doing?' and sort of half introduced me, while still having her fingers entwined in mine, so I knew it wasn't that she was ashamed of me or anything, just that she didn't want to get wrapped up in another group, because she had me, and didn't, right now, want anything else.

There was a big glass bowl with the orange punch in it. White flowers were floating on the punch. My mum would have said that was unhygienic.

'Stay away from that shit,' said Sophia. 'Spiked with absinthe . . .'

'Oh, yeah, I heard. What the hell is it?'

'It's what they used to drink in Paris in the 1890s. Gets you drunk, makes you mad, kills you. Not necessarily in that order. Drink that and you'll be seeing snakes coming out of the walls, then you'll hurl your guts up, and that would be a terrible waste of a perfectly good party.'

'OK.' I didn't mention that I'd already necked a beakerful.

'Let's try here,' she said, and pulled open the fridge. While she did that I surreptitiously put the cheap vodka I'd picked up at the corner shop on the table, behind some half-empty bottles. I was glad to get rid of it. The fridge was big enough to climb inside and have our own party in right there. Except it was full of beer. No, not full of beer. Full of everything. Sophia stuck in her hand and pulled out a bottle.

'Is that Champagne?' I said, seeing the bulging cork.

'Nah. Just Prosecco. But the bubbles are the same. Come on.'

And then she took my hand again, and led me out into the garden. It was cool outside, cold even, and dry, and a huge relief after the noise and wet heat of the party. I felt the sweat chill and then dry on my back, and I liked it.

It was one of those complicated gardens with hidden zones, and unexpected paths, and the candlelight made it look like we were wandering through a fairy tale. Where I live, a garden, if you have one, is a square of grass, with a washing line across it, with your dad's underpants fluttering in the breeze.

I could hear other voices out here – whispers, muffled laughter – but nothing was distinct, just shadows and the shadows of shadows. There was a tree, one of those with branches that droop down till they brush the ground. I opened the branches, like a curtain, and we ducked inside. It was even more dreamlike inside the lattice of the branches, with the garden lights breaking and dappling through the leaves.

I sensed a shiver from Sophia. A shiver or a tremor . . .

'Are you cold?'

She shook her head, and smiled.

'Take my jacket,' I said, slipping it off.

'No, you'll be . . .' she began, but then I laid it on the damp ground for her. It was just big enough for us both to sit on, if we squeezed together, and so we did. And then I felt a bump under me, and remembered the book.

'I've got you something,' I said.

'I bet you have,' she replied, and it was such a funnily un-Sophia-ish thing for her to say that we both snorted out some matching crude laughter.

'It's . . . I had to think about it. I was trying to find something . . . *right*,' I said, and handed her the untidy parcel.

Even through the darkness, I could see, or maybe just sense, her look of, well, glee. Yeah, glee, like a child.

'Why?'

'Just because . . .'

'I love presents . . . Oh. Sorry, that's dumb. Everyone loves presents.'

'I don't.'

'No? How can you not love presents?'

'Well, I suppose because my parents can never afford to give me anything really good, so it's always a disappointment, but I have to hide it because I know it's the best they can do.'

I could tell that Sophia was making herself listen when what she wanted to do was rip into the parcel.

'Open this,' she said, giving me the Prosecco, 'while I . . .'

And I fiddled with the foil and the wire, and then prized off the cork with a satisfying *pop*, as she took the paper off.

She looked a bit puzzled, for a second or two, and my heart sank, and I thought, This serves you right for thieving it, you dumb shmuck. And then she spun the book round and read the stuff on the back, and then opened it up, and read a bit from the front. And then you could see from her face that she realised what it was, and she looked at me, with her mouth half open in astonishment.

SOPHIA

Saturday, 10 p.m.

He hands me the package as if it's the Arc of the freaking Covenant and I flinch like I'm Holy Mary. Because even though it's light and small and looks like it was wrapped by my kid brother, this is big. Grand gesture and heartfelt declaration big.

It's not a CD, because if there's one thing I know he knows, it's that you do not take on someone with a thousand-strong vinyl back catalogue at their own game, not when you've never heard of Nina. I fumble with the layers of Sellotape and finally manage to work it loose enough to push in my fingers and pull out a plum of a present. And as I do my heart leaps its way into my throat so I couldn't speak even if I wasn't lost for words.

It's a book. But not just any book. It's *the* book. *The Great Gatsby*. No, it's actually better than that.

'Is this . . .?' I finally manage to choke out.

'It's, like, his first draft, or something. I don't know; not my field. Maybe it's no good,' he says quickly. 'Took some getting. But after the CD, you know . . .'

And I do know. And I'm shot through with a cold wash of guilt – at all the presents that I've had handed to me, shop-wrapped with ribbons and bows and a dusting of ostentation, presents I've played with or worn for a day or less, then pushed to the back of a drawer or let moulder in the backyard. Because they were worth money, but nothing to me. But this . . . This isn't a duty gift, a 'you got me something so here's something back'. This took time and effort and money I'm pretty sure he doesn't have. And, Mr Darcy, I am undone.

'Come here,' I say, taking the bottle from him and taking a mouthful of the sweet stuff. And then my lips are on his and I'm letting the liquid slip-slide from my tongue to his. And then I'm pulling him closer, pushing my tongue deeper. I want to be in him.

I want him.

His hands on my head, he pulls me away, but only to ask if I want to. Here.

And I look at 'here'. And I realise I don't care that this is the same yard I've played hooky in with Lexy; croquet with her parents; sat at high tea with her high-maintenance grand-mother. I don't care that we're only a few metres from Dawse and whichever Olsen twin is this week's friend with benefits; several more from an entire student body whose prime purpose in life seems to be to capture Kodak moments like this and share them with their three thousand closest follow-ers. I don't care that it's still March-cold outside and my arms are already stippled with goosebumps let alone my tits. I don't care about anything but him and me. Because, forgive my clichéd heart, but right now we are the only two people who exist on this frick-fracking planet, and, hey, we might die tomorrow.

'Do you?' he repeats.

And as I feel him hard against my hip bone, and feel my body do its thing right back, I know there is only one answer.

I pull him further into me. Push one hand up under his shirt. As my finger brushes his nipple I feel it stiffen; hear someone – myself – gasp. Because this is me and not me. I don't do these things. I don't seize the moment, let alone the day. But here this girl is, doing stuff; daring stuff. Daring to push her hand down to his crotch, feel how badly he wants this. Daring to pull down the stiff zip of his new trousers. Daring to slip her fingers inside, feel the cotton of his boxers, the hot, hard flesh underneath.

And this girl is about to go further, all the way, when there's a crash and a cry from somewhere inside the house, and he jumps, and his cock flinches, and as swiftly as this began, he's slipping away from me. In every sense.

'You have to be kidding me,' I breathe, hearing the desperation edge my voice, half liking it, half still wondering who the fuck has taken Sophia and what they've done with her. 'It's nothing.' I'm begging now. 'The punchbowl probably. It won't be the first time or the last. Come on. Please.'

But he's shaking his head and pushing himself down so that he can pull himself together.

I don't get it. Then I do. Or think I do. 'Is it . . .? Have I . . .?' I half ask.

But if I'm expecting the standard 'it's not you, it's me' in return, I am sorely disappointed. Because what he says instead is, 'Jango.'

'Huh?' I grunt, words failing me for the second time in almost as few minutes.

But the look on my face must be pretty articulate because he sees what I'm thinking – or at least a vague interpretation of the whole repressed Gay Best Friend scenario, probably with fewer short shorts and no jazz hands chorus – and says a panicked and emphatic, 'No, NO, not that . . .'

'Then what?'

'Listen.'

And I do. And then I hear it. Someone shouting – an echo of a voice I've heard before but can't place. And another above it. One I do recognise and only too well. One who would have been way comfortable in that last scene, and brought his own costume.

'Will?'

'Jango.'

'Fuck.'

And then my hand is in his and he's pulling me out of the cool of the yard and the peace of us, into the heat of the kitchen, and a writhing mass of bodies, some dancing, some drinking, but most of them focused on the primetime entertainment that's being played out on the thousand-pound Persian rug.

Matt pushes us a path to the pit but even from the front row I still can't make out what's going on. Not properly. On the floor, on his back, is some kid I'm guessing is Jango. But the body astride him, pinning him down, isn't Will. Whoever it is is too blond – too built, too. And besides, since when did Will wrestle with anything more than which shade of eyeliner matches his baby blues?

But he's in on this somewhere, because, as if reading my mind, I feel him push his way so he's standing beside me, his body shaking, his face pale.

And he doesn't need to say anything. I know from one look what's happened. Will's made a move on this kid – this Jango. Or maybe just looked at him the wrong way. Whichever, it amounts to the same thing. And now Jango's gone all Southern States on him, only Will has no moves, no muscle. So the Hollister hounds have stepped up. Because they might hate Will for being gay. But they hate Jango more.

For talking wrong.

For wearing the wrong shoes. And I mean seriously wrong, one of them at least two sized bigger than the other like some giant clown shoe, if clowns wore Hi-Tec.

But most of all for going to the wrong school. Because he isn't and will never be a Penn boy.

Not like Will, who may have left a year ago but there's still some Penn in his blood mixed with the glitter and shots. And whoever this is, wailing on the outsider, is Will's knight in shining A & F. But just who the frick-frack put on the armour?

'Jango!' Matt yells, his hand slick with sweat in mine now.

The kid on his back seems to hear him but instead of losing focus it's like he's been handed a shitload of kryptonite, because he gives this strangled battle cry and manages to flip himself out and over so that he's the one on top now.

And in that split, slick second I realise two things:

1. That I do know that voice, and that gaunt face, and the cheap, mismatched wrong shoes. And though they're white again now, and he sure as sugar looks better without the patina of shit and decay on him, he's still not a pretty sight to me.
2. That only minutes after I maced this former swamp monster, I kissed the kid who's now writhing underneath him.

Because the knight?

It's Lucas.

MATTHEW

Saturday, 10.45 p.m.

I didn't know what the hell Jango was doing at the party. I couldn't see him hanging out with any of the Penn lot – it'd be like a ferret hanging out with the rabbits. For a second I wondered if he'd followed me there, with some weird scheme in mind. And that made me feel sick. At times I'd half forgotten the way this whole thing started. The stupid raid on the hospital. All that. But Jango doesn't forget . . .

Even if his presence at the party was a mystery, you didn't have to be Sherlock Holmes to work out what had happened once he'd got there. Not if you knew Jango. Someone had looked at him, maybe glanced down at the big shoe. Or *he'd* looked at someone, and snarled out an insult. Either way, he'd taken offence, or given offence, and it had turned into a punch-up.

That was the outline, but the details of what was happening in front of me were fuzzy. I couldn't make much sense of the swirling mass of Penn kids, some yelling the fight on, some trying, ineffectually, to stop it, some just gawping. I made out Sophia's hot friend, Lexy. And she was one of the gawpers. Except gawping wasn't the right word, because that implies a kind of vacancy. No, Lexy was watching it the way you see a cat watching goldfish, and there was a word I was looking for, and it wasn't quite hunger, and it wasn't quite lust, but it was something that combined the two of them, and it made me almost frightened of her.

And then I saw that gay kid, Will, and his look was sort of the opposite of hers, as if he was hating what he was seeing, and his eyes were red, like he'd been crying or was about to. And I felt a kind of contempt for that, because you shouldn't cry because something shit happens at a party, not with the world the way it is, providing all kinds of real things to cry about.

But all those ideas flashed through my mind in, like, a second, because what I was mainly seeing was Jango, my mate, being sat on by some hulk of a Penn kid. Jango is tall, and Jango has the guts of a tiger, but this other kid had that defined look you get from private gyms, and posh-school sports coaching, and good food, not the sort of shit Jango gets given by his space-cadet mum.

And this kid – well, he looked more like a man than a teen-ager – was on top of Jango, pinning his arms with his knees, fighting hard to get a hand free to punch Jango, and Jango was bucking to get him off, his face red with rage and frustra-tion, and I reckon if the other kid had put anything within range of Jango's long teeth he'd have bitten him.

But, anyway, all I could think was, There's my friend, getting beaten up by a posh kid, and my duty was as clear as spring water, and I moved towards the two of them, getting ready to kick the posh kid in the head.

And if I'd done that then I guess everything would have been different. Better? Who knows. There's more than one way to lose at life.

So I let go of Soph's hand and surged through the crowd, elbowing some kids aside none too gently, because basically I was steaming, and all I could think about was helping Jango, and not even the love of my life, standing back behind me, could get in the way of those thoughts and the deed.

Plus, well, I'd had a lot to drink by that stage – the weird aniseed drink, the Prosecco – and the alcohol was singing a war song in my veins, and it blended with the *BOOM BOOM BOOM* still coming out of the speakers.

But the moment before I got there, and introduced my foot to the side of the other kid's head and triggered what was likely to be a mass brawl, with me and Jango taking on the whole of the party, Jango managed to spin the other kid, using, I don't know, rage and willpower and his innate Jango-ness. So by the time I reached them there was no one left for me to kick.

Well, apart from Jango.

The thing is that even though the other kid had Jango down, and maybe could have punched him, I'm not sure he actually would have done. It takes a special kind of person to go through with a full-on nose-crunching punch to the face, and not many rich kids have it in them. I don't mean that they're better in some moral way, just that their experiences haven't given them what they need.

But Jango's experiences had. And once he was out of danger, my urge to protect him vanished, and I saw things more coolly, and realised what a shit idea it was for me and Jango to take on the world. It was a party full of sweet kids, mainly, who didn't really want to fight us. It was a party full of Sophia's friends. It was a party full of Sophia.

Now, with Jango on top, things got a bit more . . . visceral. The kid was strong, and it was as hard for Jango to keep him down as it had been the other way round. But Jango is a dirty fighter, and kept putting in quick, humiliating slaps and half punches. And his eyes seemed to scan the floor, looking for something . . .

I glanced quickly around, and saw that some of the other kids were getting ready to back up their guy. One came forward, and made as if to hit Jango, doing pretty well exactly what I'd planned to do a few seconds ago. I stepped in front of him.

'Fair fight,' I said, looking him in the eye. He backed down, but I sensed the room's hostility, which up until then had been directed at Jango, now spreading out towards me.

'Fucking scum,' said one kid. 'Why are they even here?'

There was a murmur of agreement, but then I heard another voice say, 'Soph,' and the noise kind of stopped, as if the very mention of her name stumped them.

And then I heard a girl scream and looked back at the action. I don't know how, but Jango had got hold of a bottle

– a green bottle of Becks, with some of the lager still swishing around in it. The kid was hanging on to Jango's wrist, so he couldn't smash the bottle into his face, but then Jango spat in the kid's eye and, as he flinched, he wrenched his arm free, and began to bring the bottle down.

I moved then. But even as I went to grab the arm I noticed, or thought I did, that Jango hesitated, and his face became puzzled for a moment, and then he half smiled. But I think he was still going to bottle him and, anyway, I was already committed. I plucked the bottle out of his hand, and shoved him off the other kid, so they were sprawling side by side.

But not for long. They were both up again in an instant. But the crowd had had enough. A couple of the Penn kid's buddies grabbed him, and I got in front of Jango. He looked at me with the same black hatred I'd seen during his run-in with Fernando.

'What the fuck are you doing here?' I said.

He forced himself to grin.

'It's a free fucking country. And I got an invite. From sexy Lexy there.'

Without looking at her, he pointed with his long finger, almost delicately, as if it were a conductor's baton.

'Anyway,' he continued, 'I was looking out for my best bud. Worried about you with all these posh shits. Stab you in the back, cut your balls off, shove 'em up your arse. That's the way they work. METAPHORICALLY.'

He said the last word at max volume, in a kind of fake professor voice, nodding and grinning at the appalled partygoers, showing that he knew the word, but also somehow taking the piss out of them for knowing it too. Someone had turned the music off, and his voice was huge and clangourous.

'And there I was innocently checking out the action when that poof comes on to me.' Another contemptuous gesture, this time aimed at Will. 'Should have known – all Penns are poofs, except the lezzers and the trannies.'

He was obviously trying to rile the Penn jocks. It was working, but not enough, yet, to force them to punch his lights out.

'Shut up, Jango,' I said. 'You're an embarrassment.'

And I was thinking, You're making us all look bad – all the kids like us. No, it was pettier than that. I was thinking, You're making me look bad. Because they all think I'm just like you.

But those were the thoughts that Jango could read like a *Janet and John* book. He grinned, but it was as fake as a set of eBay Beats.

'You fucking slithery shit-licking traitor,' he said, trying to keep his voice cool, which he knew would add to the force of the foul words. 'Do you want to know why I was really here, what I was actually trying to fucking achieve?'

The room now was deathly quiet. Everyone wanted to know.

I didn't.

But it wasn't up to me. I shrugged.

'That bird of yours,' he said, his eyes sliding towards Sophia. 'She's a slag.'

The kid Jango had been fighting with tried again to struggle free, but his mates had a good hold. No one had a hold on me. I took two steps towards Jango and punched him. It landed on the angle of his jaw, and it should have put him down, but Jango hardly flinched. Maybe I was too drunk to punch properly. Maybe he was too drunk to feel it. In fact, it seemed to help him, giving him what he needed to do what he had to do. And now the grin seemed a little less forced.

'I'll give you that one,' he said, cool as anything. 'A freebie. For old times' sake. But next time you hit me I'm going to kill you. But that's not why I'm here. Yeah, that girl, Sophia – she might not know me, but I've seen her before. Outside her house. With this jerk here – the ladyboy I was teaching how to dance. She had her tongue so far down his throat she could have tasted what he had for dinner.'

I felt suddenly empty, like I'd been unzipped, and all my insides scooped out.

'So what?' I made myself say. He could have seen her anytime, before she even knew I existed.

'Five days ago, dickwit. FIVE. DAYS.'

SOPHIA

Saturday, 11 p.m.

Of all the choice names I've had hurled at me in my seventeen years of life on earth – freak, geek, tumour tits (thank you, Henderson twins, for that gem) – slag is the last I expect to be thrown. A cheap word. A word that we stop ourselves thinking because so what if we do sleep around? What's it to you?

Only I don't sleep around. I've barely slept anywhere. Yet the sting of it when it hits is hard as a slap, reddening my cheeks and sending a wave of nausea surging up from my stomach. Or maybe it's the poor man's champagne. I shouldn't drink, I think. Not on tablets. It blurs everything too quickly, makes me hallucinate, so bad I see Matt – my Matt – land a punch on Jango's jaw.

Jango laughs. And the sight and sound sobers me like a shot of Joe. This is real. This is actually frick-fracking happening. I am being fought over. Like I'm in one of Lexy's messed-up fantasies. Only I'm pretty sure her dream scenario does not include what comes next.

'She don't remember me,' Jango says. 'But I remember her. I've seen her. Outside her house I was, trying to do her a favour. Only she – Lady fucking Doolally – goes and maces me and then runs straight to lover boy here and sticks her tongue down his throat.'

Drink and fear grip me again, and lift me, weak and giddy, out of myself, so that I'm seeing this skew, watching it happen to another girl who just happens to walk and talk like me. Because the one he's riffing about I don't recognise. Not the way he says it.

'Five days ago,' he continues. 'FIVE DAYS.' Then he turns to me. 'Or have you blocked that out too, love?'

I shake my head. 'Matt . . .' I choke out.

But he's not looking at me, won't look at me. And besides, someone else wants in on the action.

'Seriously?'

I whip my head round quickly, too quickly, feeling the room pull and spin in another direction. I lean on someone – Will, maybe – and focus my eyes.

Lexy.

'You and him,' she says, nodding at Lucas, who's upright now, flanked by the baying Hollister dogs; *Game of Thrones* played out in casualwear.

'It wasn't . . . real,' I manage to mumble. 'It was . . . I was proving I didn't feel anything.'

Lucas snorts.

I turn to him, and then to Matt. 'It's true. I didn't feel anything. Not like with you. It was never anything like it is with us.'

I plead with Matt, my eyes beseeching him. Then my lips, when the eyes fail. 'Jesus, can we go somewhere?' But Matt drops my gaze and flicks back to Jango, whose eyes are wide with malevolence, pupils dilated with something harder.

'Well, she is fucked up.' He turns back to Matt. 'Oh yeah, didn't she tell you? She's sick. In the head. Why else do you think she's slumming it with you? Just visiting, she said? She's one hell of an actress.'

I want to speak but I think I'm going to puke so my mouth's shut for safety reasons and I watch helplessly as Matt's eyes on mine well with tears and disbelief, and his hands ball into fists and he flails in his head to work out what the fuck is happening. For a minute I think he's going to try another punch, but he's too slow, held back by trying to decide who he wants to hit, so Jango gets his shot in first.

'But then that's the only reason you're with her anyway, isn't it, Matty boy?'

And it's my turn to flail. 'Matt? Matt, what does he mean?'

I'm looking at him, into him. Willing him to talk to me, to explain what his dancing monkey is jabbering about, and then I can explain to him. All of it. The swamp monster, the dick picture, the mace, and the kiss that wasn't. Wasn't anything other than proof that Lucas is so last season. If that. The tumour too. That it's not as bad as anyone thinks. Not as bad as Lexy will have told Jango.

But he doesn't say a word. Instead he wipes his eyes quickly on the sleeve of his new jacket, turns, and starts walking, slowly, deliberately, through the crowd, which parts like he's Moses himself.

I take a step forward to follow him but my legs are weak and Jango's on a roll and isn't going to let me go without playing his trump card.

'You know you're a bet, don't you?' he says. 'That's all. A bet.'

I swing my focus back to Jango, and feel vomit rise again as disbelief, then reality, sink in. Because it makes sense. It does. Because why else – how else – would something as crazy Hollywood as that canteen kiss happen. I *am* a bet. I am *She's All That* and *Ten Things* rolled into some shitty British remake. This is Lexy's wet dream come true, only I'm pretty sure the cast is way uglier than she was hoping.

'Oh yeah,' Jango continues. 'He was heading to the cancer ward to find some dying girl to fuck. But he only had to go as far as the canteen and you were that desperate you let him kiss you there and then. Isn't that right, Matty boy?' he says.

I turn my head, scanning the crowd desperately to find him, to call him back to look at me, so I can see in his eyes if this is real or some messed-up Jango prank. But he's gone. Slipped away. Everything seems to be slipping away.

'Here,' Jango says, sticking his hand in his pocket and pulling out a note. 'I should probably pay up. A deal's a deal.' He thrusts a fiver into my hand. 'Plus services rendered and all that. How did it feel when his cherry went pop?'

And as I hear that word dissolve on his lips it hits me. All of it, in one thunderous tsunami of shit. And it's like the Persian rug has been pulled out from under me. Because my legs start to buckle and the room flickers in and out of focus. The light's too bright. The crowd too loud.

I'm on all fours now. And that's when I hear it. *Tick-tock. Tick-tock.*

This isn't just what's happening – drink and dumbness in some toxic Penn party mix. This is something else. Something that shouldn't be happening if I'd taken my . . .

Tick-tock.

I scrabble for memories, try to play the morning back in sharp and detailed high definition, but all I get is soft-focus snapshots. An Instagram feed of fooling around and fuck-ups. Me waking late, sex sore. *CLICK.* Will on the doorstep. *CLICK.* Harvey Nics. *CLICK.* Shots. *CLICK.*

Tick-tock.

I try to picture the pillbox, open, the day marked Tuesday empty. But it sits stubbornly in a drawer, staying resolutely shut.

Tick-tock.

I ask myself one last time. 'Did you take your pills?'

And my body, weak and useless, yet alive with it, answers back, 'No, you fricking didn't.'

I feel the fiver in my hand. And say the words as the first pulse takes me in its electric grip.

'You. Stupid. Slag.'

MATTHEW

Saturday, 11 p.m.

I looked at the faces in the room. They appeared weirdly distorted – twisted, compressed, elongated, skewed. Somehow not really human any more. I turned to Sophia, hoping to find something there, but she had become ... *other*. The turmoil – the guilt mingled with fury, the hot anger and clammy regret – all scrunched together.

But there was something else in her too, something that didn't seem to belong in this sordid little situation, something darker, stranger, deeper.

My head was pulsing and throbbing with the music. I squeezed my eyes closed, hoping that when I opened them again all this would have gone away, and I'd be back in the garden with Sophia.

But no, they were still there. Jango – leering, grotesque. The Penn kids looking like they were enjoying the drama of it. Especially Lexy.

And Sophia again. Something was happening here that I didn't understand. Happening to her. There were things that I didn't know ... that I *needed* to know. Something in her. Something she knew. I wanted to reach out to her, to make contact. If I could know what was in her head, and show her what was in mine . . .

And then I saw her face. It had a look of horror. As if she'd just found out the worst thing you could ever find out about someone. That they were a murderer, or a sicko. Something foul and disgusting. She *had* seen into me, and what she saw made her sick to her soul.

It was too much for me to bear. I had to get gone. I felt a hand on my arm. I looked for a second, and saw it was Jango's, and I shook it off, not knowing what he wanted, what further vengeance he was after, and because of the way we were, all I could do was deliver a back-handed slap, and it felt good to me; good as cool water to a dry throat.

I strode towards the front door, but then swerved to the kitchen. There were still a few people there – talking, drinking, carnivorously snogging – oblivious to what had gone on elsewhere. I snatched at the half bottle of cheap vodka and was out of there.

'Matt!'

I looked back. Jango again. His face weird. Happy or sad? Who knew? I wanted to kill him.

'Fuck you,' I said. 'Stay away from me. You're a freak.'

For a second I felt good, felt free for having said it, having stood up to him. But then it turned to acid and bile in my throat, and I spun away before I could register his expression.

I began swigging the vodka in the street. There are times when you have to think your way out of a problem, when you can yoke up your brain and whip it, and it'll drag you out of the shit. But the shit now was over my head, and thinking wasn't going to fix anything. It was time to get drunk, properly drunk, and forget.

With the first swallow I felt the horror of the evening bubble and surge inside me, and up it came, bitter and foul, into the gutter. I coughed and spluttered and gagged, and emptied out the rest of what was inside me. I vaguely felt people pass by me, hunched, appalled. I didn't care.

I took another mouthful, swilled it round, gargled, spat. I walked on, not really knowing or caring where. I watched my shadow cast on the pavement by the orange glow of the street lights, saw it stretch out before me, contract, and then fall behind. I gulped more of the vodka, warm from the party, thick and resinous, and retched again, but there was nothing left to come up, except for the mouthful I'd just swallowed, and some acid bile from my guts.

I came to a crossroads. Home was one way. Town the other. I tried to use the shadows to guide me, but when I looked down the lights at the crossroad meant that the shadows went in every direction, crossing over each other, giving no clear signal. And the light was shattered and refracted from the water in my eyes – the bitter tears of puke and regret. And so I headed towards town. The closer I got, the more the streets were filled with people. As they saw me come towards them they veered out of my way. I wiped my face on my sleeve, smearing the tears and snot and watery vomit.

'Mind it!'

'Fuck you!'

I swigged the vodka again. It stayed down. It was starting to feel good. No, good isn't the right word – no, not at all. I was getting an energy, but it was a dark energy, the sort that tears things apart.

I saw again that look of disgust on Sophia's face. And there was only one way to cope with that. I sent it back at her. All I'd done wrong was to follow Jango up to Micky's, but Sophia . . . she'd snogged that floppy-haired fuck. Others, too, probably. She'd snogged me in the canteen after ten minutes, so who wouldn't she snog? And it's never just a snog. Girls like that, they don't stop there, do they? Who else had she screwed? Screwed, yeah, that was it. She was screwed up. Sick in the head.

Something about that phrase haunted me, coming back like an echo in a nightmare. And all the words were bouncing around inside the walls of my skull.

I'd betrayed her before I even knew who she was . . .

But she'd snogged him.

But she was a liar.

I was a liar.

Back again to Jango's words.

Sick in the head.

That was what she was. She was some kind of psycho bitch just fucking with me.

I hated her.

I hated me.

I hated.

SOPHIA

Saturday, 11.30 p.m.

Some seizures I can keep walking, keep talking even, though what I say might not make sense. Sometimes it's no more than a twitch of my hands and a blank stare. So small that only the mother ship and Lexy can tell I'm having one.

This one is not that kind. This one is a full-fat, hit the floor, freak-the-room-out fit. The kind that starts with the acrid smell of the wrong things on fire, segues through a horizontal mosh, and ends with me peeing my Calvins in front of my peers – so not the party trick I had in mind.

The kind you wouldn't even wish on your evil nemesis, at least not on someone else's Persian rug during peak Pennington party.

It could have been worse, I guess. I could have upchucked, downchucked, swallowed my tongue. Although, as Dr Gupta told my ashen-faced white-knuckled mother, that's pretty much folklore.

And then there's the noise – a guttural, animal sound. Ugly. Scary, according to my friends and enemies. And I have the evidence to suggest they're not wrong. What? You think no one would slip their smartphone out and sneak that one on to their memory stick? So they never uploaded it to YouTube, and I am grateful for that small mercy, but it got passed far enough round school to make it back to Lexy and then me.

And this is bad. Seriously bad, in kudos stakes. But if this is the payoff for a benign tumour, for not being in one of those mortuary drawers, then I will take it. Because what no film captures are the three words that manage to make it above that grunting. That ring loud and clear through the haze and the headache that will last for hours, if not days:

I. Am. Alive.

MATTHEW

Saturday, 11.30 p.m.

Town now. Pub throwing out time, again. Some going on to clubs. Crowds of lads, laughing. Girls in short skirts and high heels and big hair. In the distance a police siren, going away. My face tight with the dried stuff – the tears, the rest. I looked at my hand. It was sore, and the knuckles were grazed. Had I punched a wall, on the way out of the party? I must have done. It felt . . . good.

I finished the vodka. Sucked the last drops from the neck, sticking my tongue into it, the way I'd . . . the way she'd . . .

Screw it. I threw the bottle at a bin, but it bounced off the lip and skittered away across the street, not even smashing, avoiding somehow the cars and taxis. I watched it, glittering in the street lights, coming to rest against the curb on the far side of the road. A group of lads on the pavement looked up.

They didn't really see me, didn't notice me. But I noticed them.

It was the gang from that night, a lifetime ago. Four of them now. Two smoking, the way kids smoke, making a big deal of it – see, look what I can do. The fat kid, the one with the knife, he wasn't there. But the short skinhead was. Couldn't miss him. He had no shirt on. Tats on his arms. That look of vacant anger, as if waiting for something to enrage him, the way normal people wait for a bus.

He looked again at the bottle that had bounced across the street. And then back the way it had come. Back to me.

Our eyes met. Still he was vacant. Then a thought flickered. A memory.

Flickered in him; flickered in me.

He half smiled. So did I. He thought he was going to chase me through the streets; thought he was going to corner me somewhere and kick the shit out of me.

Well, he wasn't.

Just as he turned to speak to his mates, to say, 'Look here, we've got prey,' I was running.

Not away: towards.

Fury, heat, murder. I made an animal noise, a bellow or a roar. But the roar might have been in my head. I heard a car screech to my side. I didn't care. Come and kill me, car, I thought, if you can. But it couldn't. Nothing could touch me. And in a second I was on him, on them. I saw the surprise and fear on his face. Feet first, I took him. He half turned, so my feet went into his hip, and not his guts or his groin. It threw him back against the wall, and if he'd hit a shop window he'd have gone through it, and this would have ended. He made a sound when he hit the wall, a *gnnnnth*.

I was on the ground, and then I was up, and he came back from the wall, and he'd almost recovered, almost got his fight back, but I was quicker, and I was madder, and I punched him with my hurt hand, and it was a punch I'll never land again, so perfect, so true, like a superhero, and the kid's face vaporised before it, turned to nothing, so my fist seemed almost to pass through it, painlessly, and I'd have thought I'd missed him if I didn't see him fall, and lie there, like a toy.

And then I remembered the others, but I wasn't afraid. I was going to growl at them, and they'd flee before me. I turned around, and they were there, and the fat kid had joined them. He had an open kebab in his hand, and I would have laughed, was, in fact, in the early stages of laughing, when he somehow managed to punch me in the stomach with the hand not holding the kebab. And the punch hurt so much, more than you'd have thought was possible. The wind was out of me, but it wasn't just that. There was cold and heat in it, too. I doubled over, and then for the first time felt fear. They weren't surprised any more. And now there were four of them, unhurt. And I knew I had to run. So I staggered away, still folded over my guts, and I heard them jeer behind me, but didn't yet hear the sound of them coming. They must be looking after their leader, I thought, making sure he's OK. Then they'd be coming.

Suddenly the night was cold. Hot and cold. I wanted to puke again, but there was no time. I felt it coming up into my mouth, but this time the puke tasted different, and I spat as I ran. I dodged in and out of the crowds, swerving on and off the pavement. More car horns. More curses. And now I felt them after me. The whole gang. My legs were tired, so tired after the . . . everything. I wanted just to be home. A taxi. That would save me. No money, but I could get some from my dad. I saw one. Stepped out in front of it. Brakes screamed. The driver stared at me, mouthed something, pulled around me, put his head out of the window.

'Pisshead.'

I didn't really know where I was. The town wasn't the town any more. It was hell. The circles of hell. Everyone around me was dead: dead and damned. Except the devils. Devils chasing me. And then I knew where I was, and it was right that I was here. The shit-fight alleyway. My refuge.

I staggered into it, sending metal bins clanking, empty boxes flying. The brick of the wall was good to touch, its textures satisfying, comforting. I worked sideways, both hands on the wall, feeling my way along in the dark.

Somehow I was soaking. Sweat dripped from my torn shirt. It had soaked my trousers. So much sweat . . . Had I pissed myself? I laughed, but it hurt to laugh. Who'd have thought a fat kid could punch like that? But that's a mistake you make, underestimating fat kids. Who says fat kids can't punch? Fat kids can do all kinds of things.

And then I was sitting on the floor of the alley, and I didn't mind the slime and shit. It was quiet. There was a cat. It came slowly along the alley, sticking close to the wall. A shadow cat. It stopped and looked at me.

'Come here, puss.'

No.

'Please yourself.'

But then the cat did come closer, and sniffed, almost like a dog.

And then silently it turned and ran away.

'Thought you'd be here.'

There was a smile in the voice of the kid. Not the fat one this time. The shirtless skinhead I'd clattered. He didn't look angry at all, just sort of workmanlike. He was going to beat me up in a thorough and professional way, now he'd had the chance to calm down. Make a nice job of it. Take pride in his work. I put my arms up over my face, thinking that I didn't want him to break my nose, take out my teeth. Maybe he'd just stomp and kick me for a bit.

But then nothing happened for a while. I don't know how long. A couple of seconds. So I looked up at him, through my hands, hoping maybe he'd gone, or that I'd imagined him. But he was still there, and his face was sort of funny. His mouth was hanging open, like someone acting in a play, someone who was supposed to have seen something terrible, and was trying to get that through to the audience without words. And then he used some words, because he was a shit actor.

'You're all messed up,' he said, and pointed at my front.

And then he ran off. Not the same way as the cat. The other way.

I looked down at my shirt, at the sweat. The sweat was dark, and sticky, and the dark and sticky was on my fingers when I touched it, and I knew what had happened.

The fat kid had stuck his knife in me.

SOPHIA

Saturday, 11.45 p.m.

I'm out for a couple of minutes, no more. I know this because the first sound I can actually make out, understand, is a boy and a girl arguing over the timing.

He says something about an ambulance.

She tells him I'll be fine, that she's seen way worse than this before and this has only been, like, one minute fifty seconds and I just need to sleep.

I try to speak but all that comes out is a strangled, twisted mess of vowels, coated in drool.

'Babes,' I hear.

Lexy. It's Lexy, I think. And with that name a sliver of memory slips into my head, of Lexy screaming something at me.

We broke up, I think. I know.

Only whatever I did, whatever my transgression was, is forgotten now. She's got a new role, a better one than Hurt Best Friend. Now she's Florence fricking Nightingale, kneeling over my wet, wounded body.

'We're supposed to tell her what happened just before,' she says.

'Why the holy fuck would you do that?'

Will.

'It orientates them,' she insists. 'Otherwise they panic.'

'And where did you read that? Tumour dot com? Or is there a handy YouTube vlog on the subject?'

'Oh ha fucking ha,' she snaps. So that I know it's true.

She leans over, her face looming in mine, backlit by someone's camera phone – the angel of Instagram. 'Babes, you're at a party. You . . . you had a fit . . . Seizure, I mean. Grand mal.'

I feel a hand take mine, the fingers long, fine, moisturised, one encased in a cold ring of metal. 'I'm going to call your mum,' Will says.

'Nnnnnnn,' I manage.

'She says no,' says Lexy.

'But—'

'Nnnnnnn,' I repeat.

'See?'

For a second I feel a wash of relief. I can sleep this one off here. Pretend it never happened. Pray she doesn't check the Penn blog, or find me tagged on her Twitter feed.

But the reprieve is short. And the second shot harder and truer. A punch to the gut, and the twist of a knife. 'Matt then,' he says. 'I'll call Matt.'

It doesn't come in floods but flashes. If speaking is a stutter, then thinking is like swimming through treacle. Words and images getting caught in the thick syrup that seems to coat my synapses.

A fight. FLASH.

A boy with a sneer and a too-big foot. FLASH.

Matt walking out. FLASH. Walking out on me. FLASH.

'You know you're a bet,' the boy with the big foot says. 'That's all, a bet.'

Fade to black.

'Nooo,' I say. Slurred, still, but two letters now, and emphatic.

Don't call him. Not Matt.

If that's even his name.

He's a liar.

A deserter.

A cheat and a charlatan.

I hope he suffers.

I hope he treads in dog shit.

I hope he trips and falls and pees his own fucking trousers.

I hope he hurts.

I hope he gets hurt.

Fuck living for the moment. Fuck living each day like it's my last.

Look where that got me.

Lying on the floor with cold sodden denim clinging to my legs, and the smell of ammonia drifting out into the crowd.

I don't want to do this any more.

I pull myself up so I can lean on my hands, Will's arms slinking quickly under mine, holding me up. 'Bed,' I say. 'I want to go to bed.'

MATTHEW

Saturday, 11.45 p.m.

I was frightened then and I tried to get up. But I was too tired. I was going to call out for help, but I wanted to wait until the skinhead kid had gone away, because I didn't want him to hear it, and to laugh about it with his mates. 'You should have heard him squeal, the poof.' So I rested my eyes for a minute.

When I opened them again it was freezing, and my teeth were chattering. I thought I must have gone to sleep. It was funny that, because I've always been rubbish at going to sleep, and now I'd just dropped off, the way old people do, watching the telly or reading the paper. And that was when I realised that I was probably dying.

All the rage had gone out of me, faster than the blood. I wanted to tell Sophia that I was sorry about the hospital. I wanted to hold her face in my hands, with my fingers reaching into her hair, so that I could say to her, and she'd have to listen, 'I love you; I really love you.' And I would tell her that she was the greatest thing that had ever happened to me, and that I wanted to love her until we were old people, falling asleep together. And I didn't care about her kissing that kid. It didn't matter. I didn't own her. We hadn't even done anything, then.

And as I was thinking about her, and how we'd met, and that first kiss, and other things we'd done together, I started to feel uneasy. And I didn't want to feel uneasy, because I needed the sweet and the soft things, now, at the end, and not the hard, bitter things. But the thoughts wouldn't go away. There was something I'd been missing. Some obvious fact, right there in my face.

Visiting.

She said she'd been visiting. But who? Why hadn't she ever mentioned it again?

And then what Jango had said. Messed in the head. Sick. I'd taken it to mean that she was twisted – a nutter or whatever. But sick had another meaning. And wasn't there something on the floor, that day, in her room . . .? The foil from some kind of tablets. Not aspirin or anything like that. Strong medicine.

Sick. She was properly sick. That was why she was in Mickey's. That was why she had that oddness about her. Not just that she was clever and beautiful and posh, but that she had the resonance of something deeper. The feeling that she was hearing secret harmonies when all you heard was the noise of the world.

And so what I did, I mean her knowing what I did . . . It was too terrible. I had to make it better.

And then I thought about my mum and dad, and how even if they'd gone to bed they would be lying awake, thinking about me, worrying. I had to get back to them as well. I shouted out now, but my voice cracked, and I coughed and I felt fresh wetness on my shirt. I closed my eyes again, just to rest.

And when I opened them again, I knew the world was different. I had a reason. A reason to be. A reason to live.

SOPHIA

Saturday, 11.50 p.m.

Lexy puts her palms on my thighs, studiously skirting the damp patch.

'You can have my room, babes,' she says.

I nod; let Will haul me upright; let myself lean into his shoulders; smell deodorant and cologne and the tang of shots.

My head hurts.

I don't want Matt.

I don't want to party like it's 1999.

I. Just. Want. To. Sleep.

MATTHEW

Sunday, 12 a.m.

The stars were sprinkling a crystal light, like rain, and I could feel it. I had to move. I had to find Sophia. She was sick, and she needed me. It hurt so much, but I heaved myself on to all fours, so I could crawl. But I couldn't remember which was the way out of the alley. I looked in one direction, and there was light there, and shapes moving dimly before the light, like shadows cast on the wall of a cave. And I was going to crawl to them, but then I looked the other way, and saw that there was light there, too, even though that couldn't be, because one end was blocked.

And so there I was, with light from both sides, and I didn't know which way to go. And then a wave of pain came, and the only way I could ease it was to fold in on myself, and lie there, with my face sinking into the slime until it reached the ancient cobblestone at the bottom of the world.

SOPHIA

Sunday, 1 a.m.

MATTHEW

Sunday, 1.30 a.m.

I've escaped from the black stink of the alley. But I'm not in charge of where or how. I want to be with her, back in the warmth of her.

But that's not where I am.

It's Year 7. I've gone to Jango's flat for the first time. It's a different Jango. He hasn't had that growth spurt. Apart from the big shoe, he's pretty normal, to look at. He comes in for a lot of shit at school, but he's funny, and usually manages to get people laughing. He brags a lot about his Xbox, and the games he has on it. Brags so much that people think it must be bullshit. I don't really know him. I don't really know anyone. So I'm surprised and flattered when he invites me round to play on the Xbox.

He lives in a rough part of town – two steps down from our street. Maybe when it was built in the '70s it was OK, but now every wall is sprayed with a giant cock and balls and little kids with filthy faces wander around and angry dogs look at you and the stairwells stink of piss and you can see the glint from used syringes in the morning light.

Jango's flat is on the ground floor. I ring the bell, and nothing happens. I ring it again, and suddenly there's a woman there, in a dressing gown. She's holding a cigarette. You can't tell how old she is. Her hair is so blonde it's almost white, and it makes her tan look even darker. Or it's the other way round, and her fake tan makes her hair look paler. She looks out of place on this estate.

'Jango's friend – you're Jango's friend,' she says, smiling, and gives me a squeeze. I can feel her chest against me, and I'm worried she's going to burn me with the cigarette, which makes me awkward and clumsy. I've never been hugged by anyone before except my mum and dad.

'Come through,' she says and she sounds kind of posh, but not quite right, as if she's putting it on. Despite the fact she's in her dressing down, she's wearing shoes with heels. I can see her toes. The nails are painted red. She's got pretty feet.

Jango is sitting in front of a big telly. Part of me was thinking there'd be no Xbox, and he'd give some excuse, like it was being fixed or something. But it's there. He's got one controller in his hand, and he tosses me the other, without saying hello or anything.

'Duty calls,' he says, and it takes me a few beats to realise it's a joke, because we're playing *Call of Duty*, which was the big game back then.

I'm useless and keep getting killed.

His mum brings us some juice.

'Your mum's nice,' I say. Am I thinking about the way her chest touched me through her dressing gown? I don't know.

Jango snorts.

'Yeah, nice. Sometimes.'

Jango, still normal.

We play all morning, then his mum gives us a tenner.

'Treat your friend,' she says.

We go to McDonald's. He tells me his dad was a sailor who died. It sounds like a made-up story. But if the Xbox was true, then everything must be.

I don't really care if it's true or not. I'm not alone. I've got a friend.

But the pleasure of that, the warm feeling, I can't keep it. Because the pain is terrible now, surging up like a real thing, I mean a thing made of stuff, or like it's an animal. It's an eel, eating through me, and I open my eyes again. It's black and cold and mortal.

It's hell, and it's my fault.

SOPHIA

Sunday, 2.30 a.m.

It's automatic, a learned response, one that will genetically imprint on future generations: we open our eyes, roll on to our sides, and reach for our iPhones; the flash of screen lighting up our faces, flickering our brains into focus, letting us know what we've missed while we've been wasting time sleeping.

So when my lead-weighted arm sluggishly hits an unfamiliar bedside table and pulls out not a plum but a book, I feel momentary panic, not at the disorientation of my location, but the dislocation of my life-support machine, and let out a pathetic cry of desperation.

'Hey, Sleeping Beauty.'

I turn my head, and see him slouched in the easy chair, Magic 8-Ball in one hand, a toy monkey I happen to know is called Dave in the other.

Will.

'Feeling better?'

'Where's my phone?' I say by way of a yes.

He nods at the mantelpiece, where it's now the centrepiece of some kind of Bratz tableau. 'Out of bounds. Until . . .'

His voice trails off and my overactive imagination fills in the blanks again, conjuring up a Twitter feed of bitch slaps, a candid camera crotch shot and, worst of all, not a single word from Matt.

Not that I give a flying frick-frack at a rolling doughnut what he has to say.

I take in the rest of the room; clock the pile of clothes in the corner; reach automatically between my legs. I'm dry. But the relief is momentary. My jeans and knickers may be gone, but I'm wearing pyjamas now. I glance down. Not even pyjamas.

A onesie.

With rabbits on.

I reach behind my head.

With a fucking hood and ears.

My humiliation is complete.

'I . . . we got you changed,' Will says.

'Into Bugs fricking Bunny?'

'It was the only thing we could get on you easily.'

I picture myself, a giant baby, my arms and legs being fed into the fabric, then poppered up.

Who cares though, right?

The sound of a party still in full swing reverberates through the floorboards and the shagpile. I picture Lexy holding court down there, playing up her part, relegating me to a walk-on. Or fall-down.

'What time is it?' I ask.

Will shrugs. 'Two? Three maybe? I texted the mother ship. Told her we're crashing here.'

'As me?'

'Natch. You're not that hard to get right. Attitude. A few too many adjectives. No ex-oh sign off.'

I smile despite myself; roll back on the pillow; realise I'm still holding a book.

The book.

THE book. *Trimalchio*. Its cover scuffed, its pages foxed and creased with time and . . .

Love.

'Where was this?' I ask.

'In your pocket.'

'I . . .' But I don't know what 'I' anything.

And I don't have time to work it out because the door clicks open and in walks the boy with the big foot stage right like he's about to deliver the speech of his life.

Jango.

'Seriously?' Will stands and blocks him before he can get near me. For the campest cowboy on the ranch, he's surprisingly leading man when he needs to be.

'I need to—'

'You need to get the flock out of here, Bo Peep.'

Jango looks at me over Will's shoulder. 'He's not answering his phone,' he says.

I feel myself crest a wave of something. Love, maybe. Hate, probably. 'And?' I say.

Will pushes him back towards the door. 'Let's take this outside, shall we? You know you've been dying to, sweetheart.'

Even in the half-light I can see Jango bristle. But he lets himself be steered on to the landing, the door clicking softly shut.

And, scene.

Only it's not, is it. Because in one hand I have a book. A book that tells me maybe, just maybe, I wasn't a bet. Because what would he have won? Not enough to pay for a first edition. Not enough to even bother to go out looking for one.

My phone is a metre away, two at most. I can reach it before my bodyguard gets back. Besides, he's probably persuading Jango he does bat for the other side after all. Although something in me wonders if he needs that much persuasion. Something in me wonders if his only doubt is that it would be Will, not Matt, showing him how boys will be boys.

And with that royally screwed-up thought in my head, I stand and make it the four steps to the mantelpiece.

And there it is. A text from Matt.

Only not from Matt too.

It takes me a second to see the subtlety in the missing word 'mobile'.

It's from his old phone. The one that sent the dick shot.

The one that got stolen in the fight.

The one I blocked, and then two days later unblocked because Lexy said we should hoax call it sometime. Only we never did.

I side swipe and click on it, my breathing laboured, and not just from the need to sleep that is drugging me, dragging me back to bed.

It's a photo. Of a boy hunched on the ground, face contorted, features flattened, overexposed from the glare of a flash. But recognisable still. It's Matt. He's hurt, I think. Or being hurt. Being hit, maybe. I peer harder. He's clutching himself. The white of the shirt behind his hands darker, stained.

I scan down to the words underneath and the blurry lines come into sharp-as-a-blade focus.

'Fancy him now, do you? Fucking prick.'

It could be fake, I think.

He could have rigged it up himself.

I look at the book again.

This isn't fake.

I feel vertigo begin to pull my legs out from under me, reach for the mantel to hold myself up. I have to stay standing. I have to walk. Run, even.

I check what time the message was sent.

11.48 p.m.

I check the time now.

2.53 a.m.

Shit.

SHIT.

And then, bless my badly wired brain, because somehow, the sheer volume of adrenalin that gets pumped into me at the moment overrides the post-seizure sleep-fest, tells the tick-tocking time bomb in my head to just frick the frack off, and sends me flying out of the room. And I don't care that I probably still smell of piss. I don't care that I'm dressed like a giant toddler or a wannabe extra in *Watership Down*.

I just care about him.

I need to find him.

And I need to find him fast.

MATTHEW

Sunday, 2.30 a.m.

I ran away from the pain, backwards, into time. But still I couldn't get to where I wanted to be, in her arms. There was a black star pulling me in, the gravity too strong to resist.

It's one of the parents' evenings at school. My mum and dad there. Dad awkward in a tie, because he thinks he's got to look smart. Mum in new shoes that make her feet hurt. There are three or four teachers in each classroom, and you move between them. The teachers don't have much to say about me. I'm not bad. I don't muck about in class. I'm good at English. Maths, so-so. Everyone murmurs, mutters, mumbles.

And then there's shouting. I look up. It's Jango's mum. She's yelling at Mr Stottard, who teaches geography. Her hair's black at the roots and something's gone wrong with her mouth. I can't work out what it is, but then see it's that she's missed her lips with the lipstick. She's almost scream-ing now, and waving her hands in the air, then jabbing a finger at Stottard, who's a dry, boring man, but not a bastard, like some of them. Jango is in the next chair, trying to make himself invisible, or at least that's what I guess, as that's how

I'd be feeling. Everyone's staring, the room silent except for Jango's mum.

'My boy ... he's gifted. My boy is special ... You people don't see it. Me, I see it.'

Jango turns his head slowly until he's looking at me. I'm feeling every particle of his horror. And I suppose I'm expecting him to look depressed or humiliated. But then he gives me the grin – the special Jango grin that makes him look like a devil from an old painting, but the sort of devil you might want to know. And it's the first time the other Jango shows through. But, no, now I see it isn't something from the inside that's been exposed, but something he's put on, for protection. A mask. And then, there in the room, he makes a gesture so obscene that my mum says, 'Don't look, Matty. Don't look.'

SOPHIA

Sunday, 3 a.m.

People move out of my way as I come pell-mell down the stairs. Well, you would, wouldn't you. A frick-fracking rabbit who was last seen throwing some shapes while horizontal. I can't see Will or Lexy and that's good, I think. Because they'll try to stop me. Put me back to bed. Jeebus, even I know that this breaks all the neat, convenient NHS handout seizure rules. But I figure this is a no-rules situation and, besides, how much worse can it get?

I need one person though. And this, ironically, is my lucky, lucky day, because he's halfway through the front door already. So that when I grab his arm and drag him with me, he doesn't seem that keen to resist.

'Where are we going?' he asks. Though I'm pretty sure he knows the answer.

I wait until I'm out of earshot and camera-phone-shot of Lexy's, a good hundred metres, before I stop and tell him the answer.

'To find Matt,' I say, and show him the picture.

'Effing hell,' he says. Then to emphasise his eloquence and insight, 'Effing hell,' again.

'Do you know who did this?' I ask.

He shakes his head. 'No . . . hang on. Maybe. I—'

'Come on. Maybe will do.'

'We had a fight. In town. He told you about it, yeah?'

I nod, one ear flopping into my eye. I push it back.

'These twats,' he spits. Then adds a quick 'Sorry.'

'What? You think because I'm posh I can't swear? Well fuck you.'

He raises an eyebrow. 'Oh, I know you can swear.'

I see me then, mouth full of filth, my fingers on a can of hairspray, aimed at his sneering, leering face.

'I'm sorry,' I say. 'I thought . . .'

'I know what you thought,' he says. 'Water under the bridge. Got to find my boy.'

'*Our* boy.'

He stares at me. Considers it. '*Our* boy.'

He holds out his hand for the phone and I don't hesitate in handing it over, or in putting my head next to his, so I can feel his day-old stubble against my cheek. Yesterday – Saturday – seems a long time ago.

'There,' I say.

'Where?'

I point at a word, a blur of neon in the right corner. The 'e b a b' of a cut-off cut-price fast-food outlet.

'I know that place,' he says. 'It's on one of those pissy little roads just off Great George Street. We've got . . . *history* around there.'

We don't know if he's still there. And even if he is we don't know if he's still alive. But we have somewhere to aim for. And right now that feels like a prize.

There's no bus. Not at this time of night. And neither of us has a car or even keys to one. So we go old skool. And run.

'Are you, like, dying then?' he asks between breaths.

'Like, no,' I answer. 'Well, maybe. If it grows, you know. They can't operate. It's not in the right place.'

'Didn't know there was a right place for a brain tumour.'

'Me neither,' I admit. Until I got one.

'Is it growing?'

'It was. But not now.'

He's quiet for a while after that. So all I can hear is the night air rasping against our throats, the thud of his big shoe, the slap of my slippers, the sounds of a city sleeping.

Please don't let him be sleeping, I pray. And then I pray that there is a God. And I say sorry for not believing. Even though I know I'll take it back tomorrow.

'You weren't just a bet,' Jango says then.

The book, lying face down on Lexy's bed now, comes into my head. Then other images too: his laugh; the way his hair must have been longer once, fallen into his eyes, so that he pushes invisible strands back even now when he's nervous; the taste of his tongue – Doublemint and whatever he's trying to hide. The way he looks at me; the way he feels to me, feels inside me.

I'm not a bet. Not now, anyway.

That first kiss floods my senses. A week ago, just over. Even that, that wasn't a bet kiss, a show and tell thing.

It had promise rolled in it.

He had want on his lips.

'I know,' I say.

Jango grunts in acknowledgement.

'Want to know why I kissed Lucas?' I ask.

He says nothing, so I take it as a yes.

'To prove Matt was the real thing. That was all.'

He thinks about this. Nods. 'He's the real thing.'

We've slowed now, getting close now. The lights from the kebab shop blur and buzz ahead.

But the door's shut. There's no one about, not now, not this late. The club crowds are still safe on dance floors, or on the main drag. Down here there's nothing. No one.

We reach the spot Matt must have lain in. Expecting, I don't know, a note? A treasure map? But all there is is dirty pavement and an empty Marlboro packet that isn't even his.

I sink to the floor, adrenalin fading, failing; crouching like the rabbit I've come as.

'No, that's good,' he says. 'Means he could move.'

'Or someone's moved him. To hospital. Or—'

Jango shakes his head quickly. 'I'd know,' he says. 'I'm his ICE.'

I open my mouth to correct him, then think better of it. Instead, brush my fingers over the floor as if the cobbles are braille, as if they'll yield up secrets, a story.

My finger trails through something wet and sticky and I recoil; stare at my skin in the sodium glow of the street light. It's dark brown.

I sniff it.

Not shit.

There's a metallic smell to it. Faint, but there.

The coloured bulb's skewing the truth, slanting it.

This isn't brown.

It's red.

It's blood.

I look over at the pavement next to us. There's another stain. Then another.

Tiny drops. But unmistakeable.

This will lead us home.

This is our trail of breadcrumbs. Of pebbles.

And like Gretel must have done, I take this Hansel's hand, and lead him, swiftly, urgently, into the woods.

MATTHEW

Sunday, 3.10 a.m.

The last time I saw her.

I'm outside his flat. He said he had a new game. I knock on the door. Nothing. I'm annoyed. I shout through the letter box, thinking he's still in bed. Then I move to the left and look in at the window. There's a gap in the net curtains. I don't understand what I'm looking at. Almost think I must have got the wrong flat. There's nothing in the room. No chairs, no sofa, no telly, no Xbox. Just a space. Except an empty pizza box.

And as I'm still staring through the window, trying to understand this new world, the door flies open, and she's there, Jango's mum. Wearing the same dressing gown from two years before, but now it's stained with . . . I don't know what . . . blood and sweat, and torn so that you can see parts of her underneath it, flesh falling heavily from her bones.

And her hair. Looks like she's cut it herself with nail scissors, or a knife. Clumps of it. Raw scalp. Her face at the same time both fierce and terrified, too much of the whites of her eyes showing.

'Jango,' I say, 'is he . . .?'

'Jango?' She waves her hand in front of her face, as if bothered by flies. And then she repeats, softly, almost as if she isn't sure who he is. 'Jango.'

I don't know how to cope with this.

'Can you just tell him I called?' I say, turning away, not wanting to see any more.

And then her mind seems to clear for a moment.

'You're his friend. The nice one. Look after him. He doesn't have anyone. Only you.'

And I don't know if I imagine it, or if I've remembered it wrong, but then she says, 'You can help him . . . fly.'

I walk back a different way. There's a desolate children's playground, everything broken and vandalised. Of the four swings, only one is still attached to the frame. There's a gaunt figure sitting on the rubber seat, swaying rather than swinging. It's raining, not hard, but enough to wet you down to the skin, if you let it.

I walk over to Jango. He's staring down at the ground between his feet, though I know he must have sensed me coming. He's wearing the first of his long coats.

'Push you?'

'Yeah,' he grunts.

I give the swing a push. Another. Each one higher. Jango starts to laugh. And then he jumps off, flapping through the air like a ruined crow. Later, we sit back to back on the broken roundabout. We don't talk about his mum. That isn't what he wants. It isn't what I'm for. I'm there to help him fly.

Another reason. Another reason not to. Not to . . .

But now the playground is dark. And I'm alone. And I can't help them. Help Jango to fly. Help Sophia to . . . what?

SOPHIA

Sunday, 3.15 a.m.

The trail runs out less than a road away.

'He'll have staunched it,' Jango says, squeezing my hand, as much for himself as me, I guess. Then, slipping his phone back into his pocket, 'The police are coming. They reckon. They'll be able to find him quicker than us.'

But that might not be quick enough.

'Matt!' I scream into the emptiness of an alleyway.

Jango echoes me, an octave down. 'MATT! Come on, Matty boy. Your fucking taxi showed up.'

But the only reply is a gull that flaps indignantly from the food wrapper it was feasting on.

I feel panic rise, pushing out his name again. 'Matthew!' I yell. 'Matt—' But the word gets cut off by a sob that heaves through me, fuelled by fear, too many shots, the fucked-up-ness of it all, trailing tears and snot in its sorry wake.

'We'll find him,' Jango insists.

But his voice is too high, his vocal chords strained with the effort of not falling apart too. And I know it's a lie.

'Matthew!' he screeches. Then opens his mouth to echo himself but stops, gape-jawed, and turns to me. 'I know this place,' he says, quieter. 'I know it. This is where . . .' He trails off as realisation hits him a second sucker punch. 'I know who did it.'

'Me too,' I say.

But we don't have time to exchange our moments of clarity, because Jango's jaw sets and his fingers tighten round mine as he pulls me down the ginnel.

'Fucking come on, you cunt. Come out, come out, wherever you are!' He laughs but I can see tears rolling down his cheeks too now, feel the slick of sweat in his palm.

My turn to squeeze.

'Matthew,' I shout, forcing my voice to hold steady.

Jango looks at me, his face ugly with crying. I, a rabbit in tear-smeared drag make-up, nod back.

'Matthew!' we shout together. Then again. 'Matthew!'

And again.

And again.

Until it contorts and no longer sounds like a word, let alone a name. It's taken on an ethereal quality. Become a strange mantra we have to repeat until we find peace.

'Matthew! Matthew! Matthew!'

And then I don't know any more if it's God or my tumour talking, or something we've conjured with our devilry, but I hear a sound.

Not my name.

Nor Jango's.

Not even a voice speaking.

But a strange exhalation. Like the breath being knocked out of someone.

Like a dying breath.

'Matthew,' I whisper.

And I drop Jango's hand and I run towards it.

I run towards the light.

And it's there. He's there. I see him now. Lying in the filth on the cobbles.

Matthew.

My Matthew.

And for the third time in what feels like as many minutes, I pray that there is a God, and that she is merciful, and that I'm not too late.

MATTHEW

Sunday, 3.20 a.m.

To live. To help Sophia to live.

I opened my eyes. The pain had changed. Now it was like a hunger. A hole. There was nothing in the middle of me.

I was leaving. I was leaving Sophia. I couldn't quite work out why that was important for a minute or two. And then it was obvious. Funny, that, the way a thing goes from unknowable to crystal clear in a second, like when you suddenly get a poem, and all those words turn into a thing, a swan, a god, a war.

It was important because Sophia needed me. She needed me because she was sick. Not sick in the head, but just plain sick. Very sick. And when you're very sick you need someone to love you better. And here I was, lying in this place, letting myself die, because that was easier than the alternative.

Well, I was going to live for her, and because I was going to live, then she was, because I was going to make her, and she couldn't stop me. So again I rolled over so I could crawl. And the pain wasn't as bad as the last time, so I looked up, trying to work out which way to go. And I looked to the left, and I saw the light again, but this time I decided not to look the other way, but just to trust that first light. And as I began to crawl, I sensed that I was lighter, too, as if I had balloons attached to me, balloons just lifting me a little, making it easier, and I thought how nice it would be to let the balloons lift me up into the night sky, with the stars and the warm moonlight.

But that wasn't right. That wasn't the way. And I heard shouting. Or was it the baby crying? Yes, that was it. I had to get the baby, because the baby was going to die. And I looked up at the light from the end of the alleyway, the light from the end of everything. And again I saw figures, shapes, shadows.

The bad lads.

Shouting in rage. Screaming.

They'd come back.

Or if it wasn't the bad lads then it was no one, a dream, because I was dying.

Or the dead, because I was dead.

But the dead don't hold you like this, with their heavy hair in your eyes, and their wet mouth kissing the tears from your face.

Sophia.

Sophia.

Sophia.

SOPHIA

Sunday, 3.25 a.m.

That's when I feel it. When I'm sat in the gutter, his head in my lap, his blood on my hands. That's when I know it's true. That for all my railing against Lexy and her love-is-the-higher-law schtick, when it comes down to it, this – me and him – is all that matters.

And as his eyes flicker open briefly, I lean in close, so that my breath desperately trails love, and life, into his own mouth, and I whisper the words between sobs.

'I love you.'

Then sirens serenade us as saltwater blurs my vision. And I hold his hand tight; tight as the world closes in.

MATTHEW

Sunday, 6 p.m.

The thing about being dead is how much it hurts.

A weird thing, pain. When it's happening live it's all that matters: when you've got toothache the rest of the world, even the rest of your body, just disappears, and all you are is one giant, rotten tooth, throbbing and pulsing. But then, when the pain goes, you just forget it. It's like the fluff from a dandelion clock, blown away in the wind, and there's nothing left of it.

So, there I was, in some kind of hell, circling round my pain, the pain in the middle of me. And for a time I thought that the pain was the pain of my soul, and that's what being damned meant, and I was in hell, with all the other shits and knob-heads: Hitler, Attila the Hun, all the murderers and paedophiles and thieves and liars.

But then I realised that it wasn't my soul, but my guts that were aching, and I didn't think the soul was in your guts. But because it was my guts, my actual guts, and not my soul, didn't mean it didn't hurt, and didn't mean I wasn't in hell. I wanted it to stop, the agony, and would have done anything to make it go away.

It was like there was a fist inside me made of nails and barbed wire and razor blades, and it was churning around, the way I'd seen my mum washing clothes in the sink, squeezing and mashing and wringing. And everything outside the pain was grey, and I thought this was it, for ever, the pain and the grey, the grey pain like a monster eating me. That story, whoever it was, some hero, chained up to a rock, and every day a vulture, or an eagle, I don't know, came and tore out his liver, and ate it. And then in the night the liver would grow back, and the whole thing would start again. Who? Prometheus – that was it. He was me; I was him: Prometheus, chained up and eaten.

Of course the hurting was going on for a while before I knew I was in hell. I don't really know how long. And I don't know how long I was in hell before I heard sounds. And I don't know how long I was hearing sounds before the sounds turned into voices. It was hard to understand them, but they didn't sound like the voices you hear in hell, the screeching of the tormenters, the crying of the tormented.

And I opened my eyes, not into the red and black of hell, but into a searing whiteness that hurt almost as much as my guts were hurting. And then in a rush, I knew several things:

That I wasn't in hell.

That I wasn't dead.

That I was in a hospital bed, and that my mum and dad were with me.

'I think he's come round,' said my mum's voice. And then she did some crying, while my dad mumbled words, not making much sense.

It took a while for my eyes to get working again properly, so I could see them. And then it was a while before I could say anything.

'It hurts,' I murmured, and murmuring it hurt.

My mum went out and got the nurse, and the nurse got a doctor, one of the young ones who looks like a sixth former, with acne and the works, and they sorted out some pain relief that, as far as I could tell, went into the drip that was in my arm.

Until then I couldn't really think straight because of the pain, and after that I still couldn't think straight because of the pain drug, but it was the best feeling I've ever had, the feeling of not being in pain, and I could have kissed the spotty doctor, and the nurse, who wasn't even one of the hot nurses you see on the telly, but just normal looking, like anyone else.

'Sorry, Dad,' I said, when speaking didn't hurt any more. I'm not sure exactly what I was apologising for. Maybe I was just practising, because I knew I had a lot of apologising to do.

I held up the sheet and saw that the middle of me was wrapped up in bandages, like a mummy.

'You're going to be OK, son,' said my dad, guessing my thoughts. Although you didn't need to be psychic to read my mind. 'You lost a lot of blood, and your innards were a mess, but the doctor sewed you up.'

I looked again at the bandages, and had a sudden feeling of panic.

'Am I going to have to shit in a bag, Dad?' I asked.

That made my dad laugh, which in turn made my mum hit him, which made me laugh, which was too much for the pain drug, and it hurt a lot.

'I don't think so, son. Not unless you want to. I suppose they could manage that. They can do most things these days.'

And then my dad looked serious again.

'You were lucky, son, you know. If your friends, that young lady, and that pal of yours, Jingo or whatever you bloody call him, hadn't found you in that alley when they did, you'd have ... well, no sense talking about it in front of your mother. I already wish I'd bought shares in bloody Kleenex, she's got through that many of them.'

I hadn't even thought about how I'd ended up here. All I'd remembered was the lights in the alley, lights at both ends, when there should only have been light from one. And then the pain. And then being here.

Sophia. She'd come to look for me. After everything. What did that mean? Jango must have ... Or she'd just seen how it was, how I felt.

And then I remembered again what I'd understood in the alley, as I lay dying. About her, and about why she had been in the hospital, about her pills, about her illness.

My dad was still talking, not noticing that I'd faded out. I tried to zone back in again. He was saying that the police would want to speak to me, when I was a bit better, and I felt a wave of dread, which melded with a wave of pain from my middle. I knew I was going to have to explain how I'd started the fight, and it wasn't going to look good. I didn't even hate the fat kid, the one who'd stabbed me. In fact I felt bad because the police were going to catch him, and he'd be in some kind of young offenders unit, and that would make him worse, not better, and it would be my fault.

But that was all for the future.

Later that day I had two more visitors.

Jango came in first. I knew he'd come, but thought he'd bring something stupid: cider or boiled eggs, or a massive spliff the size of a chair leg. But he brought a bunch of flowers. Purple ones, with complicated faces.

'Irises,' he said, handing them over.

I didn't really know what to do with them. There were just two other beds in the ward. Both the other patients were out of it, which was a relief – I'd have been embarrassed otherwise.

'Cheers,' I said, and put the flowers on the table by the bed.

There was a plastic chair by the side of the bed. Jango sat down on it. It was angled slightly away, so we didn't have to look right at each other.

'Daft sod,' he said, softly.

'Yeah, I know.'

Then there was a silence, but it was OK.

'It's all right in here,' he said eventually, looking round.

'Yeah, not bad.'

'What's the grub like?'

'I don't know. Got a knife in the guts. Put me off my pizza.'

'What time do they collect the dead ones?'

I snorted.

'Not like the other one,' Jango continued, 'the one with . . . the one we first went to, you know . . .'

'Yeah.'

'That was all little kids, teddies, dolls . . .'

'Yeah, Corky told me.'

There was another silence as I thought about what Corky had said – Jango playing with the little kids, all that. I suppose Jango was thinking about it, too.

'I'm sorry, Matty.'

'It's OK.' It was getting hard to speak again. I needed another shot of the good stuff. 'My dad said you found me.'

'It was Sophia, really,' he said. 'She's a piece of work, that one.'

'Yeah, she is.'

There was another silence, and one of the other patients coughed. Then Jango scraped the chair around so he faced me properly.

'I want to tell you what I was . . . what was going on, in my head. You know, before.'

I just nodded.

'Things got out of control. My life . . . it hasn't been good. Mum, and . . .'

'I know, Jango.'

'Let me just get all this out. The day of the shit fight, when you were supposed to meet her. Well I felt pretty piss poor about the whole thing, so I thought I'd go and explain to her what had happened. I'd got you in the shit so I'd pull you out of it sort of thing. I texted her – got the number off your phone before I lost it. Then I followed her, waiting for the right moment. But then when I was about to tell her, she effing maced me in the eyes. Well not mace, maybe perfume or hairspray or something. But then I saw her snog that bloke, and I just thought, What a bitch. And then you didn't back me up when I had that thing with Fernando . . .'

'It's all right, Jango. I don't really care.'

'No, please, hear me out. After Fernando, I sort of flipped. My only friend was gone. You've probably sussed it, but I've got to tell you something.'

'You don't have to, Jango. I know.'

'Really?'

'Yeah.'

And I did know. That Jango's bullshit and bluster was just a front. The mask, put on for the first time, perhaps, back at that parents' evening. That stunts like the hospital raid were designed to fail. That he was hiding the truth from himself as well as the world.

'I'm going to say it now, and then we never talk about it again, OK?'

Maybe I should have let him say it, and someone with a bit more maturity might have. But I didn't want him to. Didn't want him to make things more weird between us. Anyway, I'm sixteen years old, not effing Jesus. So *I* said it.

'Shut up, Jango. I said that I know. And I do. You're a wanker, but you're my brother, and I love you.'

And after that it was OK.

Sophia

Sunday, 6 p.m.

If I thought any stunt the mother ship has ever pulled before was big, I was kidding myself, because the one she conjures up in the wake of that night is truly *Titanic*, complete with railing at the world, and wailing like the sea itself. All that's missing is Kate Winslet's tits.

I am forbidden to drink.

I am forbidden to wear short shorts, sequins, skinny anything, and especially rabbit onesies.

I am forbidden to go out for the foreseeable future.

And I am forbidden to see him today, tomorrow or ever again.

But like the knight in shining tweed he can be when he wakes up from his American literature dream, Daddy rides in on a white steed, or at least in our Audi, and drives me back to the hospital himself, leaving her with her eyes so wide and her mouth gaping so low you'd think she was a Liebovitz print of *The Scream*.

I'd barely slept, definitely not washed, and must look like seven kinds of shit, with a dose of almost-dead girl on top.

But when I walk on to that ward, he looks at me like I'm a goddess.

Or a mermaid.

Or a girl with a dolphin mouth.

Whichever.

He looks at me like I'm someone with all my life – our lives – ahead.

And so I walk up to his bed, and I sit down and I take his hand in mine.

And I tell him everything.

Matthew

Sunday, 6 p.m.

Then Sophia.

She came towards me, shyly, and I thought for a second of the cat in the alleyway, while I was bleeding. And for the first time I saw something about her – that the life and energy and brightness were the flaring up of a fire that was burning out – and I saw the paleness underneath the gold of her skin. And it made her more beautiful. And I knew that she was going to say something perfect.

'On the pull again? There's a senile dementia ward down the corridor if you're feeling lucky.'

And I laughed so hard I thought the stitches holding my liver and kidneys and god knows whatever else was in there together were going to burst.

I'd meant to say that it was all Jango's fault, but there comes a time when you have accept that the shit you get into is the consequence of the choices you make.

'The big boy made me do it,' I said.

And then she sat on the bed, and held my hand, and we told our stories.

SOPHIA

Sunday, one year later

So I've scrubbed number five from the list. I still don't believe in any god, or snake oil salesman, or a fake-tanned tooth fairy.

But love at first sight? I'm willing to give that one the benefit of my quite substantial doubt.

I'm not dumb enough to think my loving Matt kept him going, even less brought him back. I didn't save Matt's life. Paramedics and doctors and nurses did that. But I know what I felt that day in the canteen in Mickey's.

I know what I felt that night in that alleyway with his head in my lap, and me and Jango holding his hands, telling him jokes, singing songs.

And I know what I feel now.

Death, or almost death, even when it's not our own, teaches us something. Maybe that's why we flirt with it: lap it up and gulp it down like it's no more harmful than candyfloss or Coke. So we can try it out for size from the safety of the back row of the Roxy or paperback pages; work out how we'd handle it. Or how we wouldn't.

And I flirted closer than most. So this is what I know now; what I've learned since the night my boyfriend almost bought it:

1. That the infamous dick (in every sense) that kick-started this whole story belongs to a kid called Kai, who's now facing eighteen months having to compare his in the communal showers of Westway Juvenile Detention Centre. The fat kid, Dean – the one with the knife, the stooge, the one who's doing five years for GBH – agreed it'd be a laugh, only I don't suppose either of them is laughing now. Ha fucking ha. And I should feel sorry for them and repeat Lexy's big speech about how it's society's failing and poverty is the real criminal and yadda yadda, but that dick nearly killed someone. And death by penis is no way to exit, my friend.

2. That the glass is always half full. Sometimes it's half full of pee, but even pee has its uses. And so the tumour may not be going anywhere, but it's not getting any bigger either according to Dr Gupta's latest Kodak moment. And hey, it's no kitchen knife to the stomach.

3. Which is why living each day like it's your last is dancing with the devil. Taking your pills on time and telling yourself tomorrow always comes is way cleverer, plus you don't have to mess with dolphins or any of that bucket list Disneyland shit. You just do the normal stuff. You go to school, you take your tests, you play cowboys with your kid brother. You read *Gatsby* for the seventeenth time and decide Fitzgerald was a bitter old cynic after all. You text your boyfriend to meet you down Vinyl

Revival later for his latest lesson in what's really important. Dull stuff. Normal stuff. Good stuff.

4. That shop owners forgive thieves when almost-death is
   on the excuse list. We fessed up – together. Besides, my
   dad stumped up for it – early Christmas present, he
   said. I guess money can buy some stuff. But stealing for
   the sake of proving devotion? That trumps it all in my
   book.

5. That kissing a stranger in a hospital canteen is fool-
   hardy at best and fucked up at worst. But as stories go,
   it wasn't a bad opening shot, and neither of us is yet to
   exit stage left so maybe that's telling me something
   after all.

Just stay away from the burgers when you go to recreate
the scene for your one-year anniversary though. Because
dicing with those things really is a death wish.

SONGS FOR MATT

1. THE MOOCHE - DUKE Ellington
2. I LOVE ROCK 'n' ROLL - JOAN JETT & THE BLACKHEARTS
3. Folsom Prison Blues - JOHNNY CASH
4. KNOCK ON WOOD - AMII STEWART
5. Think - ARETHA FRANKLIN
6. Suspicious Minds - Elvis Presley
7. WHY CAN'T I BE YOU? - THE CURE
8. diVINLS - i touch myself
9. Pleasant Valley Sunday - The MONKees
10. THIS YEAR - THE Mountain Goats
11. Pills and Soap - ELVIS COSTELLO
12. IF you Go Away - MARC ALMOND
13. TERRIBLE LOVE - THE NATIONAL
14. Please, Please, PLEASE let me get what I want (THE SMITHS)
15. I DON'T CARE IF THERE'S CURSING - PHOSPHORESCENT
16. To me you are a Work of Art - MORRISSEY
17. "HEROES" DAVID BOWIE
18. TO LOVE SOMEBODY - NINA SIMONE
19. I want you - BOB DYLAN
20. EVERYBODY HURTS - R.E.M

Acknowledgements

Our thanks to Sarah Castleton and the team at Atom, Julia Churchill, Sarah Elle Weston, and the ping-pong spectators who cheered this experiment on over many months.